D1135288

STATE OF
HAPPINESS

STATE OF HAPPINESS

STELLA DUFFY

Virago

A *Virago* Book

First published in Great Britain by Virago Press in 2004

Copyright © Stella Duffy, 2004

The moral right of the author has been asserted

A CIP catalogue record for this book
is available from the British Library.

ISBN 1 84408 113 3

Typeset in Bembo by M Rules
Printed and bound in Great Britain
by Clays Ltd, St Ives plc

Virago
An imprint of
Time Warner Books UK
Brettenham House
Lancaster Place
London WC2E 7EN

www.virago.co.uk

For Tom, who mapped the stars for me.

One

Dis-Location: Introduction (March 1999)

We care greatly about beginnings, need to know where and when we were born, how we met, and at which precise point does longing turn to love – and yet searching for the end is as valid as finding the source. For generations men talked of the origin of the Nile, the beginning of the Amazon. They believed they had already seen the end, the flow into the ocean, and marked that as the finishing point. Their true goal being to score down the exact nature of the start. But that finishing point is an arbitrary construct. Is the end of the Nile the spot where the water turns from fresh to salt? What is the salt-saturation level at which any one river becomes the ocean? We must be as interested in end-points as beginnings, for it is certain that both are required for mapping, just as the finality of death is vital to life. As a species we have made it our work to mark the point at which one becomes another. And yet our decisions can only ever be man-made. Whose taste buds will provide us with the ultimate definition and dare to say the precise point at which fresh water turns to salt? And then where are we when the tide comes in?

Two

The man was standing at the window. Cindy could tell he was foreign – his body wasn't perfect, his clothes weren't so sharp, but most of all he was smiling at the view. True, her friend Kelly's new apartment had an incredible view both south and west, but it was a long time since she'd seen anyone gaze with a tourist's smile on the pin-prick of red light the statue held aloft in the harbour. Cindy watched him watching, her concentration not on the man, or the statue, but on the line connecting the two, the co-ordinates that joined them.

She had been standing behind the man for a couple of minutes before he noticed her. 'Sorry. I still find it exciting. The statue.' Then he smiled and acknowledged their hostess hurrying into another room with plates and glasses, 'I still seem to turn up way too early at parties as well.'

She held out her hand, a forty-five degree angle to touch, 'I'm Cindy.'

'Jack Stratton. I made a feature on Kelly's work. I'm a news producer. It's probably why I'm always early. Never want to miss anything.'

His accent wasn't the hard London she'd been expecting. There were other tones, a twist, something not-quite-Lennon – but near.

He had dark skin, a cool hand. She added, 'Kelly and I went to high school together.'

Jack couldn't remember the last time he'd seen anyone from his secondary modern. Nor did he want to. 'You must have got on well?'

'We had no choice. It was Baton Rouge.'

'Yeah. Of course.'

Baton Rouge meant nothing to Jack. But he put it away as a possibility for later. The woman in front of him looked interesting, he had an evening of strangers ahead, he could always ask her what she'd meant if discussing Anglo-American relations became too tedious.

Kelly came back into the room, a full glass in each hand, 'That's good. Cindy Frier – Jack Stratton. Meet. Talk. Enjoy.' She passed over the glasses, spilling only a little on the shiny floor, and twisted on a bare heel to answer the entryphone.

'Frier? You're the one who did that book?'

Cindy bit her top lip. It wasn't the first time she'd heard this description of herself. 'Yeah. I'm the one who did that book.'

Cindy – who had loathed her own name from the moment she realised the frothy appellation applied to herself – was understandably interested in names. This developed into a fascination with place names – particularly when her father began to follow various girlfriends across the nation; Cindy learnt more about the geography of her homeland through his amorous adventuring than she ever had in a school room. In time, Cindy embraced her childhood fixation on the naming and placing of things and turned it into her career. Cindy Frier became the author of *Dis-Location – the function of space over time: Naming as Generation*. Usually distilled into the simple phrase – you name it, you make it. And the colonising spirit of every reader thrilled at the twenty-first century possibility that they might yet re-make the world in which they found themselves.

Jack struggled to twist the conversation back to something that made him sound less like a stalker and more like someone who just happened to have read her book. The most difficult part being that he hadn't read it, had just picked up half a dozen theories from various articles and programmes.

'I haven't read it.'

Cindy noted she found honesty quite attractive.

'Plenty of people haven't. But with the sort of press attention it got, way too many think they have.'

Cindy was twenty-six when her thesis was published. It was written with research and results but also with passion, an awareness of the mysticism and history her subject carried. And that was what tantalised the hungry public – measured truths with potential magic. Her excitement burned through the paper, across the Internet, filtered through magazines and supplements, chatrooms and chat shows. She'd spent eight years in a wilderness of study and come out blinking into the light of a hundred digi-cameras. She looked good, answered questions easily and always managed to include at least one nugget that provided a headline. Clever girl but not too smoothly articulate – she was perfect media fodder. And she was called Cindy. And she still had young-girl skin. And she carried pistachios in her pocket. She was bound to do well.

'So do you get that a lot?'

'What?'

'People pretending they understand what you do?'

'All the time. You?'

'I make news programmes. They don't think there is anything to understand.'

'Is there?'

'It's mostly just about finding the point of interest. And then following it through.'

'That's more or less what I do too.'

Jack and Cindy were saved from getting into any more blatant flirting by the arrival of four other guests, four rounds of handshakes and introductions. Small talk magnified by four, six, eight, ten. Dinner was ready.

Further evidence of Jack's foreign status emerged as the meal progressed. He was certainly not a classic Englishman abroad. Not the idealised American version anyway. More Mancunian-at-large. But he was clearly British. He didn't work out, he stayed in the city during August and he still couldn't remember how many martinis it was safe to drink before he fell over. In addition to his relaxed attitude to alcohol, Jack discussed occasional drug use as if he was talking about something purely recreational, rather than a practice not dissimilar to slitting the throats of newborn babies. To a table of people easily jaded by the finest Manhattan had to offer, Kelly's new friend was a tasty distraction from the treadmill of the acquisition-and-success routine.

Cindy, who could think of little that was less fun than spending an evening with one best friend and eight virtual strangers, had managed to wriggle her way out of Kelly's last three invitations, but tonight she could think of no excuse more valid than a pressing engagement with her latest theory. Not good enough for the woman with whom she'd shared all her school, parent, career and lover traumas for the past thirteen years. Kelly's new apartment was costing most of her salary and she needed to give at least two dinners and one party a month to better expose her good fortune – and, vitally, what a fine catch she was. Unfortunately for Kelly, while the paucity of straight men had been exhaustively analysed for the past decade – often by Cindy – what was yet to be widely catalogued was the lack of available lesbians. She'd invited three possibles to dinner, but two were rapidly

5

becoming more interested in each other and the third seemed to have re-discovered her heterosexuality the minute Jack opened his mouth. Which discovery prevented the poor girl from noticing that Jack was way more interested in Cindy. Kelly was irritated at first but figured she might be in with a chance by dessert.

Despite his offshore charms and charming honesty, Cindy had a hard time keeping her mind on Jack. She was deeply involved in an internal discussion about points of intersection: dissecting paths and converging roads, tracks running vertically parallel to the road above. And while several of the other guests had attempted to engage her in conversation about her work, Cindy was far more interested in the tines of her fork. Did they end at the pointy bit she'd used to spear the glazed carrots, or where all five joined to form a platter for her oil-drizzled mashed celeriac? Jack, though, found himself wondering if Kelly had a copy of Cindy's book he could borrow. She was clearly different from the others, which made her quite attractive. And she was pretty. Which made her more attractive. And when she heard him say he was from Manchester, she mentioned that at college she'd had a friend who'd once dated a man who supported Man City. Which made her fucking gorgeous.

Now thirty-two, Jack had arrived in New York almost six years ago, wangled himself a green card on the strength of his charming demeanour, a passion for his work, and the sister of a friend who worked in Immigration. Jack blagged some, outright lied a little more, and launched himself into a brand new career while pretending all the time he'd been doing it for years. He relied on his belief that he probably could do the job if only he was given a chance, but that was unlikely to happen at home given his parents' lack of foresight in being a mixed race couple with a working class income and no

6

Oxbridge acquaintances. Any faltering steps he put down to differences in US/UK practice, and when it came to outright mistakes he endeared himself to his superiors by admitting fault immediately and taking the new-boy blame. Some people sleep their way to the top, Jack dragged himself there on insomniac hours.

Jack loved his work and he was driven. Enough to cross the world and set up home in an unknown metropolis where Manchester City games were only available in the middle of the night, pre-recorded, on a far-too-expensive cable channel. He was perfectly happy to have a few good friends, the occasional evening out if he knew the food was going to be good, followed by a long double espresso to start the new working day. Cindy loved her work and was driven. Enough to spend most of a meal fiddling with her fork and infuriating her oldest friend. She was rarely in bed before three in the morning because she usually found that the latest concept occupying her fevered brain was just too damn interesting. Of course Cindy and Jack were going to get on.

They left Kelly's apartment together, the under-paid doorman in over-tight uniform dozing at his desk. Jack indicated a car parked on a side road. 'Can I give you a lift home?'

'You have a car? You really are foreign.'

He smiled. 'I try.'

Cindy would have been happy to travel home alone on the subway – the journey below the streets was not only faster than the stop-start traffic, it also gave her an opportunity to consider the possibilities of parallel lines, both horizontal and vertical, finally meeting at a fixed, if random, point. But Jack was smiling and the air was heavy and it was a hot walk to the nearest subway stop.

They drove up the Westside Highway and Jack tried polite conversation, 'So why do you live way the hell up here?'

Cindy looked at his wide hands on the steering wheel, the thick traffic ahead. 'I like it. I tutor at Columbia. Have some research work at the Natural History Museum. And when I go down to NYU I enjoy the journey. I'm working on an idea about subway interchanges and civic paths.'

'Oh.'

'Anyway, I'm not so interested in neighbourhoods, the shops, bars. I care about the routes, how they move, not really what they lead to. And I'm happy in my apartment. It's small and it's messy and it suits me. I like to feel contained by what I do. My place is a security blanket.'

What she didn't explain was that while her public profile suggested she should move to somewhere grander, public profile didn't understand second-publication-tied advances and an income that was only just making headway into the years of debt she'd accumulated while turning herself into an overnight success.

Then they turned off the highway and Cindy clapped her hands. 'I love this bit, look – it's an over-locking grid with a two-road interchange.'

Cindy explained her reference as she directed Jack to her building. She clarified a little more when he came in for coffee. She illuminated her point perfectly when the two of them bent their heads together for a goodnight kiss in her doorway; vertical beings, individually turning upper bodies semi-horizontal due to an inner and outside force affecting and directing each one, creating in a single moment a unique united point of both axis and access. Eventually pulling away, returned to their original parallel paths. And at the point of returning to stasis, left to decide whether repetition of such union should be left to accidental or intentional forces.

At least that's what Cindy thought about their kiss. She sent Jack on his way with her home phone number, her cell phone number and her email address. And a request to meet for breakfast on Sunday. Fixed points following an unmarked trajectory with inevitable collision as the only certain outcome. That much Jack Stratton understood all by himself.

Three

On meeting points (March 1998)

It is in our most ordinary actions that we begin to blind ourselves. We place street markings side by side and insist that they can never join, they must always run in parallel, stop at the junction, continue on, until we end them with a click of the keyboard and a name change, a cross street, a t-junction. But what if we choose not to end that road? It is our naming that has given us arbitrary divisions – the right angle at the corner between Texas and New Mexico was not so perfect before we agreed it should be so. When we acknowledge that this naming is our own work, we can envisage new ways of looking at what we already know. How much further are we then capable of travelling? We could re-place our world if we really wanted. If we weren't so scared by change.

Cindy and Jack thought that change, in the form of Jack and Cindy, looked pretty good. The evening's journey home from Kelly's apartment became a far lengthier journey to each other.

Cindy developed a mild interest in news and current affairs, was surprised by a warmer enthusiasm for British soccer, which she learned to call football, and found herself a cross-town route to Jack's apartment in the East Village that took twice as long as necessary and gave her time and content for her thoughts: if one side of Manhattan was East and the other West, what was it about North and South that the city fathers believed these compass points to be of less relevance in the naming of their new home? Was it a trans-American thinking, one that, while nodding acknowledgement to the South, primarily divided the country into East and West? Was this notion of movement imported directly from the westbound journey by the Europeans to the New World? And further, was the trek from like to lust and deep into love part of the same path, or would she be required to make itinerary choices along the way?

Jack's route to Cindy was far simpler. He fancied her, he liked her, they had first good and then – with a little more practice – great sex. And so he fell in love with her. Simple and sensible.

But they did need to make decisions on their journey to each other. Jack's first choice was not to tell Cindy about his ex-wife in England. Initially this was a wise move – in Jack's experience, most women, confronted with a once-divorced man, saw him as a serial adulterer. Or, when he admitted that Nicole had left him, a loser. Six months later Jack realised he couldn't tell Cindy about Nicole until she could trust that, unlike her father, he did not intend to regularly trade her in for a younger model. For her part, Cindy chose not to talk about her mother's serial relationships – five major and three minor at last count. She thought it best not to scare him off too soon. They continued making choices, taking new routes, finding themselves together with little effort and only occasionally faked ease. Things looked good for a continuance of desire.

In their second year together Cindy made what appeared to be a definite move towards commitment. Her way of showing she cared was to turn down the offer of a year's secondment to

Chicago in favour of an in-depth analysis of the contours of Jack's flesh. Actually, Cindy was only mildly interested in the particular field of study offered in Chicago – laser analysis applied to the already-charted Grand Canyon – and she was well aware that she'd have more time to get on with her own research in New York. Nor did she think she could cope with the Chicago winter. But she didn't tell Jack any of this, rightly assuming that her apparent selflessness would give her ample leverage to insist on the holiday in England he'd so far been denying her. She got the holiday, though not because Jack felt guilty about Chicago. It was the second year of their relationship after all and Jack was already aware of his partner's manipulative skills. There were gains to be made on his side as well. His mother had been complaining about never seeing her youngest son any more.

Cindy and Jack went to Britain – one week in London, another in Scotland and a six-day stopover in Manchester. (To Cindy's joy, Jack's mother and father were happily married. Five kids married. Properly married.) They had an uncomfortable first night in his parents' house – sleeping in the space that had once housed Jack's football posters and the teenage fantasies of three boys, with his father's snores piercing the old pinholes in the wall. Cindy could usually sleep anywhere, immediately, for nine or ten hours at a time, but not with Jack fidgeting and moaning and grinding his teeth beside her. The next day she discovered the real reason for Jack's sleepless night. He took Cindy on a surprise visit to meet his ex-wife. Both women were incredibly polite and absolutely furious with Jack for not giving them more notice. Time to prepare a speech of female solidarity in the face of bloke-ish thoughtlessness. To give Nicole an opportunity to make up a story about the glories of the relationship for which she'd left Jack (now past the initial flight of fancy and settled into a dull, immutable rut). An hour or so at least to allow Cindy to change into something slightly more threatening than the old pair of jeans – pistachio shells cramming the pockets – she preferred to travel in. There was, however, plenty of time for Cindy to notice that Nicole was still wearing the wedding ring Jack had given her. Not on her wedding finger, but definitely on her hand.

That night both Jack and Cindy admitted the truth of their scheming, leading them to take another route in their relationship. Promises of future honesty were offered as proof of undying devotion. After the first flush of lust had faded, the occasional agonies of total truth easily overcame any problems of potential boredom, leaving them with the basics of desire and friendship. Whichever was most enjoyable.

Jack left for work at six in the morning, seven at the very latest. He ran out of whichever apartment they'd spent the night in, grabbing emails and answering cell phone messages on the way, shoving a dry raisin bagel in his mouth as he jumped into his car and out to meet his crew. On a shooting day he'd spend fifteen hours getting in the raw material, hassling and harassing both subject and crew until he had enough to cut into a good version of the story. Jack was successful because he never let the camera operator get away with just one shot of the victim, or a grabbed walk-away of the conqueror. Two reporters were part of Jack's regular team, several others both queued up and were terrified of working with him. They could make their name on a piece directed by Jack Stratton, or they could find themselves in the firing line, the mouthpiece of a harsh truth that brought down the shamed businessman, the cheating workmate, the blamed councillor. On days when there was no shooting, Jack left the house first thing anyway, eating as he ran, happiest spinning from bed to office to location and back again with no time-wasting in between.

Cindy continued to work from home when she could, and to blossom whenever faced with a lecture hall, microphone or camera. She did want to write, but it seemed everyone also wanted to hear her speak, to offer her opinions on their interpretations of her work, to get her to talk in the slightly stilted, sometimes brusque, and occasionally completely arcane manner she was known for. Re-booked for. Her courses were over-subscribed from the moment they were announced. Cindy was too busy being successful to get on with doing again what she'd become successful for in the first place. And she was happy to be busy, glad people valued what she did, astonished at how much they liked her work, but she was also tired.

Cindy Frier and Jack Stratton, both successful and highly likely to become more so as long as they continued to work at the frenetic pace they'd adopted up to now. Actually much too busy, but loving the work anyway. And keeping going.

Four

Cindy didn't know where she was. This was not normal. She knew how to consider the streets, the conjugation of buildings, to follow the unmarked givens that create a location, even when none of the places were named and nothing was familiar. She might get lost, but never for long. Not this time. This time Cindy was definitely missing. She thought that maybe she would have found it exciting, this fresh sensation of being elsewhere and needing to find a new way back, ought to have been almost able to enjoy herself – and probably would have, if not for the pain.

'The glory of maps and mapping is that what eventually becomes our chart, this thing we call a map, is not static. Most people assume the map is an explanation of place, of space. But the map is also a route-plan of time. It is time that we note down when we map out a location; time we commit to paper, to disk, to memory even. When I say this river bisects that ridge, I am stating a moveable truth as if I believe it might exist forever. And yet we know for certain that one day the hill will collapse in a mudslide removing both ridge and waterway. It is an accepted truth that the ground we stand on continually moves beneath us. We are not merely mapping place, but time as well. You can only ever chart the individual moment. And it matters that you get it right.'

This was the speech that always ended Cindy's second lecture. First-year geography and earth sciences majors, the sixty-strong group would stare blankly at her throughout the first lecture. Once she'd got past source materials and class times, she then gave them a brief overview from Mesopotamia to satellite imaging. While the students waited for Cindy Frier to get on with what she was known for – the weirdy hippy stuff with a touch of self-actualisation and a few pistachio shells thrown in – she figured she might as well acquaint them with some of the concepts they would return to in the years to come. The course requirement was one lecture a week covering the very basics of the subject. Her lesson plan also took in Chinese cartography, Greek and Roman world views, and the influence of Islamic mapmaking on Western culture. She further touched on trigonometry as truth and the beauty of the spider-silk-strung theodolite. It was just five hours a week with a full weekend's marking maybe once a month, but it gave her a small steady income and a place to experiment aloud with new possibilities of theory. For the students it offered a whole lot more. While all around them were succumbing to the twin dances of excess alcohol and the discovery that life without Mom and Dad might be almost as terrifying as it was exciting, Cindy's students had intangible possibilities and convoluted theoretical constructs to comprehend – clear proof that university study really could offer the staple of a three a.m. conversation. Just as they'd always hoped it might.

In each year there were usually a handful of real students. Those who were there not merely to cover course requirements, or to use the four-year space to grow up, but consciously present for the process of enquiry. And Cindy loved them for loving her subject. The remainder stirred themselves from their hungover stupor long enough to notice

Cindy's good looks, her passionate chaotic delivery, her disconcerting habit of dropping a handful of pistachio shells on the desk at the end of the class, and, more often than not, they were forced to acknowledge she had some good ideas. She knew how to make her own profession sound like the search for the Holy Grail. Because to her, it was.

But not that particular afternoon. That day she paused just after delivering her coup de grâce about mapping time. Stopped short where she would normally have launched into a vision of herself and other cartographers as fine-tuned missionaries of terrestrial truth. Instead she turned away from the massed ranks of students, back to the white board where she had sketched a medieval view of the world – Jerusalem as central point – and tried to catch her breath, fighting against the ragged pain cutting down the centre of her chest. Faced away so that she could double over without the curious stares of sixty eighteen-year-olds confirming the suspicion that she was about to throw up. Then the pain was too much. She passed out. Vomited. And naturally choked.

When she woke up, Cindy did not know where she was. She looked down at her right arm – a thin canula was inserted into the vein at the crook of her elbow and a plastic bag hanging above her head dripped a clear fluid down the narrow tube and into her body. Cindy followed the key line of the gently throbbing blue, pictured the quiet liquid travelling through her arm and into her own pathway of blood vessels; arteries and veins taking in something she couldn't identify, her liquid-hungry heart pumping it through regardless. Her body felt stiff and uncomfortable, there were other wires attached to discs she could feel stuck to her chest, a monitor to her left, a thin stream of oxygen passing through a nasal canula at her nostrils. Body placing briefly analysed, Cindy turned her attention to the room. Moving her head was difficult, she felt heavier than usual. The room was white. No windows. She lay in a high-raised bed, no chair for a visitor, no curtains to draw for privacy. She was alone in a quiet room for one.

Jack was there five minutes later. Back to stand beside her again and wait until she woke up. Angry with himself for missing the moment of the opening of the eyes. Angry with Cindy for being there at all. Angry with fear. Holding her hand and interpreting the white room for her. Then he left her again just long enough to announce to the corridor that Cindy was awake. Three doctors in almost-white coats followed the young nurse in.

'You collapsed.'

'Why?'

'We don't know yet. Do you remember what happened?'

'I remember hurting.'

'Where?'

'Chest, stomach. All over.'

Cindy couldn't find body specifics. Sort of her chest. Sort of her stomach. Sort of everywhere, nowhere. She did what she trained others to do. Took it one step at a time. Tried to look at the individual moments rather than the whole, building from small certainties to a total unknown.

'I was teaching. It was the afternoon. My class was nearly through. Introduction to the Self in Mapmaking.' The assembled medics didn't bother to pretend comprehension. This was not new to Cindy. She continued, 'It must have been ten, five to three. Then there was the pain. I couldn't breathe. I don't think there was anything stopping my breath, but the pain took my energy away – my attention away – from breathing in again.'

'You stopped breathing?'

18

'No. I mean I didn't know if I could. There wasn't any intention in it.'

'And then?'

'I didn't want them to see me like that. The students. I didn't want to scare them. I thought I might throw up, I didn't want to embarrass myself. I turned away from them . . . and then I woke up. And I didn't know where I was. I still don't know where I am.'

They nodded and promised to come back, to keep an eye on her tonight, begin tests tomorrow. They offered no explanations and left Jack to make it better. He named the hospital, told her the level, explained about the room. This was closest to the nurses' station, that's why there were no windows. The drip was saline, in case she was dehydrated after the nausea. He held her hand and they traced the route of the ambulance from classroom to hospital. Jack's journey from work, leaving behind a camera crew and nervous reporter. He'd left messages for her parents. The doctors said they weren't too concerned – they didn't know anything, but as yet, with vital signs stable and no obvious problems, there seemed to be nothing definite to worry about. Jack kissed her carefully and left the room to phone the good news to Cindy's parents, his forced ease at this new turn of events fooling neither of them.

Cindy lay back and closed her eyes. Much of her work was about the process of understanding – not merely where, but also why. But this was not her work, this was her self. This was a new place in which to feel lost. When Jack came back and held her hand again, she felt a small degree of safety. Her father's girlfriend had taken the message and sent her love, her mother's boyfriend had done likewise. Not unusually, the route to Cindy's parents was indirect. With Jack beside her, Cindy lay still, breathing slowly, and eventually drifted back to sleep, comforted slightly by his assurance that he would stay there all night if she wanted, and anyway the nurse had told them she would remain under observation for the next day or two at least. No chance of getting lost again.

Five

Cindy underwent comprehensive testing during three full days in hospital, and then another week visiting various clinics around town, and was eventually sent away with a clean bill of health. She was not measurably unwell, therefore there was nothing wrong with her. Clearly this could not be true, or she would not have collapsed in pain and a pool of vomit in front of sixty first-year students. But, apparently, there was nothing wrong with her. Because the cause of her pain and collapse could not be found, it could not be named, and without a name it could not exist. Not as a medical fact. Going home again with no diagnosis was in some ways better than leaving with any of the numerous answers both she and Jack were terrified of. On the other hand, the uncertainty didn't make for much improvement to Jack's insomniac state; his barely-contained anger every time another junior doctor raised a questioning eyebrow simply made Cindy all the more certain they were wasting her time, the doctors' time and the insurance company's money. Which was certainly easier to say aloud than giving voice to her own terror.

Cindy's health insurance had paid for the CT scan, the MRI and the blood tests. Jack paid for a round of ordinary x-rays just in case. Cindy endured hours being photographed and x-rayed from all angles, spent most of a day radioactive for the bone scan, and put up with her own semi-claustrophobia while lying in various 'stay-perfectly-still-for-me-honey' poses for the greater good of getting results. She went for a list of blood tests that rivalled any acronym-heavy mouthful spouted by uncomprehending actors on a TV soap. She spent half a day running and jumping and puffing and breathing hard, all the while hooked up to a heart monitor. By the end of it all, though, there was still no answer. The doctors were not saying Cindy had not collapsed, or that she had not been in extreme pain – her heart rate and physical state when she was brought into hospital testified that something had definitely happened. They just couldn't say why. Or what. As far as the hospital and doctors and specialists and haematologists were concerned, there was no specific cause. And, having tried every avenue they could, the city-wide contingent of health practitioners was forced to tell her to go away and forget about it.

'Forget about it' was a phrase not easily spoken by a professional body that prided itself on accurate diagnosis as the root of efficient treatment. More than most, Cindy understood the dilemma the medical staff was presented with. They had been given an incident occurring in a single moment in time and then asked to extrapolate truths from it. Whatever had occurred in Cindy's body had indeed taken place, but where it had come from, and where it was going, were quite different questions which no-one seemed eager to answer without some factual base as a starting point. Least of all Cindy, who couldn't bear the thought of being at the mercy of other people and needed no further encouragement to simply ignore what had taken place. Much to Jack's alarm and irritation, once the tests were over and she was sent on her way, Cindy decided to carry on as normal, no rest required, no break in routine necessary. She may not have been able to forget about her collapse, but she was determined to ignore it.

*

22

'I really think you should take some time off.'

Cindy's top lip twitched slightly but she kept her tone calm, 'There's nothing wrong with me.'

Jack hissed back, trying to keep himself from shouting, 'They can't find anything wrong, that is not the same as there being nothing wrong.'

'It is to me.'

'You're hiding.'

'From what?'

As the doctors had no answer to this, neither did Jack. He tried another route, one that allowed him at least to seem positive. 'We could have a holiday. I could make time . . .'

'Jack, you've always said you hate taking vacations. "One week off to get over work and one week more to start panicking about what they'll have piled up for you when you get back." That's what you said to my father last year when he said we should take more time off.'

'That's because his idea of a break involved us going down to stay with them. You were very grateful if I remember rightly.'

'I was, I am. Once a year with him and the current Barbie is more than enough. But don't try to pretend now that you'd like to go on vacation just because you want me to rest.'

Jack acknowledged the pointlessness of his attempted subterfuge and tried again. 'You could go somewhere by yourself.'

'Where?'

'The coast for a few days. Long Island? That's not far.'

'I just threw up in front of my entire class. If I don't get back in there soon they'll never take me seriously.'

'They won't take you seriously if you collapse again, either.'

'Don't snap, Jack, it doesn't help.'

'Helps me.'

'Baby.'

'Chicken.'

But Cindy was not to be diverted. 'Stop fussing. It happened, they'd know if it was something that really mattered, now let's get on with it.'

Jack stretched back in his chair, scratched at the hair on the nape of his neck – he needed a haircut, the almost-curls were starting to irritate him. Cindy watched his obvious body language, his raised arm signalling a clear desire to reach out and grab her by the throat and pull her away on holiday, held back by his concern for her. He gave it another go. 'You could give up your class, I'm getting in enough for both of us. Then there'd be more time to concentrate on your own work.'

'I'd just start thinking about another project.' Jack groaned and Cindy leant across their half-touched plates to pick at his bitten fingernails. 'I like teaching. It reminds me of how much I still don't know. It's a good way of getting in the raw material.' Jack shrugged and Cindy continued, 'And you know I never like you paying for me. I don't want to be looked after. It's not something I'm very good at.'

He knew this was true – paternal responsibility in their relationship was something neither of them wanted from Jack. At least they hadn't wanted it. Jack had never wanted it. Until he stood beside Cindy in the hospital bed and saw how pale she was, how the wired monitors and artificial veins which pumped controlling liquid into her body dwarfed his normally heroic lover and made a girl of her. He was surprised to find himself feeling so protective; in all their time together, despite his in-built desire to always make it all right, Cindy was usually two leaps ahead of him and he was running to catch up. Now it was all Jack could do to stop himself grabbing her and holding her down, his concern a soft blanket to dampen her enthusiasm and keep her close to him. Tethered maybe, but safe.

Jack said none of this. He didn't want to keep arguing until his concern came out in thoughtless anger. Nor did he want to admit that he felt differently about her now. Good different, but certainly different. Instead he let her pay for dinner, drive them home, where they climbed into bed and each other's arms, Jack tentatively making love to the porcelain doll-woman he now found himself scared of breaking. He careful and Cindy fucking blindly, violently, all her sensations engaged in the single task of trying to shut out the nagging questions piled in the pit of her constantly tense stomach.

Worries suffocated into silence, Cindy fell into her usual deep sleep and Jack listened to her regular breathing, sending out an agnostic prayer that something might come along to clear out this newly installed apprehension, his fear.

Six

Jack was offered a promotion. Jack was offered exactly what he had moved to the States hoping to get and never really dared to imagine he'd be allowed to have. His boss asked him to lunch with three other company chiefs and, when they had finished praising his work methods – their analysis not entirely correct, but Jack knew better than to contradict four bosses over a fifty-dollar steak – they made the offer. His own programme, twice weekly, networked, guaranteed – at least for the first season. His own small newsroom, his own small team. And Jack in sole charge – well, just the four of them to answer to. Really a very serviceable amount of accountability, a tiny chain of command, especially when weighed against how much was his alone to make. Or break. And Jack was offered this perfect, once-in-a-lifetime chance in Los Angeles. He was expected to start hiring three weeks later. He was expected to take the job. He called Cindy.

'Oh. Really?'

'Yeah.'

'Wow, that's great.'

'Yeah. It's fantastic. Brilliant . . . well, for my career, for work . . .'

'Not just your career, for you, Jack. A big deal for you. Congratulations.'

'Thanks.'

'When?'

'Soon as possible. Three weeks.'

'Oh . . . right . . . that is . . . soon.'

'Yeah.'

'Three weeks?'

'Mmm. So, what do you . . .?'

'God, Jack, I hate LA.'

'I know.'

'Fuck.'

'Yeah.'

Cindy sat in Kelly's apartment and stared out the wide window that ran across the west wall of the room. In her left hand she held a martini glass – emblazoned with a silver playboy emblem and heavy drops of fat condensation – containing Kelly's speciality: vodka martini, straight up. In her right hand Cindy held Kelly's other speciality: a fine-rolled joint of delicate Californian grass, couriered cross-country for one of the senior partners in her firm and occasionally passed on as part of the unofficial bonus package. Kelly would have preferred a weekend at her boss's house in the Hamptons, but the irregular few ounces were a perfectly pleasant substitute now summer was nearly over.

In a steep vertical drop from Cindy's gaze, the Eighth Avenue traffic was a hot metal crawl. Each just-packed car trying to get home before the sun disappeared, hoping to catch a solar-illuminated glimpse of the object of desire that made it perfectly understandable to spend almost twelve hours a day at work – I love you, therefore I go to work to earn for you, therefore I hardly ever see you. Doomed lemmings in an upstream salmon-leap run, home to spawn or die. Cindy's slightly fuzzy gaze travelled out three blocks further west and the river threw a blind of reflected light across her watering

27

eyes. She squinted against the glare and looked out from heavy eyelids, flickering lashes filtering a fit-inducing strobe glow. She sipped her drink, chewed an olive. Then, as the orange turned to red and a bright star slowly became distinct from the setting aeroplane to its left, the low band of thin cloud on the horizon started to break up. Shining lines of neon pink switched themselves on against a background of electric blue. More stars glittered, the sun curled down behind Jersey City, and eventually, with nowhere near enough fanfare, Cindy made out Liberty's torch, invisible through the sunset, a tiny red matchstick against the fat cruise liner coming home.

The light show over, Cindy stubbed out the joint and sidled over to the bench where she was sure she'd left half a shaker of martini waiting for when Kelly came back from work. But the sunset spectacular seemed to have stolen Cindy's drink. She put her glass down and reached for the freezer, had her head inside it when Kelly arrived.

'Cinna! I'd know that arse anywhere. You know, sweetie, most people prefer to use the gas oven.' Kelly dropped her bag, took the empty glass Cindy was offering her, frowned at the joint stub and sat Cindy down. 'Last time you let yourself into my place we were celebrating, right?'

'My father and his Barbie cancelling their Thanksgiving visit.'

'This time you've been smoking by yourself?'

'I didn't think you'd mind.'

'Of course I don't mind. But I take it this means bad news?'

'The joint means bad news?'

'Smoking alone does.' Kelly looked over at the array of empty wine bottles she'd left by the door, ready to take to the recycling bin. 'Drinking alone on the other hand is a sign of complete maturity. Come on then, what is it? You're not crying.'

'I'm too angry to cry.'

'Oh good, no-one died.'

'Not yet.'

'Ouch. So what? Is it work?'

Cindy said nothing.

Kelly tried again, 'What? How bad can it be? Jack forgot your birthday? No . . . You're pregnant?'

Cindy put down her emptied glass. 'Jack wants to move to California.'

Kelly sucked in her breath. 'Oh my God, Cindy. I am so sorry.'

As it turned out, Kelly's exclamation of semi-religious concern was less to do with her distaste for Californian sunshine and more because she automatically assumed Jack leaving New York meant the relationship was over. In Kelly's life, one partner declaring a desire to live elsewhere invariably signalled the end of the affair. It didn't suit her self-view to have to negotiate that much, and spending every other weekend flying cross-country looked like a compromise too far. Kelly often declared that she never wanted to work at a relationship – if it couldn't survive simply because it was meant to, she wasn't interested in throwing hearts and flowers at a dying passion. It had occurred to her that this might be why she was single and Cindy was attached, but it also occurred to her that at thirty-two she didn't plan on changing anytime soon. Kelly wanted a regular lover; she wasn't sure that meant she wanted a partner as well.

Cindy fixed another martini and patiently explained that she had no intention of breaking up with Jack. In fact, despite his irritating concern since her collapse, they both felt the threat of illness had made their commitment to each other even clearer.

'So what's the problem?'

29

'I hate LA.'

'Then visit LA.'

'I don't want to only see him every weekend.'

'So live in LA.'

'But I don't like LA.'

'You said that.'

'Well?'

'Live near LA. Find a little town up the coast and rent a beach house. He can go to work every morning and you can stay home and work and have a cool cocktail waiting for him when he walks through the door in the evening.' Kelly sipped her martini. 'Actually, I like that picture myself. I've trained you well.'

Cindy shook her head. 'Three things wrong with that. One – it's a new programme, he'll be working the whole time.'

'Like that's any different from now.'

'Two – we might not like living together.'

'Cindy, you already live together. You've been living together for almost three years, you just do it in two apartments. And you just said he's never going to be home, so you'll probably have more time apart than you do now. Anyway, you're so joined at the hip or heart or wherever it is you got joined since you were sick—'

'Wasn't sick. Fell over.'

'You'll be doing both in a minute if you keep drinking at this rate. The point is, you say you feel totally committed to each other – about time you lived together, isn't it?' Kelly nodded, pleased with her logical reasoning, 'Number three?'

'I don't like it out there. People talk to you in supermarket lines. And it's so damn sunny all the time.'

'Babe, you're right. It sounds awful.' Kelly fished the last olive out of her glass and chewed it, licking the salty alcohol from her fingers. 'This is a good move for Jack, right?'

'Of course it is. It's what he's always wanted.'

'Right, and it'll make no difference to your career, might even give you more space for your own work. There is that follow-up book you still haven't produced . . .'

'Yes. Thank you. That's what he said.'

'It's what anyone would say. What's the time limit on Jack's contract?'

'Two years minimum.'

'And then?'

'He can come back here. If he wants to.'

Kelly shook her head, stood up and put her arms around her friend. 'Cinna, you're just scared. Get over yourself. Have an adventure. It's not as if you're being asked to do it alone.' She looked round the room, seeking out the empty pitcher. 'Now that's solved, are we drunk enough for another?'

Seven

Dis-Location lecture notes: Mapping the Unknown.

As a species, we map. We chart. Both the land on which we are born and the seas bordering that land. We also chart the sky. Without the star-mappers, those who worked on land – and more particularly on sea – had no reference point for their labours. Each civilisation thought it had learned something new. Contrary to popular belief, many Greek cartographers knew the world was far from flat, long before Columbus 'discovered' America. Sometimes knowledge is lost. Other times denied. Our scientific revolutions of the last millennium trained us to think we could do anything. But the most recent century taught us otherwise. The skills that made us masters of our earth, when turned outwards so we could learn about our place in the universe, have finally revealed how very small we are. So we find ourselves at a crossroads in our subject. We continue to look outwards and we see the universe as never before. But there is something else we can study from out there. We can turn our gaze on ourselves.

Kelly was right, of course, it was just fear. Sinking into the back of the cab, her head swimming in a martini fog, Cindy allowed herself to acknowledge what she was really scared of. If she moved with Jack, if she had all the time in the world to work on her new project, then she had no excuse if the second opus didn't turn out as impressive as the first. She hadn't consciously taken on her teaching work to distract herself; she'd already been teaching when her thesis was published. But the difference was that now she was very aware of how much was expected from her. She'd written her thesis thinking maybe twenty academics might read it. And a handful of devoted friends. Purely by chance, lack of expectation had oiled her ascendant path. Now, though, she knew that every pronouncement she made would be screened through the censor of her previous success. Was Cindy Frier delineating the negatives of satellite imaging studies because that's what she truly believed, or was she after another spot on a talk show? And this convoluted theory about the inevitability of converging parallels – did it mean anything, or was it simply self-reflexive babble intended to get her written about in the more upmarket women's magazines? Worse, if Cindy could come up with these paranoias after four-and-a-half Kelly specials, how many more attacks could a real backlash specialist compile?

But Kelly was wrong when she said Cindy wouldn't have to do this on her own. With only a thin experience of relationship behind her, Kelly held on to the single person's dream: that with a partner to participate in the trials of life, one need never face trauma alone. Cindy knew this to be false. While she loved Jack, she was well aware that her work was her own. Just as Jack's was his. In the middle of the night, in the moment of least certainty, all she really had to rely on was Cindy. Cindy in her own bed, Cindy in her own head. She was very much Jack's partner and he hers, which simply served to make it clear that they were two people, not one unit. She hadn't yet come to a definite conclusion on her thoughts about converging parallels, but while she believed all valid theories should be applicable in any field of endeavour, she had yet to find a way to bend this idea to fit her own life.

Cindy struggled up four flights of stairs and let herself into her apartment. She wasn't surprised to find it empty, despite their plans for Jack to come over that evening. Practice had taught him that persuasion didn't work with Cindy, any more than it worked for him to be the persuader. Jack didn't know what to expect, had no idea what Cindy's decision would be, but he'd been very clear he was prepared to accept whatever choice she made, and he would almost certainly take the job anyway. Having been very specific about what he'd do to keep them together, Jack knew he'd just have to wait for Cindy's response. He expected she'd get some serious drinking in, most likely with Kelly, and took himself home hoping to hear from her by the weekend, if he was lucky. Cindy tended not to make most of her life decisions quite as spontaneously as the first night they'd met.

Jack went home to his own apartment and, thanking the new-building Gods for a sound-proofed home, opened a bottle of Sam Adams, dragged out a random selection of favourite books and started to read aloud to himself. A paragraph at a time, he shouted out the phrases of his comfort writers to an accompaniment of 70s English glam rock. John Updike to Marc Bolan. Salinger to David Bowie. David Lodge to more Bolan, T-Rex guise this time. Le Carré to Sweet. Lacan to Slade. The latter was something of a mistake, edging him from comfort into confusion. Finally he settled for reading *Halliwell's Film Guide* from the beginning to a loop-playing compilation tape he'd made when he was still stealing from his middle brother's LPs. Bad-quality recording and some of the tracks even worse choices, but by the time he got to *Bad Day at Black Rock* he was dulled enough to almost-doze.

Cindy lay in her own bed, sipping alternately from a cup of warm milk and another of strong coffee, slowly sobering up.

Kelly had fixed it. She didn't have to live in Los Angeles. Cindy was drawing herself a future. Pictured an office – a wide, light room with smooth walls and perfect shelving. A wooden table for her desk, looking out over a raised deck and the Pacific beyond. The constant hum of air conditioning units that was her Manhattan lullaby replaced by an irregular surf-beat. Getting on with her work. Watching the tide re-map the shoreline four times a day. Staying long enough to uncover the encrypted codes of a territory largely new to her. Getting on with her work. Maybe she would analyse how the geographical uncertainties of life in an earthquake zone created the need for a new form of mapping. Or what it did to the people to live on a shifting body of land. Getting on with her work.

Cindy reached for her phone and called Jack. His insomniac head allowed the phone one ring before he reached it.

'Do they have nut shops? I'll need a good nut shop. Organic. No salt.'

'Cindy, are you pissed?'

'I was. Anyway, I'm coming.'

'Where?'

'To the land of the setting sun.'

'Really?'

'Yeah . . . I have a plan and . . . well, I'll come with you.'

'Fuck babe, that's brilliant. Can I come over?'

'Do. I'll tell you all about our new house.'

She replaced the handset, felt a twinge in her upper stomach as she reached down to the side of the bed to lay the telephone on the floor, and remembered the other thing LA would offer her. A place to run away from the scene of her collapse, the fear in her body. Something she wouldn't tell Jack about later.

When Jack arrived, Cindy was laid out down the centre of

her bed, half-undressed, half-drunk and fast asleep. Jack kissed her smudged-makeup face and found a space beside her, curling himself round her comatose form, pulling the duvet over the two of them, his spirit punching the air in excited anticipation. And a little appropriate fear.

Eight

Jack went out to Los Angeles after a frantic three weeks of packing, sorting and arranging schedules. Cindy took things at a more leisurely pace, completed a month of lectures until her replacement took over, arranged a sub-let for Jack's apartment and tentatively agreed that a friend of Kelly's could stay in hers – as long as she promised to stay out of the office, not to fill up the place with plants, and to leave the minute Cindy found the West Coast too much to bear. Giving in to a big new adventure didn't mean she also had to give up her safety guarantees.

Then, packed and parcelled into something resembling enthusiasm, she followed. Having agreed to go West, Cindy attempted to change her orientation and do it as well as possible. Which meant agreeing, at least in principle, that the West was warmer, sunnier, wider. Climatic truths were part of Cindy's subject, she had no trouble accepting them. She just hadn't yet given herself over to the idea that longer hours of sunshine meant greater happiness for the human heart. Cindy boarded the plane at La Guardia, vowing she would be as loving and supportive a partner as humanly possible. And if not, then she'd keep her mouth shut much of the time.

When Cindy met Jack in the arrivals hall at Los Angeles airport she noted the thrill of fresh lips. Kissing in the airport and the car like the beginning of their relationship, when they had still edged their way around each other, sometimes blind, sometimes sure, as yet uncertain of who the other really was. Jack looked tired and over-worked already, though she didn't mention either to him. Nor did she comment on his driving – his British tendency to veer to the left and his more recent New Yorker's habit of catching close behind the car ahead was hardly ideal for a Los Angeles freeway. She stretched out in the warmth of the sun-shaded passenger seat and looked about her with genuine interest. She took in the hazy blue sky, what might have been pelicans heading down towards the coast. If she could see that far without squinting. If she'd known for certain what flying pelicans looked like. Noted the palm trees dotted among the pines, the dry gardens of the distant hill houses watered for hours on end by lazy sprinklers. The wide cars on either side of them with pretty, blonde drivers, their smiles Disney-broad. Cindy had made the decision to be with Jack, she was excited and nervous about officially living with him, but, having committed her-self to being there, she was determined to get the most from it. She had brought with her thick files of notes for her new project and was enthused – if a little scared – about starting all over again from a different place. With an old wooden table for a desk. And a sunny deck. And a wide sea view. In a home that was spacious and bright and California-typical.

They hadn't spoken much about the place Jack had found for them. Cindy had been sorting out her own things. And drinking something over the requisite number of going-away martinis on several extended goodbye evenings. Jack had been required to get on with his new job as soon as possible. Home hunting hadn't been high on his list of priorities. Once he actually began work on the programme, home hunting wasn't on his list of priorities at all. He was far more concerned with new-office politics and finding staff, and working out just how much of the promised 'free hand' he'd really have. He was pleasantly surprised at the latitude the new bosses appeared to be giving him – and not at all surprised that it wasn't as much as he'd hoped for. Jack's game plan was no different now than it ever had been: take things at face value, go with the system that was in place, and while doing so work from inside to change the structure to suit himself – preferably far sooner than any later.

Cindy didn't know any of the specifics about their new home. She knew Jack had rented a house outside Los Angeles, somewhere to the north. She knew it was within hazy viewing distance of the coast. She knew it took him three-quarters of an hour, minimum, to get to work. She knew the property was outside one of those small towns that work at keeping themselves individual despite actually being a dormitory for commuters, with the city boundaries encroaching year by year. There had been no time to shop and the furniture was basic so far, but Jack had set aside a room for her to work in. It had empty shelves, one corkboard, one chalkboard, and a wide wooden table as requested. And Jack had promised that it had a view. Cindy was ready and eager to watch the sun setting beyond the ocean as she went to work.

For centuries maps were drawn oriented towards the East – the East at the top of the actual picture instead of the North of common usage, hence orient-ation. The moon might wax and wane, the stars cross the sky in their nightly trajectory, but the sun always rose in the East. For Europeans, the East was the fabled land, where other communities thrived in exotic fashion, different languages were spoken, dozens of them in a single market place. From where cargoes were carried home – spices and silks and heavy chests that opened to exude the heat and enigma of their journey. A star will rise in the East, a child will be born in the East, the water grows sweeter the farther east you journey. This held true for hundreds of years. And then the west yielded up a new continent. And now North American folklore – and therefore the whole movie-going world – fixes on the West. Heading West, going West young man, making for the Western lands. Striking out, not for the rising sun, but to follow its path across the land. A north–south grid is used to map flight, but sunflower bodies follow the light. Cindy was ready to do the same. The sun was just about to set when Jack pulled in to their new driveway.

The table was from IKEA. There was no setting sun. There was a deck, but it didn't face the sea. There was a freeway between the house and the ocean. A tract of half-built houses. There was a hill view and beyond that a mountain view. Then more mountains still. Cindy had come to California ready to go West and learn to love the sun. Jack had rented them a house that ignored the sea and faced east. It was the best he could do given time and money and the constraints of Cindy's embargo on any house that was sited in the official city of LA. He didn't expect her to love it, but he had thought the mountain view might help. Cindy's smile fell from her face at the same time the heavy sun fell into the sea – not that either of them saw it. The only window of any size that faced west was the one in the shower room. Dark orange light splattered against cold white tiles.

Good girlfriend burst into tears, plans and determinations replaced by what-the-hell-am-I-doing-here and this-isn't-jetlag-this-is-fury. Then apologies and promises to move again if it really was that bad, and not even a suggestion that Cindy go outside and look at the stars beginning to crawl over the hill, the stars that, despite the proximity of the bright-night city, were sharp and formed into recognisable, if not readily named, constellations. The over-worked boyfriend hurried

Cindy into bed. The over-tired girlfriend had no choice but to let sleep blanket fire.

Jack was gone silently to work two hours before Cindy faced the morning. She woke to a cloudy day, a blue-free sky and a too-brief, scribbled note of love and apology on the kitchen table. Cindy made herself coffee and watched the mountains light up as the climbing sun eventually burnt off the morning mist, raising her drained cup to the midday east.

Nine

Jack wanted Cindy to be happy in Los Angeles. He wanted to do the right thing. Jack always wanted to do the right thing. It was part of who he was. It was much of who he was.

Wanting to do the right thing was why he'd married Nicole in the first place. She'd had a dream of happy ever after. Jack loved Nicole, she wanted to be married, they might as well do it. And then, just eighteen months after the wedding, five weeks before they had finished paying for it, Nicole realised Jack wasn't her fate after all – how could he be, when Simon so clearly was? They divorced as amicably as possible in the circumstances, Nicole guilty and Jack forgiving. He was also secretly relieved, a feeling which first surprised and then comforted him. Jack knew he would never have left Nicole if she hadn't left him first, his desire to do the right thing would always have kept him with her. Too late to stop him being married and divorced by twenty-three, but still early by most people's standards, Jack Stratton began to do the right thing for Jack.

He knew that doing what felt right to him usually worked out in the end. Of course he had to be clear that he wasn't self-deluding. There had been a drunken night early on, a shoot miles from New York and Cindy, when falling into bed with an assistant he would never see again had seemed like the right thing. Fortunately, Jack noticed the truth just in time. Though it took getting close enough to the young woman to taste the iced rum on her tongue to work out the difference between what was right and what just looked like it could make itself right for the evening. It took tasting the rum. Then Jack remembered Cindy didn't drink rum. So he couldn't fuck the girl. Simple. Lucky. She'd actually asked for vodka.

Mostly Jack wanted to be the good guy. No matter how many late-night talk shows assured him that mean bastard was what women really wanted, Jack liked being the one to make it all OK. If a group of them were going out for dinner, Jack would book the table. He remembered everyone's birthday, except, on purpose, his father's sister – the one who hated his mother and never tried to hide it. He even remembered Nicole's birthday. And sending off her card in plenty of time every year always gave him a feeling of satisfaction. She had left him, but he was still generous and friendly. He wasn't bitter. But he had to admit he felt pleased that the outcome of their history had made her foolhardy and him right. He wanted to be good – that didn't always have to mean nice.

Jack wanted to make Cindy happy if he could, and at ease if happy was not possible. He wanted her to be healthy. He wanted his new job to go well. He wanted to recruit the best team. He wanted to be brilliant. He wanted too much. He was bound to fail. Of course Jack had known Cindy wanted her desk facing an open window with a wide expanse of ocean; he just hadn't counted on it being so important to everyone else as well. Too many people and too little coast-line. Jack was stuck, Cindy on her way and not even asking about the view any more, just assuming. And no view to be had. Not within commuting distance, and Jack was already looking further along the coast than he'd planned. Time screaming at him and Cindy counting on him and the new team looking forward to working with him. It was starting to look like not only could Jack not do the right thing, but maybe he wouldn't even be able to do the wrong thing. He might have to do the worst thing.

For Cindy, the worst thing would be staying in a hotel. She couldn't work in a hotel. Could barely think in a hotel. Cindy needed space that was her own, somewhere she could think without bumping into the furniture. The four days she'd been in hospital were hell for both of them, but for Cindy half the hell was that the bed was not hers. That someone else had slept in it before her and would do so afterwards. That someone else came in to clean, to wash, to dust. The room of her own was the high altar on which Cindy based her most essential requirements. And given that he had forced her relocation, Jack was only too aware that it was his job to find the new home. Five-star luxury, even with a sea view on all three sides, would not do.

Then the eager young woman Jack had taken on as his PA suggested he stop pining for what couldn't be had and take a look at what was available. If there was no sea view within the outer limits of the budget, then there was land instead. Opposing plates grinding against each other for millennia and range after range of peaked and graded and live oak-covered hills spilling out of the fault lines. The way Yvonne put it, Cindy would be delighted to wake up to green instead of blue. Yvonne put it really well, and Jack was really busy. So he opted for what, to him, was actually a better view. A mountain view. And Cindy was a city girl after all, it wasn't as if she'd grown up with an ocean expanse on her mother's doorstep. It wasn't as if she had any view at all in the boxroom where she worked – the most she ever saw when she lifted a heavy head from her screen were the carefully piled papers and open books strategically placed about her apartment.

44

Cindy wanted a deck, this house had a deck. Just not facing the water. Which meant it didn't get afternoon sunshine, which ought to have been good. Cindy was always rude about over-tanned Californians. He could have made more of an effort to prepare her. He could have done a lot of things that would have made the shock not so great and their reunion a whole lot lovelier. But he didn't have time. And he was scared.

Jack was working harder than ever before and the programme hadn't even started yet. He was finding his way around a new city that stretched from Santa Barbara down to San Diego if his 'this-is-your-new-patch' briefing was anything to go on. He was lunching new bosses and dining new contacts. And he had only three more weeks to get it all up and running. Or up and stumbling. Or even just up. He was exhausted and excited and terrified. With every prior promotion, he'd found himself disappointed almost immediately. Jack's ladder theory always proved right: he might climb a new rung of the ladder, but once there the view was always the same, essentially, nothing changed. Except this time the view looked, felt, tasted different. There would no doubt be plenty of late nights when the audacity of thinking he could do this job was shown for the idiotic arrogance it really was, when he choked on his own hope. But right now it looked like what Jack wanted. It looked like what he'd been aiming for since the start. Which was bloody terrifying. And set against that, getting a desk from IKEA rather than a lovely little store specialising in old wood, finding a house that faced east instead of west, maybe not getting it all completely right, didn't seem like such a big deal after all. For once.

Though of course, he was sorry.

Ten

Cindy had been disappointed before. And she had made it better before.

Her seventh birthday party. Cindy's parents were in a good mood, shifting furniture and moving Cindy's father's notes from the reach of grubby fingers, joking between themselves in a way Cindy rarely saw, but recognised with relief whenever she did. In the morning they opened the cards. Her mother didn't complain about the twenty dollars that arrived from her grandmother in New Jersey. And her father didn't suggest that Grandpa Frank might have made the effort to visit instead, just this once. In the afternoon the games were good, the prizes successful. Someone nearly spilt a tray of apple juice, but the tray was held by Cindy's mother and steadied by her father. Who burst out laughing and smiled at his wife. Who grinned back and winked. Cindy held her breath and let the glow of her parents' shared smile relax her little-girl shoulders. Ten minutes later everyone sat in a circle and watched as Cindy opened each present and thanked the giver. And it was a wonderful party and her parents were being nice to her, and better than that they were being nice to each other. Everything was great. Until it wasn't.

Cindy's mother handed over her present last. It was exactly what Cindy had asked for. Vouchers for two afternoons' horse riding. Cindy stood up to kiss her parents, her mother and then her father, squatting on the floor beside his wife. This was the last present, a signal to the other children that they should start collecting their coats and the goodie bags that would sustain them on the journey home.

But Cindy's mother held out her hand. 'That can't be the last gift.'

Cindy heard the edge in Hannah's voice but figured she was safe with so many others there, eager eyes picking up the tone and ready to witness. 'It is. Yours and Daddy's was the last.'

'No, that's my gift. Not your father's.'

Cindy looked at her parents. Her mother's tone was even, her arms rested gently by her sides, she was smiling. But her father's fixed grin let her know that despite her mother's outward demeanour, there was a problem. Cindy knew perfectly well that her mother asked what she would like and her mother bought the gift and her mother even wrote the card – her father simply added 'Daddy' and a kiss at the bottom of the page. But any gift or card or treat had always been offered as if it came from both of them. Now her mother had changed the rules. And everyone was watching. Carmella and Josie exchanged looks. Martin sniggered. Each tiny sound reinforced the belief that was central to Cindy's homelife – all other children lived in happy homes where the parents loved each other and always smiled and the only voices raised were those of the parents against their unruly offspring. Marcia and Greg might argue, but Mr and Mrs Brady never did. Cindy's mother was threatening to give away the secret.

So Cindy made it better. She smiled at her mother and she lied, 'I know. I wanted to kiss Daddy too, because it's been a great party. We're going to get my present tomorrow, right Daddy?'

Cindy's mother leant back on her haunches, her right

47

eyebrow shot up, but before she could contradict, Cindy's father interrupted, 'Sure baby. Tomorrow, after school.'

The world stood still while Cindy's mother considered whether to fight back or not. But she smiled defeat and Carmella had to content herself with her own parents' bitter arguments for entertainment that evening.

The next day Cindy's father picked her up from school and took her to a bookstore where she chose a collection of fairy tales. She was really too old for them, but the pictures were glossy, the pages smooth and thick. Her father wrote in the book, signed name and date in his scrawly scientist's handwriting.

Years later Cindy's mother told her that in the kitchen over messy cake plates, just before the present giving, her father had confessed to his first affair. Or at least the first affair he had confessed to. Years later Cindy understood her mother's bitterness. At the time, though, all she could think of was how to make it right. And for the first time in her life she was able to take the constant uncertainty of her parents' unhappiness and turn it to her own advantage. The sense of freedom and power it offered was obvious, even to the seven-year-old girl. The map of Peter and Hannah Frier's relationship had not changed, but Cindy's interpretation certainly had.

At fifteen she sat becalmed in a bedroom in Baton Rouge. Despising her father, loathing his girlfriend, and bitterly resenting the mother who'd agreed she should go away. Though Angelina didn't know it, Cindy was well aware that this new Barbie didn't have a shelf life beyond eighteen months. It was only a case of holding on. But her new school was another matter; negotiating the labyrinth of high-school politics was something Cindy understood really would make a difference to the rest of her life. New school, new teachers, another shelf of prettiest girls and cutest boys, but the same old system. Cindy made friends with Kelly and with practised ease they found their way into several 'best-at' groups. Within six weeks of her arrival Cindy was settled in and very welcome. It took little effort, just a basic analysis of the place – who to pleasure, who to placate. By the time Cindy left Baton Rouge she was Class President and Angelina was on her way out. Unlike Cindy she didn't know how to read the signs. Or that no amount of shared commitment to deep purple nail varnish with her not-quite stepdaughter was ever going to help Peter Frier overcome his fear of commitment.

There was the occasion Cindy lost her first research grant. After six months' work her thoughts were starting to coagulate into theory. After seven months' work the development company that had agreed to fund her for two years appointed a new Head of Projects. Cindy's baby was the first to be dumped. She cried for a day, railed against industry's fear of change, and then she gave in, re-ordered her papers, put them in a damp-proof box and into storage. She learned that esoteric concepts about the meeting point between actual land development and theoretical mapping strategy are best nurtured in a buoyant financial market. And she learned that research grants go as quickly as they come; the only reliable source was her own endeavour.

She had done heartbreak, she had dealt with relationship problems, she had grown up in a household in which to exist meant to compromise. Cindy made herself another cup of coffee. She pulled on the old walking boots that had accompanied her on much of her travels and put a handful of pistachios in her pocket. She fished a compass from one of the boxes piled up in her morning-facing office and grabbed the fresh notebook Jack had left ready for her on the wooden table, three sharpened pencils silently beside it. She picked up the cell phone with Jack's new office number first in its memory. She locked the door behind her and set off up the road that ran alongside the house. She didn't look back, faced east and home and hills. By the time she had been walking almost ninety minutes Cindy had thoroughly lost herself. Only then did she seek out a café, buy coffee and a dark chocolate bar, and sit down to catch her breath. The café window faced west. The sun was high in the sky, just arcing over to begin its midday descent. The Pacific spilled out beneath her. She opened the notebook to write her journey, mapping the way home by memory as she had done years ago for study practice, deliberately losing herself at least once a week, then checking her recollection on the return, draft map against concrete or walkway or hiking path truth. On the first page of the notebook Jack had drawn himself kneeling, mountains looming from one side, threatening waves from the other, and a cartoon bubble whispering 'sorry' above his head. Cindy looked at the picture, the ocean, her drained coffee cup. Then she turned on the cell phone. Jack was working. She left a message, hung up, ordered another latté.

Eleven

Walking notebook: Memory in mapping? (LA)

Memory is how we map who we are. The memory is the route plan of the individual personality. But just as mapmaking is selective, so is memory. When we use recall to place ourselves in the map of our own lives, we must be aware that we are relying on a dangerously unstable tool. To do so is to always doubt the veracity of one's own view. And then, having doubted, we must note down our findings anyway. Accept that we cannot ever tell a whole truth, and yet continuously strive to do so. We practise accuracy in our mapping, and hope for the veracity of memory.

Cindy walked back to the new house, past anonymous stores and wide parking lots with wide gleaming cars, hot afternoon light bouncing off the fresh chrome, and a bewildering variety of whole-food, health-food and organic-food supermarkets. Not a lot of neighbourhood delis, though. She veered on to a narrow path following the main road, though with a dammed-up stream and more litter than the main route, and every now and then the alternative way offered up a dusty pot-pourri of sun-dried late flowers to kick through or a slew of used condoms to avoid.

Cindy did not get lost, though part of her would have liked to. Instead she found her way back as the circuitous return journey dissipated her anger and the low-slung sun warmed both the sky and her feelings towards Jack. She located the house with a disappointing lack of fuss, and walked into the sitting room, noting with unwanted pleasure the dark scarlet sofa she'd failed to observe in her fury of the night before. She washed her coffee cup from the morning, further distracted by the deep orange glow from the late afternoon sun, the light reflected inside off the hills and through the green foliage into a beer-bottle amber. A gorgeous light, warm and soft, easy to come home to. If she ever chose to call the place home. Which she didn't. Not yet. The walk might have made her feel better, but she had no intention of letting Jack off the hook that easily. There was still the matter of the shock to deal with. Why he hadn't told her what to expect, dealt with the insubstantiality of her Pacific fantasies. And on the subject of the desk, how the hell he'd thought beech veneer was ever going to measure up to the old oak table of her dreams. Her list of complaints filed and ready for presentation, Cindy grabbed a towel and headed for the bathroom. She threw her clothes on the floor, cheerfully noting the absence of a laundry basket and using it as a balance to cross off a wonderfully large, two-headed shower from the pros list. She stepped beneath the massaging spikes.

It wasn't until the hard warmth had been pummelling her body for almost three minutes that Cindy opened her eyes. When she'd taken a shower last night and again late this morning, the blind in the bathroom had been down. She hadn't been interested in whatever view of the ocean-free neighbourhood it provided. Now, though, she wanted any real light she could get in the house. So she'd flicked up the blind before getting into the shower. The shower box itself was raised, almost ten inches above floor level. Certainly it was high enough that Cindy felt another complaint on the tip of her tongue as she stepped in. Yet with ten more inches, and her back turned to the water, Cindy could now see out the top half of the shower room window. The bottom half was dark blue glass, for privacy she'd assumed, but the top half was clear. A big, smooth chunk of plain glass, four feet high by five feet wide. She stood and let warm water wash down her back while a wide, flat expanse of the Pacific calmed her eyes. The dark blue of the lower window picking up the warm blue of the setting-sun ocean. It was stunning. Huge. Arms–width wide. Perfect. Then Jack was at the bathroom door.

'You should have told me!'

'Cindy, you would have hated anything last night.'

'I might have liked it this morning.'

'You weren't even up this morning. Were you?'

'Nearly. Just before midday.'

'And you didn't open the blind then? Too pissed off to let the sun shine in?'

'You might have told me.'

'Doesn't it feel better to discover it yourself?'

'Don't be smug, Jack, it doesn't suit you.'

'Oh, I think it does actually. I think, in view of the circumstances, that just-setting sun hanging precariously above the horizon line out there, I think I have every right to be smug.'

'Only about this.'

'You're still mad?'

'Hell yeah. You should have stopped me getting my hopes up.'

'I know. I'm sorry.'

'And you should have told me about the desk.'

'I know. I'm sorry.'

'It's ugly, it's thin and insubstantial and it's so . . .'

'Crap?'

'Yes. Crap.'

'I know—'

Cindy interrupted him, 'And you can stop saying sorry and not giving me a chance to be mad with you!'

Jack smiled. Cindy smiled. 'I'll get you a new desk. A new old desk. The oldest, biggest, widest, most solid and used and characterful desk you've ever seen. A desk beyond your wildest imaginings of what a desk might be.'

'It won't work.'

'Why not?'

'We'd never get it to fit inside this shower box.'

Jack's tense heartbeat slowed to a far more manageable rate. 'The sunset's good from there, isn't it?'

'Incredible. And it's nearly over.'

'So I'd better get in with you then?'

'Be soon.'

Cindy maps by memory. Since her early teens she has put herself to sleep recalling the pictures from her day and re-making them into grid-reference charts. She didn't bother with the angst-filled teenager's diary. Cindy collated an internal atlas instead, subway tokens and bus tickets hoarded in her desk drawer for reminders. She tested herself against topographic truths, played mind games with atlases. She had virtually photographic recall of almost every place she had ever been – as projection not picture. The only thing she could never remember was Jack's body. In her head the mole on his chest was above his left nipple, in reality her hands found it above his right. When she thought of Jack on the nights they slept apart, Cindy envisioned a tiny scar on the outside of his right knee. It was on the inside of his left. She could not keep Jack still in her head. He filled out, lost weight, changed skin tone, hair length, shoe size. The world around her was mutable but easily preserved, even if it was held purely as a possibility of the moment rather than an eternal truth. Jack, on the other hand, was only constant in himself. And when they held each other, when they made love, when they kissed, Cindy did so with her eyes wide open. So she remembered where she was. So she didn't get lost.

Jack and Cindy in the shower, light fallen into the ocean outside, cool water running on their hot backs, Cindy's hands and fingers and lips and mouth channelling sense-truths to her wide open eyes. His hair almost black, his Indian-English skin a dark copper, his eyes light brown. His legs tight against hers, his shoulders broad, pushing into her arms, teeth and tongue tasting and testing the possibility of Cindy being happy now. Water in her eyes and night in her gaze and Jack beneath her mouth. The wrong-way house a blip, the pathetic desk a stumbling block, Cindy's re-tracing the lines of Jack's body a truer way home.

Twelve

Cindy began hill walking, path walking, valley walking. This was new to her. She was subway girl, cross-town bus girl. Walking was what everyone had warned her against in LA. It couldn't be done, no-one walked in the tarmac city. But they were wrong. There were books and there were tracks and there were maps. Far from being impossible to get away from the roads and the seemingly endless tracts of suburban houses and the freeway bindings, there were many junctions of departure. The difference was that other times Cindy had been in LA she'd been shown the sights by locals who really did believe that the most exciting part of their town was Rodeo Drive and Melrose. Venice Beach possibly. Laurel Canyon at a pinch. But this time Cindy wasn't a tourist. She was staying.

The first journey was a peaceful return to the good coffee café, even paces following the earlier furious steps. It took her almost an hour longer to get there. She walked the immediate neighbourhood on Tuesday, a wider radius on Wednesday. Each time stopping after a few hours, speciality coffee or fresh brownie as the excuse to brake, map the return route, and then follow her own plan back, checking her memory against the apparent truths of the hand-made image. On the Thursday of her first week in LA Cindy tried waterfront walking but gave up after a few hundred yards. The plainly posted signifier cartoons, their guns and guard dogs intimating intimidation, made her all too aware of the not-so-hidden threat that what appeared to be public and open was really private and closed. Besides, for a mapmaker, the hills and the valleys running down to the sea were of far more interest than the shoreline. The beach expanded at low tide, contracted at high tide, and disappeared with the spring tide; up close she could see the surfing scum as the waves broke over her bare feet. From halfway up a forested hill, though, the ocean looked exactly as it had in her East Coast imaginings, shocking blue and sky-open.

Cindy woke with Jack every morning. They had coffee – she in bed and Jack in the car – then, hours later when alertness had fully arrived, Cindy would put on her walking boots and get outside. Much to her city-girl surprise, she began enjoying the walks. She was not changed in a month from city dweller to Beverly hillbilly, but the discipline of mapping new routes excited her in the way it had done as a student, when she'd first started to test herself against her own memory. Within a month she knew the surrounding area in a four-mile radius sweep: the old houses now abandoned, when fire or wind or out-of-season storm had loosed the foundations from their moorings and sent them flowing down the hillside to be caught on a stocky oak or pine cluster; which path would be dry after a night of rain swept in from the north; which creek-bed would overflow at the slightest provocation. She came to understand her way, creating a hand-made atlas to place herself. Re-place herself. She walked herself Home.

When word got round the campuses that Cindy Frier had relocated, she was invited to give lectures, attend discussions, even asked to be the keynote speaker at a high-profile symposium. She turned down the offers. Since her arrival, she'd discovered the pleasure of keeping time solely for her own work. Cindy hadn't escaped the fear that maybe she was, at best, a one-hit wonder, but the pressure had lessened. Her agent still sent effusive emails, but these word darts travelled from New York. Continental crossings may have changed beyond imagining since Lewis and Clark finally reached the Pacific, but the degrees of longitude against which they marked their route were immutable. New York to Los Angeles offered a welcome time gap in which the strength of nagging encouragement dribbled away. Though the exile had not been her idea, and despite her fear that she could not live without the frenetic New York pace, Cindy found she enjoyed the benefits of a fresh location and her reduced work-load. Not that she didn't feel a tiny bit snubbed when she bought her morning paper and the news-seller failed to recognise her. Or endure a pang of professional jealousy while watching a late-night TV discussion on cartographic determination of epidemic causes.

Jack noted her shift in position, irritable legs pushing him to the furthest end of the sofa. 'So how is it now? Being here?'

'Mostly OK.'

'You've got plenty of time to work.' A statement that turned into a question as he saw her eyebrow start to raise.

'Well, I didn't actually want it, not in the first place, if you remember . . .'

'No. You wanted no free time at all so you could run away from your new project and not have to worry about living up to the last one. Not to mention ignoring the major physical collapse you never talk about now.'

'Don't choose to think about it, either. Thank you.'

Though the back-off bite was loud and clear, Jack couldn't help himself from pressing further, 'So you're feeling all right?'

Cindy pushed his concern away. It was a waste of time to

think about it too much. And frightening, too. 'Physically, yes. Same as when you asked me last week. The collapse was a blip. Nothing. OK?'

Jack waited a beat. 'So where's the but?'

'What but?'

'Isn't there one?'

Cindy sighed. 'Don't know me so well. Maybe. I don't know. I'm missing something.' She wriggled on the sofa, her body contorting to push out the words she hadn't yet formed, 'I'm not teaching or tutoring, I've got all this extra time I didn't think I wanted. I can work with it, only . . .'

'You don't want it?'

'No, I do. But . . .'

'But you don't as well?'

'Ye-ah.' Cindy squirmed assent.

'I see.'

'No you don't, Jack. You think it's impossible to feel two mutually exclusive things at the same time.'

'Not where you're concerned I don't. So is there anything you'd like to do about this, or do you just want to hate me for making you move?'

'I'm not blaming you.'

'But it'll come. I'm wondering if I can get in a pre-emptive strike.'

'You make it sound like you're scared of me.'

Jack laughed. 'I wish. I'm scared of me. Of how shite I'll feel if you're really unhappy here. And it's all my fault because I wanted it and now you're stuck in this crappy house with no view. I don't mind you blaming me, Cindy, it's me blaming me I can't stand.'

'Oh. OK. So what are you going to do about it?'

Jack's response took a few days to formulate. He was working fourteen-hour days, six days a week. The first two programmes had gone out and been deemed a success, several hard news stories broken in the opening episode, some juicy revelations dug up and beautifully shot by his hastily-compiled team. An almost-routine was emerging, something stable forming around the edges of the chaos. Jack had time to talk to his colleagues about matters other than the amplified version of a simplified truth they were sending out to the world. The people he'd hired were curious about him. His past. The woman he lived with. And when he said she was Cindy Frier, one or two wanted to meet her. Some knew of her. Or had heard her name in connection with something, a name familiar enough to nudge recall, if not actual memory. Jack's solution to Cindy's dichotomy-desire for both acknowledgement and anonymity, to deal with the thing that was maybe missing or maybe being missed, was to invite half a dozen work people and partners over for dinner. At their house. That Saturday. Three days' time.

Thirteen

Dinner arrived ninety minutes before the guests. With no desire to prepare food for eight strangers, and no intention of staying sober enough in the presence of eight strangers to make cooking possible, Cindy accepted Jack's three-day-notice of dinner for eight and dealt with it like the society hostess she was not. She called Kelly, complained that her boyfriend had turned into a businessman, and wrote down the number Kelly offered from the middle of a complex and pro-tracted negotiation. Kelly didn't cook. Ever. And had an enviable list of caterers across the country.

Cindy had hoped that perhaps Jack's rash choice of eight people for dinner would not come to full-bodied fruition – but she had failed to count on the fact that it was the new boss doing the inviting. And what better way to discover what that boss was really like than to see what was in his home. Not to mention check out his partner. People brought wine, which was nice, and flowers, which were nicer, and Amber the assistant producer brought tickets to the zoo. Which was just weird.

Dinner was a dance, its moves choreographing the trian-gulation of conversation. Cindy noted the movement and listened to corners of talk. There were stories of people who'd moved out here, near Jack and Cindy, each time intending to stay for a couple of years and each time never moving again.

Sunshine and ocean and ease of life sucked in the would-be transitories with quicksand certainty.

'Everyone talks up the ocean, but half of it's private and the other's polluted – no matter what they say – but the hills. That's the real beauty. That's what you want to do, Cindy. Put those walks on the map.'

'And have the trails as tourist-infested as the shore?'

'My aunt and uncle moved up this way forty years ago, hated it at first, ended up staying until last year.'

'What happened?'

'She died, he killed himself. True love.'

Douglas winked, holding out his glass for more. 'You wait, Cindy, five years and you'll be as Californian as the rest of us who only meant to stay six months. Few can resist the lure of orange-tree winters.'

Cindy smiled possibility but poured wine with a worried glance at Jack. Each further conversation insisted Cindy's Californian conversion was imminent. Eight guests and only one of them native to the state. The others had come for work or love or love of work, planning on a year or two and then staying anyway. The four with homes closest to Jack and Cindy were the most vociferous, passionate about their chosen camping ground. Alcohol was talking. There were more empty bottles than Cindy had expected from health-conscious Californians, adopted state or not. But there were other whispers hiding in the wine. There was the usual arrogance of one who believes their hometown – native or adopted – is the best place ever, and the filtered demand for confirmation in return, that turns a plaintive 'please agree with me' into 'I dare you to contradict'. But there was another note beneath. The paranoia of the adopted émigré: 'If I say loud enough and long enough how happy I am to be here, you will have to hear me – and agree that I belong.'

And then she blanked herself from the conversation. It was too much, this deafening approbation of the land. Cindy sat back and waited until she could see the patterns in the table. People moved seats, re-arranged themselves into the next triangle, laid out in graph-paper conversations. The dinner table dance mapping the definitions of her new home.

Jack and Cindy went to bed two hours after their guests left. Before Cindy, Jack would have gone to bed the minute he'd locked the doors. Turned the lights off on the mess and taken his not-sober head to bed. But Cindy was a clean-up-at-bedtime girl. Once midnight was past, her thoughts turned to the next working day and the need to have a clear space in which to begin it. Cindy could never sit still for long. She would begin a clean page and, with just four points delineated, rise from her chair and stretch. Look out the window at the intersecting roads beneath. Sit again, more heavily this time, scratching the back of her head, leaving the research tome behind her on an armchair, her half-finished coffee cup on another table. Twenty minutes later she'd get up again, this time to make herself a sandwich – before realising that what she'd really meant to do was check a forgotten fact. Cindy would answer a call, wind the trailing phone cord around her left hand and commute into another room, sipping cold coffee as she went. Her day followed a pattern of incongruous beginnings and endings, the placing and pacing part of the process. Movement clarified the access to a magic thinking that waited beneath the activity. But whatever scattered state her home and workspace looked like three, five, eight hours after rising, the day always opened fresh and smooth.

Jack cleared the table, Cindy rinsed plates and placed them in the dishwasher – strategic stacking to allow maximum dishes washed, least left to do by hand.

'What do you think of them?'

'I'm sure they're brilliant. Hard-working. All that.'

'And?'

'And Amber's pushy, Douglas thinks he's more important than he is, Rebekah clearly wants his job, Josh finds us boring, Michele finds you too damn interesting and Glenn reminded me a little too much of my father.'

Jack took the empty boxes out to the bin, came back in, locking the outside door behind him. 'So you didn't have a good night?'

'I had a great night. It's hugely pleasurable to listen to complete strangers rave about your partner's abilities and the all-round general wonderfulness of the new boss, the new job, the new programme.'

'Of course it is. They didn't ask about you?'

'Rebekah asked what I'm working on. When I explained about the synthesis of mapping and memory thing, she told me her first memory.'

'Was that useful?'

Cindy turned off the kitchen light, led Jack into the sitting room where they re-positioned chairs, closed windows.

'Only if her dog Scruffy prompted categorical site recall. Douglas asked if I missed New York. Told me I'd love it here in time.'

'They all said that.'

'Every single one of them. And I'm sure they're right. I just find the enthusiasm a bit forced. The Californian Dream. Striving to be happy all the time. No questions.' Cindy looked around the room. 'Are we done in here?'

'Looks like it. Bed?'

'You change the duvet, I'll get the sheets and pillowcases.'

'You have so got the better half of that deal.'

'I know.'

Over the flutter of fresh sheets, Cindy continued, 'When

you left Britain, you knew you wanted to be here. It was a plan. These people just fell into it. And they don't just live here, they love living here. Like they've taken an oath of allegiance to promote it whenever they can.' Jack was smiling at her. 'What?'

'I have noticed it too. But it's what you all do.'

'All who?'

'All Americans.'

'What do we do?'

'Love it. Unreservedly.' Jack moved to the bathroom and continued, mouth full of toothpaste, 'Even those of you who get pissed off with the government or whatever, you still love it. The campaigners against the NRA or the death penalty, they love it. I noticed when I first arrived and nothing has changed my mind since. You actually believe America is it.'

Cindy followed him into the bathroom, taking off her makeup, reaching around him for the mirror. 'Don't British people think like that too?'

'God no. For a start it's not really Britain. The Scots don't want to be British. The Welsh are definitely not British, and don't even try to work out where Northern Ireland fits into that. And the English are tired and fed up with hoping for the best.'

'But keep going anyway?'

'Of course. Blitz spirit. Whereas I'm certain that while you lot might complain about your country . . . scratch an American and underneath you'll find he really does believe it's the best country on earth.'

'What's that got to do with tonight?'

Jack got into bed, placed his lecturing head on the pillow and continued, 'They're the same, only they've distilled that certainty and made it California-specific: the best state in the best country in the world. They move here and they give in.'

'Give up?'

'No – give in. Yield. Cede. Acquiesce. Because it is sunny here and the sea is incredibly blue and the hills are the greenest green.'

'And then they put it on celluloid and show it back to the rest of us in glorious technicolour.'

'Exactly. And we – the rest of the world – buy the image. You guys are all shiny and glossy and hopeful . . .'

Cindy climbed in beside him, turned off the light. 'And stupid?'

'Maybe. Whereas we're dark and cold and worn—'

'But wise.'

'Exactly. It's why you elected a movie star for President when we picked a grocer's daughter. California is just the extreme of the American dream. They have to buy into it. Because if they don't—'

'The whole thing comes crumbling down?'

'Something like that.'

'I love you when you're drunk, Jack.'

'Why?'

'You make such a lot of sense. And you've made me feel so much better.'

'I have?'

'Yeah. Next time I listen to a bunch of adopted Californians praising their homeland, I'll just remember they're only protesting too much because if they didn't then the American dreamers would have to wake up.'

'And the Free World would crumble. Don't forget that.'

'Hell no, we mustn't forget that.'

Fourteen

Cindy turned from her personal maps to those of the area she was now living in. On one journey in the hills she discovered a perfectly positioned bookshop-café, marked it in her own route map. While the book section was so limited that its shelved stock actually amounted to less than Cindy's still-boxed own small library, the café part offered fingerprint-gooey home-made brownies. And the winding trail Cindy took to find the shop gave her ample enthusiasm to indulge once she was safely sitting down in an enveloping armchair with an iced latté and two brownies by her side. In her hand. In her mouth. Gone. She could have reached the café in less than half the time by taking a direct route along a gentle gradient of ordinary roads from their home, but the trail offered oak-enhanced views and the delicious scent of bay trees. Not to mention the thrill of dodging poison ivy. The preferred route also appeared to be working strange magic on her body. Something about this daily walking was making a difference to her flesh, re-positioning her body in a way she wasn't sure she really liked – thinner legs, calf muscles more obvious, small round of her belly floating away, cheekbones still more prominent. While many women might have rejoiced in the change, Cindy was a little disturbed. She was used to her body as it was, had no fight with it. Her flesh was not something she was interested in re-mapping. Then again, she didn't want to give up on the walks. Took another brownie instead.

The bookshop owner proudly displayed in his window a selection of hand-drawn maps, printed and lovingly bound by children from the local grade school. The half-dozen flimsy booklets were on sale to guilt-accosted parents. And visiting newly local cartographers. Cindy sat with the children's maps laid out in front of her, one weighted down with a chocolate muffin, another with a coffee brownie. They clearly drew what was important to them – their school, homes (Mom's and Dad's), the closest mall. But they also included details significant to the specific cartographer. Some drew iconic line drawings of the largest buildings or their best friend's house, others shaded in areas of special interest for wildlife, fire breaks, places where the land was re-claiming itself after flood or fire. The pictures an act of reclamation in themselves.

'Are they that interesting?'

Cindy looked up to see the shopkeeper leaning over her, a fresh latté in his hand.

'Your coffee's probably warm by now. I brought you another. You've been stuck here for more than an hour.'

'Oh right, well, I like maps. One or two of these kids have a really good eye.'

The man stepped back; clearly he'd only expected a grateful smile for the coffee. 'You an artist?'

'Cartographer. Mapmaker. At least I have been. Now I write about it.'

'So you're a writer?'

Cindy sipped the latté, testing the temperature on the tip of her tongue. 'I guess.'

He looked from Cindy to his sparsely populated shelves. 'Published?'

Cindy smiled. 'Um, yeah. I wrote a book about mapping. Cindy Frier? I think you have a copy.' She nodded towards the reference section where she'd noted her book incorrectly stacked with a thin range of atlases.

Matthew Amos nodded, plainly disappointed to have found a real writer in his shop, only to have her turn out to be a non-fiction nerd. Then he muttered that he had something she might like to look at, and wandered over to a cluttered desk at the back of the shelving units. The desk rivalled Cindy's for papers, though not for dust. Clearly he hadn't needed to touch anything in the past year or so. Cindy picked up her coffee and took another mouthful, wondering as she did so about the state of the kitchen that made the great brownies. They didn't taste dusty.

After ten minutes of opening and closing drawers, the man let out a satisfied yelp and came back, an age-crackled plastic folder in his hand.

'You might want to see this.'

Cindy held her hand out for the folder.

'Mrs Antoni's class. Fifth Grade. We made maps. It's how come the kids did these ones. Their teacher's my girlfriend. I told her about it when we were out hiking one time and she thought it was a cool idea.'

Cindy held the folder half-open. 'How old are they?'

Matthew shook his head, frowned at the yawning gap between his child-self who'd completed the original project and the adult who now hoarded a tattered folder in the back of his very own store. 'It must be nearly forty years.'

'And you kept them all this time?'

He shrugged. 'Sure. Mrs Antoni was hot.'

Cindy nodded, remembering brown eyes and a long blond ponytail, a first-year teacher enthusing over Wallace Stevens. 'Yeah. I had one of those. Mr Werber.'

Both smiled, complicit in faded fantasy. Cindy pulled out the old pages of newsprint. Twenty or more maps, each one easily as detailed as those she'd just been studying, each one decades older than its counterpart. She gazed at them for a moment and then asked, 'Look, I know you don't know anything about me, but this is what I'm working on. Memory, the individual mapmaker – how, where, when changes happen. I'd love to look at these properly. Can I see them again? I'll be coming back anyway.'

'Yeah, not that many people come in and eat my brownies right after breakfast.'

'I like them fresh.'

'Morning's best for fresh.'

Cindy left the shop with two more brownies, toffee and plain chocolate. She took an alternate route home, a new path she'd been directed to by the café owner. Who watched her go from his shop window, brownies clutched a little too tight in their paper bag, oil already starting to stain the paper, striding out in walking boots and old jeans. A Mrs Antoni lookalike, her messy bob bouncing as she headed downhill.

The trail Matthew had pointed out to her was far more winding than the one she was used to. And secluded. And stabbed along the way with flawless jewels of hidden ocean sightings. Having spent so long looking over the maps it was now midday, the least appropriate time for walking. Any early morning mist had been cleared by the sea breeze, only to be quickly replaced with a pale wrap of amber smog as the sun heated the already dry earth. She watched the glittering city towers assume their customary shroud, a pale pall hung over the reaching monoliths, reflecting back a diffuse light so that the swathe of land falling fast a hundred feet below her and then rolling more slowly down to the ocean took on a soft-focus glow, stained-glass tints spilling on to the hills. Even knowing the catalogue of ecological disasters behind the colouring, Cindy had to admit it was pretty.

Today, though, it was just hot. While some of the leaves showed the shallow slide to autumn had begun, there was as yet no hint of welcome chill in the air. As she left the road and headed on to the trail it felt even hotter, trees acting not as shade but almost as a canopy, the heat of a summer tent when the canvas is cooker not cooler. Cindy's legs were attacked by scrubby chaparral, while every now and then her eyes were assaulted with the strength of the sunlight shining directly on to outcrops of bleached sandstone and reflecting back into her face. On her journey home she passed only three people on foot. One kid of twelve or thirteen, who had clearly spent the morning hiding away from school and looked as unhappy with himself as his parents would be when they found out. And then another couple of walkers, these ones dressed from head to toe in all the proper gear, a far cry from Cindy's old jeans and Jack's Manchester City shirt. But that was it. No other flesh and bone souls passing her on the way.

Cindy reached the house, put her key in the lock, and as she turned off the alarm she gave in and acknowledged just how much she missed New York. Not for the bars or the nightlife or the famous-only-to-tourists delis, or any of the buildings or the sights or the subway. But for the crowds of people. She missed walking down the street and dodging strangers. Wanted the sticky, uncomfortable rub of someone else's hot skin against hers as they squeezed into the quick cold of the subway carriage. She missed the fat tramp with the skinny dog who sat on the church steps near her subway stop. In the scented hills, in the little house above the Pacific, enjoying the constancy of sunshine, Cindy found herself longing for the confirmation of self that strangers gave her. And so she climbed into the shower and washed and cried and dried and then followed the hillside shadow of the setting sun from her office window until Jack came home and she could yield to the safety of skin.

That night she told him about her afternoon.

'It wouldn't work even if there were loads of people on your trail.'

'Why not?'

'Look at your helpful café bloke.'

'What? I liked him. He makes good brownies. And his map was good.'

'Yes, but he disoriented you. As we said about my colleagues, Californians are different – the new ones in particular. By the time they eventually settle in with the pool and the view and the two cars, they're so grateful for the sunshine and the easy life, they completely forget to complain. And a shopkeeper should be too busy to chat, too disinterested to help out. It's what you're used to. Moaning. Complaint.'

'Oh, New Yorkers complain now?'

'More than occasionally. It's that melting-pot thing. They've managed to mix feeling pissed off with everyone else and socially superior at the same time. They're practically Liverpudlians they're so good at it. No wonder John Lennon felt at home there.'

'And Mancunians?'

'Sweetheart, we expect nothing. So when we get anything at all, we know to shut up, sit back and drink in the good life.'

They finished dinner and went to bed early, heavy stomachs and slow kisses, warm bodies and a quiet, gentle sex that turned into a hotter and faster place than they'd found recently, bodies re-making the stretched seams, filling in the time they'd had to spend apart. Cindy fell asleep with a smile on her face and sweat on her back. Not complaining now.

Fifteen

The fear is nausea-inducing. Intestines protest, diaphragm rocks back and pulls itself in, rubber-band tight, breath squeezes through the remaining narrow opening, terrified to make a noise, draw attention to itself, to the in-out motion of carrying on. Breath carrying on regardless. Body primal, obscene in its refusal to bow to change. Cindy's flat stomach constricts, concave rebellion, taut against the possibility of more that is presently unknowable and yet will become truth the moment it is spoken aloud. Her tight muscles freeze in shock, an otherwise insensible body of individual cells collectively recoiling from both real and imagined dangers. For once the imagined dangers are less real than the reality beneath her hands. Cindy feels it. Incarnate terror. Fright movie flesh. Three twenty-nine a.m. Insensibility to knowledge. One minute passing.

It is the middle of the night. Three thirty a.m. The clock glows red on Jack's side of the bed, Cindy can see it clearly from the three pillows she raises herself on every night. At first, staying over in his apartment, the light from Jack's clock was too strong a scarlet through her closed eyelids. Now she welcomes the ember shade as she falls asleep, it is comforting, since they moved to California it has been an every-night reminder that they are now living together. As boy and girl, man and wife. While Jack has been working late at the office and then later still at home, Cindy has fallen asleep with the light of his absent presence filtering through her eyelids. There is no comfort from the light now. In this moment she cannot imagine falling asleep ever again. Three thirty-two a.m.

She had fallen asleep, half in Jack's arms, half collapsed on both her own. After sex they had turned to kissing as usual. Whatever the vagaries of the act, like every other time-lapsed couple, they had their pattern. For Cindy and Jack the post-coital mouth to mouth was more insistent and pressed fiercer than the build-up, lips and teeth biting at the other, tasting and sucking to recall individual desire, reverse the consuming process of the intimacy, bring each back to the specific face, the singular body, the two-not-one. She twisted away from him several hours later as the reality of numb limbs eventually signalled their distress to her sleeping brain, and stirred just enough to turn – without waking – to her own side of the bed, back flat to the mattress, neck bent at a seventy-five-degree angle to the perfect pillow raise, the shift achieved without either of them really aware she was moving. Right arm brushed down her naked front as she made space next to his deadened bulk. And then maybe she felt something. And then definitely she felt pain. Three twenty-eight a.m.

Sharp, digging deep into her upper centre. Catching at her breath, drawing it inwards in fast panting gasps. From a place beyond the flesh, hurting too much to stay within, Cindy notes the specifics. Upper centre of her thorax. Above the stomach. An inch or two down from the breastbone, then two fingers west to her right, the pain has a central focus. It lies in the gap just beneath two ribs. She concentrates on the stab. Not stabbing. It is continuous. There is no throb. No out to go with the in, just in, constant in. Walks her fingers up from the lowest rib, counts the cage. The pain is held intercostally between the fourth and fifth ribs from the bottom, where the two join to create a chunky bar, heading for the sternum. She can push her fingers through, up and partly under the bone, would make a rib-spreader of her hand, the better to reach the pain. Located. When her fingers meet the source, there is a release. Something unblocked perhaps. Something beginning to be known.

The pain recedes and beneath her questioning fingers she feels for the source. Dreams she finds it beneath index and middle finger. Shocked awake and knowing something new is in the room with the two of them. Something tangible. Hand runs over her cold skin again, back down, then counting up the ribs. This is no dream. Mouth swallows automatically, takes in awareness with silent gaping gasps, brother and sister body cells knowing the unknowable before Cindy does. Before Cindy can. It does not hurt now, she has succumbed to a swoon of welcome endorphins, sweat across her forehead, fight-flight animal scent from her under-arms, bitter adrenaline in the back of her throat. Engaging the brain and taking control through slapped-away sleep, past building terror, Cindy tries again to touch the site. She picks up her hand – it feels as if she is picking up her hand, the dislocation is that specific – and runs it over the skin above her right rib cage. Notes the stand-out ribs that were not always so prominent. Easily counts up the ribs through their cover of not much more than skin, pushing desperate-to-be-ignorant fingers in, and slightly under, the lowest rib. She wonders if the walking has really made her this thin. Then the next narrow strand of bone and cartilage. She wonders how long she has been skinny – and believed it was normal. The next rib. And then she can feel it. This thing that is part of her and not. It is new. Brand new Cindy. She wants to be sick. Throw it up and out. Diaphragmatic convulsions.

Jack stirs, brought to this side of awake by the deafening yell of her cacophonous thoughts. She does not want Jack awake. Not yet. Sensible Cindy takes over. Soothes the fear-girl. Makes it better. It cannot be real. It is the middle of the night. Jack is tired, has to get up early for work, soon for work. Cindy should not wake him. Not now. Not for this. They agreed in New York there was nothing wrong with her. Cindy knows her own body, she eagerly concurred with the doctors, their lack of cause. Understood and welcomed that answer of nothing wrong. This then is a dream, the inevitable nightmare dregs of her New York sickness paranoia, stirred up by the passion, the intimacy, the depth of desire, the resolution of fucking, the novelty of prominent hipbones. This is nothing. Must be nothing. Cindy goes back to sleep. Cindy is sleeping. Three thirty-six a.m.

Sixteen

In the morning she got up half an hour after Jack had gone to work. Felt the kiss on her forehead but stayed hidden in the sheets, hiding in sleep. In time the kiss worked its way to her brain, her trembling eyelids, and she was properly awake. Cindy pulled herself from the safety of the moulded mattress, poured coffee from the pot Jack had left warm on the stove. She sat on the deck in the heat of what was already an autumn chill in New York. The hills were bright, the sunshine, even now, close to hot. Jack made good coffee. Jack made good sex. Cindy smiled, remembering the slow liquid join. Ran a hand across her bare shoulder. Thin shoulder, half a dozen freckles. And bone. Nine fifteen a.m. She was in the shower before she remembered the nightmare. There was no comfort in the Pacific blue as condemning fingers brailled a flesh-fact from her fear.

She stared at herself in the long mirror. She looked the same, she looked like Cindy. Shadows under her eyes from the lack of sleep, hips and ribs covered with less soft flesh than usual, bones newly exposed from the hill walking routine. She ran her hands over her torso. No extraneous lumps or bumps. Pushed fingers behind her ribs. Nothing to feel. A slight tenderness, but that no doubt caused by the pummelling she had given herself after thinking she'd found something there in the middle of the night. Though she had found pain. Searing pain. Breath-catching pain. There were next steps to take but Cindy didn't want to move.

Cindy could not have imagined herself as a worrier. Even when she was ill in New York, she hadn't really taken in the fear. That was Jack's domain, she just wanted to get on with it. There was pain. That was clear enough. And there was also fear of hurt and fear of the unknown. Then there was waiting, and after that, when the outcome was inconclusive, Cindy had simply put it all away in the don't-look box. Leave the scab alone and the scar will fade. After the collapse and the lack of answers, Cindy turned away from not knowing and ran with Jack to the sunshine and far better things to worry about. Like a house that faced the wrong way. People who were too friendly in the supermarket. She could have worried then, back in New York, been scared like Jack. She chose not to. And she'd kept running once she got to California too, up and down the hills and canyons, exploring what had gone and looking for a future way, hidden in present signs depicting the past. Now she had a sign in the present. Something was wrong.

She let her hand run across the rib cage again, probing fingers reached for the edges, feeling skin, flesh, muscles and tissue. Somewhere in there too, her liver, heart, spleen, solid organs, chunky and dark red. Cindy did not know the mapping of her interior, did not have clear site markings for what she knew was in there. She wanted to claw in through the skin, take a spoon and, digging icecream-mouthful bites, burrow out the hidden jewel. Now there was no pain, nor could she physically feel it, but she knew its presence. She had not yet assimilated this new-grown piece of herself. (Cindy hoped she had not assimilated this new piece of herself.) She did not know what it was, this thing she had reached past her own bones to feel. But she knew it wasn't good.

She made an emergency doctor's appointment. Explained to the nurse, offered up past history, suggested recall to the notes that had been forwarded from New York, and intimated some of her night's fear. She was promised swift attention. Heard both words as omens. Would far rather be told to lie down and take an aspirin, that she was making a fuss over nothing. Cindy was not impressed with what sounded like Californian enthusiasm for a new case. She rang off before the receptionist could wish her a nice day. They were taking her too seriously. She hated them already. She did not call Jack. This was too unreal to tell Jack. Cindy could barely force herself to dampen down the fear – of pain, of possibility – she knew she did not want to have to deal with Jack's worrying as well. This was the excuse she gave herself – she was saving Jack from feeling as she was. She was saving herself from having to cope with Jack in pain.

Cindy went to the clinic. An easy drive, further out along the coast. The single-occupant car travelling at maximum-allowed speed with windows closed, silent air conditioning and no distracting music – the modern contemplative's sanctuary, where destination is all and the journey a continuum of arrival. Racing for enlightenment. She parked in front of a two-year-old building in a row of shiny new shops, all promising better love and better lives and glowing good health with the purchase of a new pair of shoes, a new computer, a designer dress, a detoxing and invigorating juice. The clinic had been recommended to Jack by his employers. When Cindy arrived in LA she and Jack had made the twenty-minute trip out here, filled in the requisite forms, taken a basic medical and, on leaving, bought an organic tofu smoothie for each to sip – and in Jack's case spill – in the car. Cindy had commented how much the doctor they saw looked like Marcus Welby. Jack wasn't sure who she meant, his US TV

79

history didn't stretch that far back, but he was pleased to have just one doctor to consult. The new Californian clinic was more like an old English version – one physician with powers of referral, rather than half a dozen specialists and none he ever expected to know by name. While Cindy found the system disconcerting, even she had to admit that the older man inspired confidence. Parking outside the clinic for this visit, inspirational confidence was sorely needed.

Jack's new employers had clearly done them a great favour. She was in and out of the clinic in thirty minutes. On to another hospital, a little down the coast road this time, clutching referral papers and a natural sesame seed bar, no salt, no sugar. Cindy had raced into the café in desperate need of a comforting catch of chocolate, carbohydrate fix, glutinous solace offering, emerged with the closest she could find – the sesame bar was carob-coated. After the first bite it was returned to its wrapper. But she wasn't yet ready to let go of its potential saviour properties, the uneaten bar accompanying her to the next appointment. According to her Marcus Welby lookalike, Neil Austin was the very best. He saw Cindy for all of five minutes. Not quite long enough for her to judge his degree of 'best'. But in those minutes he was helpful and friendly and firm and assured. Cindy liked the self-assurance. She liked that he was seeing her as a favour to the older physician. And she liked that when she'd told both of them about the lump she may or may not have found in the night, neither greeted her suggestion with the hysteria-mocking suspicion with which she accused herself. Both agreed further tests were in order. Fortunately for Cindy, Neil Austin was well connected too. It was eleven in the morning. If she didn't mind hanging around in the hospital for most of the day, he was fairly certain he could find her a few cancelled appointments, get started straight away.

This time familiarity meant the complex machines were simple repetitions of a previous reality, not the true-life images of something she had only seen before on film or TV, pictures associated with a tear-stained backing track or a sonorous voiceover. What was new this time was the absence of Jack. Jack, she knew, would want to talk about it, place this development in context. There was no context in which Cindy wanted to understand this change in her life. There was nothing here Cindy wanted to get used to. Without him she could keep this to herself. Keep it from herself. A few hours where all she was doing was offering up her body to the interests of medical research. And Cindy was very much interested in medical research. It was clear to her that the radiographers and operators and analysts were mapmaking. She had once started a paper on the correlation between medical and terrestrial research; gave it up as something that would need too much specialist knowledge in an area she had little prior knowledge of. Now, though, her body was forcing attention. Cindy Frier as the unmapped area. She was the uncharted realm, place of maybe and myth.

She travelled, not across a city this time, but from one department to another. Arrived with pink and blue and green slips of paper in her outstretched hand and in return was granted admission. She handed over her flesh and bone self, gave it up for eager inspection. Some examining rooms had a student or two; each time she was asked permission and each time she granted it. Of course they could stay and watch, if it would help them, or her. Cindy became a lecture tool, a teaching aid. No-one, of course, was crass enough to offer diagnoses in her presence. She was simply there as the live section in an explanation of how to use the equipment. Just as Cindy herself might make use of a prominent hill or a significant building to explain the practical basics of surveying to a packed lecture hall. Though she did wonder what they said when the door closed behind her.

She gave up vials of blood. Each one separately labelled and sent off for testing. Uncovered her skin for the gel-easy ultrasound. Left the small darkened room and took the stairs to another floor, another waiting room, attendant waiting. Held out her arm for the injection of a dye into her already punctured vein. Caught the nurse's irritable headshake and offered up the other arm instead. Waited while her blood carried the dye through her. Lay perfectly still for the CT scan. Counting down the forty-five minutes, breathing slow and steady, the thin beam travelling her body, each new transverse image cutting right through her. She felt nothing now, with the red-line x-ray piercing her pain of the night before. Task completed in that department she journeyed on to MRI. Took a seat in the waiting room with several others. Waited for a cancellation or claustrophobia tantrum to give her a chance of closing herself into the narrow, noisy tunnel, offering up her body to the magnetic radio waves. A crying and shaken teenage boy back in the waiting room after only ten minutes gave her the opportunity. Again perfectly still, the noise barely dulled by the thick ear plugs she had eagerly grabbed, she was rolled into the narrow chamber. Cindy concentrated on her breathing. On the process. Radio waves shimmering through her body, the powerful magnet stirring her body's hydrogen atoms, the scanner turning the atoms into images. The heavy knocking around her head was thick and close, the machinery tight fitting. She travelled with the radio waves through her skin. Serous membrane, layers of muscle and epithelial tissue, the smooth muscle tissue. Then the cells themselves, the molecules, the DNA that charted Cindy. The atoms located by the machine close around her.

Cindy dressed and undressed. Stood, sat, lay down on

command. Gave up her arms and her veins and ignored the placatory 'small scratch'. Wondered, if a needle in the vein was not invasive, what was? Then looked about her in the waiting room and realised the limit of invasion was an empty question. There were drips and bags and blood and secret liquids, people patched up and people opened wide. The two old men in wheelchairs, slowly and quietly discussing their latest operations. The very young woman sobbing openly, tears and snot and blonde hair falling down her face, no attempt to hide her distress. People clearly in pain, obviously frightened. The sick. The sicker. The sickest. The dying. Cindy was not one of them. She walked briskly. She may not have been wearing makeup, but she had showered looking out to the ocean, her hair was brushed and her toenails liquid red. These people unashamedly wore hospital gowns in the corridors as well as the examining rooms, hers was reserved only for the intimacy of the confessional. She was not one of them.

As the afternoon wore on, Cindy realised that not having Jack with her did something else. She had chosen to drive off alone purely to dissociate herself from the processes she was about to undergo, offering up her flesh but not herself. But she found that being on her own actually gave her some strength. She did not have to look at Jack's uncertain face, his mask of endurance as he strove to appear brave for her. She did not have to hide her own distress so that he would not worry for her. She was among total strangers. And comfortable.

Neil Austin had been right – Cindy was seen quickly and courteously, there were enough cancellations for her to be stalled just once, ninety minutes at the most. No-one asked pointless questions, there was no real waiting, little pain. The array of tests was offered so that her walk around the hospital followed a progressive pattern. Clearly Neil Austin had strength and position, the route his name left for her suggested power and respect. She gave a fleeting thought to the respect her insurance company might have for him and then ignored it as a minor concern. Not now. She was finished for the day, the hospital would call tomorrow. It was four in the afternoon. School was out. Cindy went to the beach.

She drove back up the coast to the nudist beach one of Jack's team had mentioned at dinner. Cindy did not do nudist beaches. Did not do taking her clothes off in public. She corrected herself – not without at least three white coats in attendance anyway. But Cindy wanted water on her skin. Wide water, deep water, rough water. The gentle beaches closer to the city were not what she was after. Cindy wanted sticky salt water and heavy waves to pummel her skin, wear away at whatever was causing her pain. She felt something was still there, lurking. But now it was under analysis. Charted and recorded and marked. The white coats had its measure, her job was to await the verdict.

The water was colder than she'd expected. There were not many people on the beach, tired couples, and a few tourists, disappointed there was not more flesh on show. Cindy left her clothes by the high tide mark, tied her car keys into the middle of three layers of clothing. A thief would have to run away with her panties to get the car. A thief would have to do more than that to get her to care right now. The bright blue morning had faded to an overcast sneer, the muggy heat making the temperature contrast more shocking. Upper body in thick liquid air, legs and lower torso chilled in the fast slicing water, cutting through her on transverse and oblique planes. The waves here were quick, every seventh slapping harder than before.

She walked out until the water began lapping at her midriff then dived under the next wave. The salt stung her eyes,

84

swam through her closed lips into her mouth, twisted sand and thin weed into her slicked-back, water-black hair. Behind her was the land and her clothes and her car keys and the clinic and the hospital and Jack and the house and her work and New York with a third of her life in storage. In front of her was a long, dark line of horizon. Low in the sky and very far. She swam towards it. Over the smaller waves and through those that loomed crush-heavy. A slow crawl: head under, up for breath; head under, up for breath. After ten minutes, when she was tired of fighting against the side-pulling current and her eyes were red with salt, she stopped and turned to look behind her. A little girl and her same-size dog stopped by Cindy's clothes. The dog sniffed and moved on. The girl was more interested. Looking out to sea and trying to spot the owner of the jeans and sandals and t-shirt bundle. Cindy wondered where the child's parents were, if they often let their daughter walk her dog on a nudist beach. Maybe it was the only beach the dog was allowed on. Cindy watched the little girl run after the dog and touched her ribs, fingering the implications. Then she stretched out her body and began to swim faster back towards the shore. Pushing against the current in the opposite direction now, losing herself in target and speed and the strength of water pumping against her skin. The horizon curled itself around and pushed her back into shore.

Seventeen

Travelling out to return home again (Tokyo, winter 1997)

Occasionally a new map comes along, a map that has no choice but to obliterate the old. Past suppositions are swept from a current map as were the illuminated dragons and monsters when the South Seas finally gave up their secrets, revealing few people and fewer demons. The lack of fantastic creatures almost as disappointing as the missing mythical world. We embark on our work assuming that the aim is to add to the sum total of knowledge, and yet often, what we have to achieve first is a wiping out of previous knowledge. New truths regularly batter old ones into submission. Or non-existence.

Cindy was surprised how easy it was to keep her day from Jack. He came home late and was full up with some new story. How Rebekah looked to have found something really exciting. Cindy kept herself in her office for much of the evening. This was not unusual and suited Jack who got on with his work at the kitchen table. They shared leftovers in front of the late-night news and went to bed, both exhausted from their long day. Three times during the evening Cindy opened her mouth to tell him what was happening and each time clamped it shut again. There was nothing to tell. There was everything to tell but she didn't want to say any of it out loud; she was as scared for herself as for him. Scared it was something and scared it was nothing. They went to bed and in a first time role reversal Jack fell asleep before Cindy, who lay awake waiting for the pain.

Princess and the pea and no lump to disturb her night, her night was disturbed anyway. The next morning she accepted her coffee and dragged herself to the office in a sleepy tumble. Jack respected Cindy's work. He would not disturb her any more than was absolutely necessary. A silent kiss goodbye and she was alone again.

The morning pulled itself through the house. She was too scared to go out for a walk. Did not want to chance a message left on the answerphone in case Jack came home early or checked in from the office. Did not want to trust that an over-worked nursing assistant would think to call her cell phone. Sat inside for long impossible hours while breath stopped and the wind outside waited for something to happen. Nothing did. Not even the present. Cindy had pictured a possibility for this day – something about finding a space for real life in this time of waiting weightlessness. With Jack out of the house and her own computer turned on, emails checked, possibilities enhanced, mind engaged, she too might create another place to be. A place that didn't have herself in it. In reality, she spent the morning sitting as still as in a scanning room, waiting to be told to breathe out.

Lunchtime came and with it a change of pace. Cindy at her desk. She had a clean sheet of paper in front of her, computer screen scrolling through ten different map projections – plane and conical and cylindrical, 3-D graphic possibilities and other variations one of her graduate students had been working on. A form of map projection intended to encompass more than topography, something for the layers beneath as well. Cindy Frier as scientific visualisation. There were dozens of ripped paper shreds on the floor by her left foot.

Cindy was imagining a mapping form that would encompass what she was now doing, feeling. The New York to LA journey, from walking the canyons to travelling with the machinery that quarried beneath her skin. It was not getting anywhere in particular, but at least she had removed herself from the place where she was chilled with worry and into an altogether more attractive locale. A position of purely academic interest in which the subject was Cindy. It felt like research. It was the closest she could get to work. It was the furthest she could get from herself.

It was half past three. Cindy had been at her desk for almost two hours. She was not making any progress on her project but she had started to concentrate on two alternative views she liked the look of. And she was certainly moving away in leaps and bounds from her terror-head. But the minute the telephone rang Cindy noticed her hand had reached to pick up before she could stop it with any act of will. Suddenly this call had come too soon.

'Is that you, Ms Frier?'

'Yes.'

'Good. It's Neil Austin. We met yesterday?'

'Yes.'

Cindy knew who he was. Nor was she likely to have forgotten the man's name. Couldn't imagine ever forgetting the man's name.

'I'm glad to be able to speak directly to you, Ms Frier.'

'Yes.'

Silence. Cindy wasn't making it easy, didn't know how to.

'Right. OK. You see the thing is this. We need you to come back in.'

Then they knew something. Something they wanted to build on. Confirm. Condemn.

'There was a problem with the scans?'

'Not as such.'

Cindy considered how much lying practice they put in at medical school. She'd heard about actors working with baby doctors, training them in presentation, how to handle difficult patients. She wondered if she was a difficult patient. She wondered if this man was lying. He'd chosen his words very carefully. Not as such. Yes and no. Maybe. Close but no cigar.

'What it is, Ms Frier, is that we need you to come back in.'

'When?'

'Well, tomorrow morning . . .'

'No.' Cindy looked down at the ripped sheets of paper on the floor, the careful drawings on her desk, the Cindy-possibilities laid out before her. 'I'm busy. I'm working.'

'This is important, Ms Frier. If it's anything that could wait . . .'

'I don't think so.'

There was a silence. Cindy imagined him twisting the telephone wire, wondering how best to strike.

'The problem is, Ms Frier . . .'

Cindy could hear the doctor suck in his breath, how best to say this, which strategy for this woman as opposed to any other patient? As opposed to the half-dozen others he'd had to call today? Cindy remembered she was not special, there had been others scared in the waiting room; Cindy was only special in Cindy's life. Only she could have this conversation, now, with this man, and these fears.

Another intake of breath then a rush of words down the too-clear line, 'Actually the results from the scans are inconclusive.'

Cindy's heart skipped and danced for joy. Inconclusive. The catcher's-mitt of possible safety that means nothing at all. Other than a tiny chance to breathe. Four syllables that in

New York had provided her with all the excuse she had needed to run away.

'So we need you to come in again. For a biopsy.' Immediate deflation of the hope balloon. 'It is the end of the week tomorrow, Ms Frier.'

And there was Cindy looking forward to a carefree weekend of beach blanket barbecues.

'So if you come back – ideally first thing in the morning – we could get you seen before the end of the day.' He paused, and Cindy wondered what new carrot he had to dangle beyond the glorious promise of no pain, 'And that means I should have your results for Monday. It means we'll know what to do next.'

The man was good. Cindy agreed an appointment time.

Eighteen

'Hey honey, I'm home!'

Jack had been calling this since California. For a split second of primary-colour comedy Cindy was tempted to turn into Wilma and yell the news in similarly ear-splitting fashion. Clamped her mouth shut on an unsayable untruth.

'Brilliant day – I have got the juiciest news. Well, the start of some juicy news anyway. Possibility of juice, how's that?'

Cindy nodded. It wasn't a nod of interest. It was a shift of her head, a soft inclination, a barely perceptible moving forward, into what stood in front of her. The spatial acknowledgement of the invisible atoms colliding before her all she could manage. Jack took it for tell more, go on. Jack was wrong.

'You know Rebekah's been working on this story? And it's really not her kind of thing at all.' He kissed Cindy on the forehead and rushed past her to the bedroom. The shower the next thing on his mind the minute he walked through the door. Kiss Cindy, let the water kiss his skin. Cold rush to sluice away the irritation of the drive and wide Pacific view to remind him of how far he'd come. 'Likes to think of herself as far more human interest.'

Cindy opened her mouth and shut it again. Human interest, tears and touching, flesh and folding.

'Anyway, I got her on to a new piece we only just got in. Much more hard news, and Christ, you should have heard her

91

a couple of days ago, she was stomping around and slamming down files and sneaking out for cups of coffee every five minutes, and then there were these big fat sighs to let me know how dull she thought it was.'

Cindy sat on the sofa, curled up knees and hidden clenched fists.

'Then, day before yesterday, she started getting interested in it herself.'

Jack dropping clothes in the bedroom, shouting over the running water. Cindy dropping tears on to her legs and screaming for him to shut up. Dry tears, silent screams. Jack clattered in the bathroom. Cindy knew he was dressing again in shorts and Man City football shirt, his everyday after-school wear. His everyday wear every day if he didn't have to go into the office and pretend to be Daddy. The towel used to dry his hair was not equally well employed on his body. Jack pulling on thin cotton over damp legs, thighs almost dry, hamstrings mostly wet, threatening to rip the weave with every irritated tug. Cindy swallowing back the bile in her throat.

'Some big irregularity to do with planning permission and building sites. The eco-warriors are going to have a field day when she gets this one out. I reckon we'll know more by tomorrow – once she gets going on something she's likely to work all night.'

Cindy looked at all night. It stretched on into forever. Constant darkness and never waking up, because waking up was having to face it all over again and deal with it and be with it. Cindy wanted to be without it.

'From what she's got so far, I think we might be on to my first major Californian scandal. Those hiking trails you're so fond of and all this greenery. Turns out there might have been a lot more if not for some sneaky work by the developers. Something about core sampling and underlying strata?

Your sort of thing really, I should get you on to it too!'

Cindy researching this new twist in her own path. Looking up overnight lumps and bumps, scans and biopsies. Jack combing his hair, back and then forwards and then to one side and then leaving it anyway, because it never went where he wanted it to, because he was not now, nor had he ever been, in control of his own curls.

Jack was listening to messages on his cell phone and shouting the rest of his story. Cindy wondered how anything other than her own flesh had ever seemed interesting to her.

'You know, she's OK, Rebekah. She's got the gall of . . . well, someone with a lot of gall. It must be an American thing. Or posh girl maybe. Rich girls never think they'll have the phone slammed down on them do they?'

Cindy looked at the phone. Considered who to call. What she might say.

'But the really annoying thing is that nine times out of ten she thinks some old movie star's latest divorce is proper news. Still, given time – and enough hassling from me – I think she's got a future.'

Cindy tried to speak and couldn't. Knees pressing too tight against her chest to let the air flow across her vocal cords, fingernails cutting so deeply into her palms that there was nothing to let out but a whimper of pain.

'Eventually she'll discover that there's news and then there's irrelevant trivia. My work here will be done.'

Jack stopped, waiting congratulations or praise or acknowledgement. He left his wet towel on the bedroom floor, came back into the sitting room. 'Cindy?'

She was pale. And, he noticed now, thin. Shaking, slightly, slowly. She couldn't look at him. She whispered into her fist, punching back the malignant words as they dripped from her mouth.

'I've got some news.'

Jack hates her. Hates her for allowing him to come home and talk about himself and be the self-concerned boyfriend he never wants to be. Hates her for not calling him straight away. For beginning the journey without him, making him the bad guy. Making himself the bad guy. And beneath the first fury is another, harder to say but sitting there and growing anyway. Jack wants her to have been more in control. This is her flesh. This pain or thing or whatever, it came from her, did not invade from the outside. He wants Cindy to have been stronger, to have made it disappear. He wants Cindy to have been less frail, less human. Less ordinary. And he hates himself for that want and hates her for being the catalyst for that want and he could never have imagined hating anything about her, despising any piece of her smooth, sweet body, but this new possibility is not soft or sweet, and she guides his hand to the focus of pain, lets him feel with tentative fingers and angry hands and he is scared to touch, scared to make it worse, scared that he cannot make it better.

Cindy does not understand the reticence, the holding back. Does not know Jack is disgusted with himself. Believes he is angry at being shut out. They sit together and the silence is not easy or companionable or even careful. It is a hard silence born of self-loathing and the searing acid of terrified bile. But they hold hands anyway.

Fear forks the route. It is true they have nothing to fear but fear itself. Nothing that is, except physical pain and emotional hurt and loss and illness and disease and death. Of course there are those to fear as well. Or rather these are Cindy's fears. Jack's terror is of standing uselessly beside her. Right now Cindy and Jack are on very different paths.

94

Nineteen

They made it through the first hour. Silent almost. Sun on its slow progression to a southern hemisphere spring, moving away on the elipse of its orbit, hint of chill in the golden haze creeping through wide open windows Cindy wished she'd had the energy to shut three hours ago when she first noticed the pale season-switch was making her cry. Then she had wanted threatening rain and heavy clouds, a thunderous New York sky promising flooded streets and a sodden, sweating subway before nightfall, people rushing home to the cacophony of worn-out air conditioning and sweltering rain battering grimy glass. A city full of party guests up on the roof to admire the storm. Now she would have settled for three in the morning dark, half-full vodka bottle and two more hours of night in which to soak it up. Bed-hidden did not suit this open evening, this quality of cocktail hour light. She was in the wrong picture. Most of all Cindy wanted to be sitting in the thick dark alone. With no Jack to have to care for and worry about and be responsible for his hurt. She couldn't bear the reflection of her own distress, magnified in the silence that stifled their mutual concern. Couldn't bear that it was her body relocating his shining eagerness to this place of stilled affliction. The pain plain. Couldn't bear, had no choice. Bore.

Jack held her hand, wanted to ask questions, force answers, held his tongue instead. He poured wine, drank his first small glass way too fast and then poured more into a larger container, wider mouth, easier to swallow. Holding it down.

Cindy held her glass as the condensation bubbles ran down into her white-knuckle hands, held the glass until her skin had absorbed the moisture and the wine inside was blood-warm, its much-vaunted green astringency turned to skin toner acid with the pressure of her touch, fingers locked tight, jaw set. Skin temperature far warmer than the chill inside could believe.

Jack went to the kitchen, the better to drink more wine while he made a meal neither of them had the will to eat. Going through the motions, forcing another hour round the clock. He washed salad leaves, cooked organic meat, peeled potatoes. Performed the tasks of caring and catering, offered to re-fill Cindy's glass, added to his own. Brought her a carefully created morsel which she accepted with a smile and then spat out the window the moment he went back to the chopping board. Performed the routines of carrying on. An hour later neither was any hungrier than when he'd started, but they sat at the table anyway. Light down low to compensate for the rough set sun, background music suggesting promise but urging panic. Seared flesh and wilting fauna laid out before them on white slab plates, gleaming tools precision-layered on either side. Cindy pushed lengths of string beans around her plate, cleared a series of paths between slices of chicken breast, measured precise distances from fork to mouth and back again. Untouched by either, food and eventually even the wine grew cold again. Jack's glass emptied and re-filled, his fears re-fuelled, the bottle emptied.

Finally.

'You should have told me.'

Jack was shouting. Cindy agreed with every word he said.

But not so he could hear. Not so she could hear. Cindy didn't want to hear.

'How the fuck could you let me go on like that? And yesterday. You left me out of this all day. Jesus, Cindy, you make me look like such a cunt!'

Jack could hear himself. Hear himself make himself look like such a cunt. He couldn't stop, it all came out anyway. The tart mouthfuls he wanted to swallow back that spilled vomit-ready from his mouth, steady flowing fury instead of the tears he was too upset to cry. 'Fuck it! I bloody knew this would happen.'

'What?'

Jack stomping up and down the room, throwing his arms around as if he could abracadabra-wave away the dread, 'I knew running away and not following up on all those tests was going to fuck us up. Jesus Christ, what the hell is this? What are we going to do?'

Cindy looked up at the 'I knew', frowned, didn't understand him. How could Jack have known this would happen when she didn't know?

'You knew this was going to happen? How?'

She wanted to ask what, not how. How he knew didn't matter. She speculated on special boyfriend body-mapping knowledge, the sensitivity of his lover's fingertips soaking in strange truths through their co-joined touch. Pictured late-night confabulations outside the Manhattan hospital room, she sleeping Snow White in the monitored bed, young doctor unskilled in the breaking of bad news pleading with Prince Jack of Man City to do the dirty deed, make the leap from Charming to Woodcutter in one forest-clearing bound. Saw him hunched up late in the office, bent over mystic readings from his imported Englishman's beverage in a bone china cup, pictured the ruptured teabag spilling her broken-bone secrets. How Jack had gained this knowing was easier to think about than the thing that really mattered. What he knew. Cindy wanted his special knowledge of her body, wanted the what not the how, wanted the real not the maybe.

All the while wanted none of it.

Jack bit back the all-knowing just a moment too late. Of course he'd known. In the part of him where all bad knowing resides, of course he had known it would come back, that the un-named 'it' would return until it was all there was, until Jack-and-Cindy was obliterated by whatever it was inside her flesh. There would be pain and blood and awfulness, that was how these things happened, and nothing Jack did ever went right, not totally right, not right without a catch-all, catch-22, catch-up, hell clause. Nothing would ever work out again because that was how it was, he had been that little bit too happy, had taken his finger off the just-in-case button a second too soon and had not kept a good enough lookout, a brave enough stance. And how the hell had they found themselves here in bloody LA with no fucking friends and no-one to rely on and of course it was all his fault. It was Jack's fault. It was his job to make it better.

Jack didn't know anything. Not really. Except a fear that lodged, gagging, in his throat; a tangible terror that could only be dissipated if he turned the horror-future into reality, made it whole, giving him something solid to beat back down again.

'Jack? How did you know?'

'I didn't. I don't. I'm sorry. I'm fucked. I don't know any-thing. Other than that this was my nightmare and now it looks real.'

'Doesn't it?'

'And I am so pissed off with you for not telling me.'

'I couldn't.'

'You shouldn't have been by yourself.'

'I know. I'm sorry.'

'Why didn't you want me with you?'

'I don't know. I couldn't say it out loud.'

'Why not?'

'I don't want it to matter.'

'But it does matter.'

'Yes, and I want it not to be important. I want it to be like all those scare stories you read in the paper, where it fills the front page and then turns out to be nothing after all.'

'Maybe it is nothing.'

'Yeah. Sure. Only this is the second time and I don't think I can believe in no cause for alarm again. It was hard enough before.'

'You didn't tell me that.'

'I didn't tell myself that.'

'I'm so sorry I wasn't with you.'

'Nothing to be sorry for. I left myself alone, not you. I stayed away from me too.'

'How do you mean?'

'I went blank. Let the shock have me. Gave in. I just went from one test to the other. Body doing it and mind put away somewhere it couldn't get to me. I couldn't tell you. I thought that saying it out loud might give it more power. I think we're giving it too much power.'

'Cindy, you don't believe in magic.'

'No. Shame isn't it?'

The self-pity wasn't pretty, but it was real, and understandable. And that it was fuelled by fear, not knowledge, made it all the more sticky, harder to keep a lid on the bloody movie-image fears. Which was fair enough. The mind can accustom itself to any number of unpleasantries, the body submit to all kinds of indignities. But not usually right away.

They went to bed then. Touching light and tentative. Jack trying to hold Cindy in his arms, contain the hurt and the fear in a willing six-foot span. Cindy eager to feel his touch. To let in hope past the scar-tissue defences of fear and crawling questions. Jack's hands on Cindy's skin. Strong and heavy on her arms and legs to reassure her, confirm her wholeness, hard on her back, kneading and pinching, then careful down her front, holding her breasts, her torso, now round the maybe, skirting the issue, dodging the hurting. The two of them willing themselves closer, each one drawing the other back into the right place, right time, right now. Eventually time and custom won out, the brain clicked shut, flesh came into focus. Cindy's body knew what to do with Jack's, his with hers. She didn't need to keep her teeth gritted tight, lips drawn into a fine line, afraid in case more unpalatable truths spilled out. Her tongue could taste Jack's skin now, Jack's mouth, his saliva wanting her, drawing her in. They were used to each other, knew what to do here, on a cool night in warm sheets with careful reach and uncaring want.

In the dark and Jack trying to find Cindy inside herself. Reaching into her with his own body and his desire, wanting to claw her back to where he waited, this side of their future. Cindy lost, map-free and no bearings. Fortune changed but not yet knowing how. Jack whispered he wanted to be in the place where her spirit might be, hold her soul. Jack didn't think he believed in a soul, Cindy had no certainty either. But it sounded good to both of them and for a whole, worthwhile moment Jack is inside Cindy and she is outside of him and he outside of her, and they are joined as tight as possible and they are together and it is union. Just as it was for the first fuck and the last. Purely physical, completely more.

They lie separate again. Holding hands in the dark. An owl calls in the night, there is scuffling, scratching in the trees, mice maybe, or the feral cat their neighbour mentioned last week. Cindy feels her limbs slow and turn dizzy, welcomes the first signs of sleep. Jack opens his mouth to speak, closes it again.

'What?'

'Nothing. Doesn't matter. Go to sleep.'

'What, Jack?'

A pause. The scratching. Distant cars, or maybe the sea, caught on a high wind.

'I'm afraid.'

'Me too.'

More waiting. Cindy prompts confession, 'What are you frightened of?'

'Losing you.'

'I'll leave you a trail.'

'How?'

'Pistachio shells. I'll drop shells as I go so you can find me.'

'You do that.'

More dark. Quiet.

'I don't want to be alone, Cindy.'

'I'm not going to die, Jack.'

'Then what are you afraid of?'

'Pain.'

'I won't let them hurt you.'

'OK.'

'OK.'

They fall, lying, into the welcome small death of sleep.

Twenty

A late night. Early in their relationship. Movie and dinner and martini and sex. More martini. Jack woke in the middle of the night, Cindy beside him, eyes wide open, staring up at the ceiling, dark amber light tracing thin strips across the high white plaster. They were in his apartment, the quieter hum of his brand new air conditioning compensating for the raucous late-night party people of the East Village.

This night, only the fifth time Cindy had stayed over at his place, Jack was disturbed by something he couldn't name. He lay there for a breath or two, waiting for reason to catch up with his focusing eyes. When it did he realised that what had woken him was Cindy – wide awake, stretched awake, open awake. Her loud thoughts had woken him.

'What is it? Is it the noise? I'm sorry . . .'

'No. I don't notice noise. There's something—'

'Where?' Jack sat bolt upright in bed, ready to leap, fight-poised despite nakedness and half-light and his complete daytime inability to even watch an action movie, let alone take part in one. Editing the reality was a totally different matter to his newsmaker's mind.

Cindy placed an arm on his back, 'No, not here. Not real. Lie down.'

Jack pressed his body back into the mattress, heart beating through to the springs.

Cindy held his twitching hand with one of her own and with the other traced a plane about three inches above her face and chest, 'Here. I can feel something here.'

'Cobweb?'

'No. Something. Some nothing.'

Jack wanted to be nice boyfriend, wanted to cope, but it was three in the morning and his heart was hammering his tight ribs and he had no idea what she was talking about. Unless he'd picked himself a mad one after all, and if that was the case then his antennae was completely on the blink, because in the past two months he had become more and more certain that Cindy was as sane and wise as anyone he'd yet to meet. He chanced truth, 'I don't know what you mean.'

'Neither do I. But it happens sometimes. Like a membrane. This thing, just above me.'

'So what is it?'

Cindy smiled, shook her head, looked above her, squinted to a site of no-focus. 'I have no idea. But I think it's something about understanding, about knowledge. I get this thing. It feels like if I could pass through here, this membrane – for want of a better word – then I'd know everything. I'd have the answers.'

'What? Like if you died?'

'No, I'm way too much of a scientist for that.' Cindy shook her head. 'It's more about knowledge. Like I need to ask myself the right questions. And if I knew exactly what to ask me, then right now, when I feel like I could almost get through this thing, I'd get the answers too.'

Jack didn't know what to say.

'You think I'm mad.'

'No. It's just as you say, you're a scientist. I've never heard you talk like this before.'

'I don't do it often. I don't feel this thing all that often.' Cindy stretched up both her arms to the ceiling. 'There, gone. I've broken it.'

'Broken through it?'

'No. Broken it. The membrane, the covering, whatever it was.'

'The spell?'

'Maybe. Anyway, it's gone. No great insights for me tonight.'

'Sorry.'

'No. It's fine. I'm hardly Newton. I'm not waiting for an apple to fall.'

'Then what are you doing?'

'Waiting for thoughts to turn into ideas. Something I can translate to others. It's how I work.'

'Right.'

Cindy curled her body into Jack's. 'Did I scare you?'

Jack thought for a moment, decided they maybe did have a future, picked on honesty. 'Yeah. A bit.'

Cindy smiled, kissed him, pushed her knee between his thighs. 'I think I like that.'

Jack kissed her back. 'Very much.'

Now. Present time. Jack and Cindy asleep in LA. Poles are shifted, bearings changed. Reference points deleted in rash uncertainty. They fall asleep holding hands and twist in dream from comprehending close to arms-length distant. They do not love each other any differently, but this new illness possibility – and its silent death-head outlook – moves them apart anyway. Cindy and Jack carry individual theodolites, each has their own distance-measuring chains. Now two individuals occupying the same space and time, mapping completely different events.

Cindy started with the first pain, back in New York. The searing lunge that brought her down in vomit and shame before a crowded class of under-graduates. Measured the time from waking up lost to the indignities of hospital tests. Trekking across the city, marking paths to previously unremarkable buildings, squat blocks now shining out in their see-me clarity. The end of their journey an inability to find anything conclusive, all the while questioning her truths, her recall. The way she had wondered if it wouldn't have been better to have had something solid to show the medics. A broken limb, an opened vein. But there had been nothing to measure then. Now there is. And now she knows this is worse. Palpable is far worse than not. Before there was possibility and pain. Now there is the potential of positive proof. This would have a name, a history, histology, pathology. This thing demands investigation. She could not stop touching the place where she'd felt the pain, desperate to find and not find it again. Wanted fine callipers to measure the width, depth, diameter and reach. Would have worked geodesic miracles to determine precisely the size and shape of this new excess of Cindy, imagined seismic readings taken from the tremors in her probing fingers. She tried to picture distances. Ribs to lung cavity. To heart. To brain. Kidneys, liver, spleen. And even though she was not completely certain of the under-skin topography, she knew for sure that the distances were too close. Cindy thought the left little toe might be close enough, next door might be close enough. Somewhere else. Plant this in someone else.

Cindy was dreaming New York, twisting in her sleep and missing coffee shops and diners, the too many people and steamy subway platforms, surging forward to the cool carriages, tourists demanding local stops on the express, locals smiling express satisfaction at the interlopers' discomfort.

Followed herself following the paths above and below, backwards and forwards, looking for a cross-route, looking for a way out. No way out but going on in. Cindy could run away but she'd be taking her body with her.

Jack also journeyed in his sleep. He was the handsome knight in shining white armour, charging to her rescue. He would scoop her up and place her carefully on his horse and they would gallop away from this fear. There was no need to stay here, no need to be in this place of uncertainty. In his dreams Jack was all the heroes rolled into one. He was the team star Colin Bell, Bogey dressed in sky-blue strip, Howard Keel singing love songs at dawn. And he could make it better and he did make it better, scored the equaliser in the last minute, held Ingrid Bergman tight and then changed his mind, keeping her with him forever. Fuck saving the world, he was saving the girl, raising the cup, taking it all back home. Too long in New York, Jack dreamed a ticker-tape parade down Deansgate, Columbus Day parade turned out just for the two of them at Piccadilly Station.

Six in the morning and Jack woke up. Cindy had been asleep for almost two fitful hours. He studied her face in the pale light, just beginning to bounce off the edge of the Pacific. There were shadows under her eyes. A darker tint, fading down to her colander splatter of teenage torment freckles. The few freckles which should have meant outdoor wholesome and healthy. They went perfectly well with her cheerleader blue, not so well with the hidden distress. He wondered why he hadn't seen these shadows before, asked himself were they there last night? Did she have them last week? Were they simply the result of twenty-four hours' uncertainty, or should he take them to mean more? Jack realised he had lost his skill in reading Cindy's face and this scared him. He'd watched her at work and in sleep many times, studied hard to gain knowledge from her when she hadn't known he was watching, when her absorption in a task meant he could see her clearly, masks dropped and truths laid out. He had decoded the vertical frown lines, two narrow ridges down to her nose, how they denoted a new problem to be understood. He had seen her bite the hard skin at the side of her thumbnails, understood this as a signpost for help-me. That he should bring her a drink or a quick kiss to her bare neck and then leave her alone. That she needed to work, but also wanted to know he was near. He had seen her chew her top lip in frustration and learned to stay well clear, that even if he was not the cause of the anger, he might still become the lightning post for whatever irritant had distracted her energy. He had lain in bed at night and felt the jiggling of her feet, one against the other, a slight tremor from left to right and back again. He had learned not to ask her to stop moving, but to use it as a lullaby. She could not stop anyway, it was not an act of will, the constant movement was a pacifier, even in half-sleep. After years of relationship Jack eventually understood that Cindy displayed her inside working-out on the outside of her body. She was the perfectly presented mathematical problem, where no stages were skipped and each individual calculation could be clearly read.

Jack knew how to be around Cindy, he knew who to be around Cindy. He had no doubt that she did exactly the same with him. This was what Jack knew partnership to be, an accommodation, a yielding, an intentionally practised understanding. This was precisely what he had not achieved with Nicole. The fireworks and feuds, desire and destruction, were all just part of it. Jack knew this now. The woman who slept beside him with the shadows under her eyes and the too prominent hipbones was the lover who had taught him these things. Cindy learned them as he did, sometimes in alternating patterns – often it seemed that she'd done so in an altogether different language – but they'd made it to this place together.

Jack followed the path of cumulative years and it brought him here. Studying his partner, checking out new lines he had not previously noticed, dark shadows that scared him, and a bloody bitten fingernail he did not expect. Weight loss neither of them properly noticed until last night, bones scraping too hard against each other. The rest – work, friends, money, family, his programme, her project – was not separate from the two of them, it all just taken a fresh-shuffled place in the current order. There was always a current order, changing daily, hourly. Right then, the only next thing to do was to watch Cindy. As was the thing after that. And the thing after that. He waited as she breathed in and out. His tears were fear and loss. He wondered if it was possible that one outweighed the other, and then he didn't want to know.

Morning began. Neither was ready for it. Cindy pulled herself back from vertiginous sleep, Jack called in to work. They should get on with whatever they were doing yesterday, take this as an opportunity not to let up just because the boss was too busy to come in. Rebekah wanted to talk to Jack about her story. Jack was encouraging and non-committal. His lack of enthusiasm was simply another spur to get her going. She snarled at the telephone and clambered over his indifference, the better to haul herself up the team ladder. They drove to the doctor's office together, holding hands on the steering wheel.

Twenty-one

They have said it is likely to hurt. Cindy is not yet used to the hospital's 'may sting a little', 'sharp-stick' lies. But given an acknowledgement that there is pain involved in this process, she knows to expect more than 'maybe hurt'. Neil Austin explained the procedure he'd ordered for her. Carefully and with reference to two of the scans taken the day before yesterday, he talked Cindy and Jack through his reasons for this biopsy. The reasons were accompanied by words such as suspected and possible. Cindy heard these words but brushed them aside. It was the next sentence she was interested in. The sentence with shadow and tumour as subject nouns. That sentence did not come. Neil Austin was hedging his bets, taking circumspect glances at a maybe possibility. He did not want to commit himself yet. He did not want to commit Cindy yet. She and Jack followed the nurse to another room.

The nurse again explained the procedure that was to come. That there was likely to be a 'degree of discomfort'. Cindy wanted to ask both the nurse and the new doctor now in the room with her if they knew this from fact or merely hearsay. But she was wearing a regulation gown of papery over-washed cotton, tied at the back of her neck and flapping open against her goose-bumped skin. Jack was sitting silently against the wall, trying to stay out of the way, conscious that most people in the waiting room were waiting alone. That his request to go into the treatment room with Cindy was met with a raised eyebrow of suspicion. He was looking over at Cindy, a curtain rail between them, knowing that at any moment the curtain would be pulled across and he would be shut out just as firmly as if he had been left down the corridor. But he was there. And he could see her, she him. If necessary he would rip the curtain aside, pick her up and run away. The possibility of rescue better than nothing.

The two other women in the room were well dressed. The doctor had a white coat on certainly, but it was left open over a smooth tailored suit of soft grey silk. She did not look like a woman who ironed her own clothes. Her hair was blow-dried sharp, the curl that would later creep out would not arrive until well after the working day. Her shoes seemed made for lunch rather than running from one medical crisis to the next. But then this woman did not need to run, crises came to her. They arrived worried and temperamental, afraid of the next moment, with disarrayed hair and tense faces. In contrast to the people she sees daily, this doctor was calm and patient. She was about the same age as Cindy. Cindy wished her both older and wiser, younger and quicker. She wanted insightful experience coupled with youthful vigour, wise counsel and cutting-edge audacity. Of course this woman had a life of her own. Cindy knew better than to take topography as fact. Maybe the doctor had relationship troubles at home, a demanding child or aged parent to cope with, a lonely bed and nights wondering where she went wrong. Cindy knew nothing of her life, the woman knew only Cindy's notes, she was the biopsy specialist, a craftswoman cutting and splicing the narrowest sections of tissue. It was this woman's job to cut carefully into Cindy, taking out a fraction of almost nothing in the hope it would explain everything. Later, with further help there would be interpretation, an extrapolation of history from histology, prognosis from pathology, suggestions to the supervising physician. For the moment this doctor's task was to make a perfect minute incision in Cindy's body and cut away a sample of the inconclusive flesh. Cindy wished she would do up the buttons of her coat.

The nurse was a few years older than both of them, heavier in body, but still crisply direct in blue and white trouser suit. She may have been less obviously sleek and seeming sweeter than her boss, but Cindy knew about nurses. The public image of vocational angel masking the hard fact that watching death and mopping blood and cleaning pus and tidying up after the messes of others creates not the gentle mother of myth, but a business woman who tasks in flesh. There are those, of course, who take the job home with them, who suffer along with the patients and relatives. The ones with the nervous breakdowns and forced early retirements, who still believe it is possible to save the world one by one. But maybe not this nurse. She looked too comfortable. Neil Austin explained that the doctor was skilled and adept. Cindy should be pleased she made herself available at such short notice. Two days ago Cindy would have been appalled that something as threatening as a tailor-suited woman in an unbuttoned white coat holding a needle-scalpel ready for her innocent body should have had pleasing connotations. But this was not two days ago, this was today, her body was no longer innocent, and Neil Austin had asked her to trust him. Cindy trusted him. She chose to do so. It was the choice of no choice.

And then both the nurse and the doctor were assuring her that it would all be over very quickly. That the local anaesthetic was the worst part. Cindy would have questioned their choice of 'discomfort' as a descriptive term, but half-naked, faced with a smiling wall of self-confident expertise, she did not feel very much like standing up to the tailored women's euphemisms. She did not feel very much like standing up. Running from the room screaming 'get me out of here' maybe, but not standing up to the weight of the medical profession and its absurd desire to under-play every invasive action with a preparatory lie.

The extensive preparations reminded Cindy of when she had her ears pierced. Cindy and Kelly had fallen through the fashion crack and both were determined to make up for lost time. In Cindy's bedroom. After school. With nothing to numb the pain but a few ice-cubes. And the vodka martini the ice sat in. Kelly held the ice against her ear until she could no longer feel the cold burn, then Cindy handed her the burnt cork to place at the back of her earlobe. Cindy held the needle in her hand, pushed it against the lobe. Saw Kelly's eyes flicker. Then the earlobe stretched into her hand, it was something separate from Kelly, a single piece of flesh and not her friend. Skin and flesh and skin again. Cindy pulled the needle out the other side and pushed the little gold stud through the hole. One yelp from Kelly and the butterfly was secured on the back. The next ear was swifter and easier. Cindy was a pro, hadn't even squirmed at the faint pop as the needle pushed out the second layer of skin. Cindy had done it. Unfortunately Kelly wasn't to add piercing to her own list of skills. Southern Barbie came home early, took one look at Kelly's burning ears and put both girls in the car, driving Kelly home immediately. She stopped off at the mall on the way home, marched Cindy to the jeweller and had her common-law stepdaughter pierced then and there. Cindy remembered her fear that day in the mall, how the Barbie had held her hand. Reached out and took her hand even though it wasn't offered, would never have been given if she'd asked. The man had said 'just a little discomfort' and he lied because that was his job and what all the mothers and the teenage boyfriends and the estranged fathers were paying him to say, and Cindy found she was glad to have a hand to hold through the repetitions of tight grip and crunch and then the throb of bloodless pain.

She wanted to hold Jack's hand but he was five feet away, behind the now-pulled curtain. The nurse was holding her hands. Cindy was laid out on the narrow bed, both arms above her head, resting slightly on her left side, a firm pillow behind her back to angle her body better for the doctor's aim. They had measured and calculated, the doctor would use the ultrasound to guide the needle to the right place. The nurse was stroking her hands. Cindy wondered if maybe she had misjudged the woman. Maybe she was soft-nurse, break-down-nurse under the crisp blue and white. Then the doctor said, 'OK, I'm ready' and the nurse stopped stroking her hands and grabbed them both tight in a vice grip so Cindy couldn't move and she realised she'd been conned, was being held down, the nurse was actually holding her down, and the needle slipped inside her. Cindy let out a moan. Holding her body still as directed, her breath steady as possible, still she let out an involuntary gasp through gritted teeth. Of course it hurt. The local had done its work but this invasion was more theoretical. The needle was hunting. Searching to cut and suck out a piece of her. Something Cindy had made within herself.

The needle slides in. Straight through the layer of skin, pushing down until the epidermis gives way. There is a swift, almost silent pop as the skin breaks and then it is into fat. Cindy is lean enough, leaner than ever, but still there is a narrow line of bright yellow globules covering the next layer. The needle is a fine drill. It is carrying on down. Through the chest wall, muscle and cartilage. Narrow, unimportant blood vessels are no match for its drive, swept out of the way, crumpling beneath the steel force. Then it meets the target. New flesh, new body. Not foreign but fresh, just-made. A new piece of Cindy that is younger than the rest of her. The doctor references the ultrasound, decides to push just half a millimetre further. Human judgement and expensive technology combine to calibrate the precise point of enough. The needle holds now. Slices soft and sucks in, pulls Cindy out of herself. She finds it is the retreat that hurts most, scraping against the already bruised body, bashing newly severed blood vessels, pulling at the torn skin. Cindy feels the unnatural movements of blood and muscle and tissue, the needle is shifting her uniquely sited Cindy-arrangement of molecules and atoms against their will, and the cellular displacement translates to her mapmaker's brain as pain, regardless of what the local anaesthetic might have promised.

Meanwhile, the top layer of outer flesh may be numbed, but her insides are not used to invasion. A dull ache begins, sliding up from Cindy's chest, through her side and deep into her shoulder. They had told her it might hurt in her shoulder. It made no sense when they said so, and less now that she feels it. But the pain is definitely there. Then the doctor holds up the needle, triumphant. They tell Cindy she is a good girl and just another two to go. Three times in total the doctor breaks through unwilling skin, each time watching carefully on the ultrasound, measuring for distance. Measuring for disease. The doctor's technique is faultless. This is what she does most days, entering bodies with ease and precision. Most days this doctor goes home and does not even think about the five or six quite dangerous procedures she has performed that day. Occasionally, though, she looks at her hands and prays nothing will ever happen to damage her concentration or her skill. Those are the days she drinks water with her dinner instead of wine.

Then the procedure is over. Cindy is sent upstairs to a quiet room to rest. The immediate pain eased, the dull ache increased.

When she has dozed a little and accepts a glass of water, feels easy enough to sit up, blood pressure and pulse are taken, the fine needle incisions dressed, she is declared ready to go home. Jack can take her home. They will have the results on Monday. Though she does not say, she is still a little shaken, surprised by the pain and surprised by the strength of the nurse's grip on her wrists. She wants her own clothes and she wants her own bed and she wants Jack.

She also wants none of this to be happening. But Cindy has already started down the path. There is no turning back at this point.

Twenty-two

Jack needed to do something. He offered a back rub, a foot rub, music or TV. Or silence. He offered to stay in or go out. Offered to offer. Cindy felt silly. It was five in the afternoon, there was nothing wrong with her, it was only a few small holes. Bruised and a little bloody but not that big. Though they were holes. Real holes in her own body. And a dull ache from her centre, through her back and up through her shoulder. Instructions to take it easy. Cindy tracked the ache that, as she followed it, turned from dull thud to painful twist, and then she gave in. The sheets were clean, Jack tidied the room they left in such a hurry that morning, made it look good. Welcoming. Cindy noticed she was tired. And hurting. And really quite small. She climbed gratefully into bed. She would be babied, read magazines, eat chocolate and pistachios. She had permission to play patient. Jack took care and was quiet, the good boyfriend. They loved each other. There was nothing much to say. This was waiting.

Cindy was soft in clean white and starting to sleep, Jack closed the curtains, left the room, the door ajar. He would be there in a moment, she only had to call. She fingered the dressing, a scab already forming beneath. Touched the bruises they'd left behind. It felt like a badge, a medal. The first scar.

Cindy slept and Jack sat in the kitchen. He picked at the fraying seam on his old shorts – so old that the logo, which was once a byword for cool go-getting spirit, had now become a signifier of all things wrong with the global inter-nation. Jack Stratton, newsgatherer par excellence and well aware of the state of Third World sweatshops, didn't even wear these shorts to walk down to the shops any more. But he did wear them at home. When he needed to. When time-softened clothes and a washed-out sky blue were the only reasons for reaching into a drawer. Cindy had wanted him to throw them out when he was packing for LA. He'd refused, fearful that he might need them, that easy comfort would be required in a new job with late nights and hard hours. Even with his unvoiced worries about living together, a slight con-cern that Cindy's proprietary attitude to his shorts might stretch into the rest of their shared days, he had still assumed any trouble would come from the office. He pulled at the hanging thread and wondered if it was naivety or bravado that had stopped him imagining trouble might come from home instead.

Cindy turned in bed, tried to rest on her side, arm beneath her as usual, disturbed the thin dressing over the new side wound and rolled again on to her back. Nearly woke, reached out for Jack, then retreated to the safety of sleep before his absence could equate with their present knowledge.

Jack quietly lifted the pot to make coffee, emptied cold liquid and old grounds, then put it back down. Opened and closed cupboards, drawers. Shone a welcoming light on the contents of the fridge and closed the door. He ripped open a box of tortilla chips, reached for a jar of salsa and then stopped himself. He didn't want salsa. He probably didn't want food at all. Maybe it was only alcohol he wanted. Dope. Coke. Something to either take the edge off or add a new one of its own. Jack studied the tortilla chips, broke one in his hand, held it to his nose, his lips. Nothing biting. Certainly his

twisted stomach wasn't hungry, and if his mouth wanted anything it was maybe chips and curry sauce. It certainly wasn't
whole grain natural blue tortilla chips, fair trade organic salsa.
There were other tastes, saliva forming, lips licking. Chicken
kebab, extra chillies. Fray Bentos meat pie. His mother's
home-made gravy, home-made with Bisto powder from a
box in the pantry. The food of his childhood and youth. The
entirely un-English food of his grandmother's kitchen, last
tasted when he was ten, before she died and his mother took
her ashes home alone. Two women alone. The box of non-
sense his team in New York had bought him once as a gift
from an outrageously over-priced British shop in the Village.
Presented it to him with pride in their accomplishment, even
if his editor did have to add that they could tell why the Brits
had been losing the war if this was the stuff they'd been
brought up on. Losing the war until America strode in to
make it all better.

Cindy turned on to her left side, rested her aching ribs
against Jack's pillow, burrowed her face into the smell of his
head, kept sleeping. Hiding.

Jack turned his home thoughts to work. Better than thinking about Cindy. Better than worrying about Cindy. Better
than bursting into wrenching tears from fear for Cindy. Fear
for Jack. He looked at his cell phone and pictured himself
turning it on. Taking the messages, checking his computer for
emails. Imagined the process and left the follow-through. He
stood two minutes in front of the machine, blinking in time to
the fast-flashing lights on the answerphone, and watched his
fist reach out, threatening to pummel the light, then flower
into careful fingers, turn the sound down, switch off the
ringer on the telephone. He could not bring himself to actually pull the plug, acknowledged that a part of him still needed
to maintain contact with the office. Umbilical to some other

safety. He just couldn't quite summon up the work ethic. He opened the huge cold American fridge for a small cold American beer. Took out the over-chilled, under-strength brew and wished for himself the comfort of a bitterly damp night and a smoky room and some stupid pub quiz where all that mattered was the correct order of Henry's wives. Divorced beheaded died, divorced beheaded survived. Felt himself bite into the sticky sweet of his grandmother's jellabees. Teeth and tongue recoiling at the excess sugar syrup, little boy mouth wanting more anyway, then still another. Wishing taste could make it better, the full cupboards seemed empty. Jack walked his beer into the shower, watched the lazy Pacific roll in and out, the moon's gravity its only concern. The big wide Pacific ignoring him as he let half a dozen tears fall to the bottle in his fist. White knuckles, salt condensation, serious blue.

Twenty-three

Waiting for results. Cindy felt sick. All the time. The silent irritation of uncertainty at the back of her stomach became a legion of anxious butterflies, moths, bats, churning digestive juices and meals uneaten. She couldn't eat, there was no room for food in there anyway, not with all the flying creatures, but then agreed to eat to keep Jack happy. And once she started she couldn't stop. Wasn't hungry, found it all tasteless, but crammed it in regardless, the stodgier the better, chunks of bread and potatoes, heavy foods, thick and grey, trying to plaster over the fear. She wanted to cry all the time, but knew that if she gave in to the fear-tears she wouldn't be able to stop. There was nothing to halt this anxiety except Neil Austin telling her that there was nothing wrong. Not nothing found, but nothing wrong. Until she heard that, no amount of probabilities and statistics and assurances would make it better. Because Cindy did not believe there was nothing wrong. Somewhere inside she had followed a cellular path to unpleasant knowledge, she simply awaited confirmation and analysis. And yet, even while she waited for the bad, she tried to keep the tiny kite of hope flying in the gales of fright that were knocking her about, waking her bruised from dreams of bad news.

Waiting for results. Not his own, though. Jack was clear about this. He was waiting for Cindy's news. Her news was both his news and something entirely separate. They were not one. They were two very much joined but they were not one. Cindy's screams – silent, passive, smiling – taught him that. He stood one remove from the epicentre. Jack was disappointed with this awareness. He admitted to himself that he'd enjoyed the single entity couple he and Cindy had seemed to create since moving to LA. They had been thrown more into each other's company, rested on each other heavier than before. Jack no more believed in two-as-one than Cindy, but he had liked playing it for the past few months. In the light of the current anticipation their outlines had grown bolder. Jack was not as certain as Cindy that the results would bring bad news. Not that she had told him her fears directly, Cindy would not give magic to her concerns by speaking them aloud, but he knew she was hibernating, getting ready for going under, building up her strength for what was to come. The weekend was immeasurably long. Jack's skin was stretched taut over electric nerves, brittle bones.

The note was pinned in the middle of Cindy's noticeboard, lit with a neon glow of apprehension, reminding her to return to the physician's office on Monday afternoon. The results would be in. The wait was impossible. And regardless, it began. Cindy tried to get on with her own work, cleared her desk, made fresh piles of paper, typed up notes, added new colours to her whiteboard. And when the ordering was complete, the make-work, fake-work finished, she sat at the desk. Wrote half a page. Began a new page. Started a diagram, a mapping potential. Tried another page. This time a more specific route from needle to shadow, shadow to truth. She stopped, mid-word. Tried to analyse her reaction. Other than the new possibility of unwanted, unwarranted flesh, everything was as normal. Except that Cindy couldn't quite breathe properly, her lungs didn't seem to be able to take in air, the terror coils in her stomach appeared to have swollen and now took up space usually reserved for oxygen, she was panting half the time, taking long, slow intentional breaths the other half. She felt dreadful. Full of dread. This was all she felt. She didn't know how to feel anything else. And yet she kept going, looked the same if a little thinner, talked the same, smiled the same. And it was not even false, forced. It was simply the other half of Cindy. One Cindy living in the world, while real Cindy waited it out in the air-raid shelter beneath the mask, the world shrinking around her, caving in on itself until there was nothing else to think about, nothing else to understand. And a wide weekend to wait.

The note pinned to her board was a summons to the Principal's office. But Cindy didn't know what she had done wrong. She didn't know how she had been found out either. Sitting outside the Principal's office at fifteen, called up for taking yesterday morning off to go and stand around at the mall with Kelly, no money and nothing to do, but far better to do their nothing there than in the classroom where they were supposed to be. But fifteen-year-old girls stand out on a Tuesday morning and they were spied on and reported by Mrs Dufresne, the history teacher. Each girl called in to the office alone, no chance to go over their story. Kelly first and then Cindy watching Kelly going home with her mother, Mrs O'Connell silently marching ahead, Kelly dragging her feet down the street, five tearful paces behind. It had taken maybe half an hour from Kelly's call to go to the Principal's office until Cindy had seen Kelly and her mother walking away. But Cindy had been called in at ten thirty and now it was almost lunchtime. She'd been waiting for ninety minutes. Every now and then Mr Gibson would go in or out of his office, barely glancing at Cindy, not saying a word to her.

Teachers and students walked past, registering slight surprise or smirking interest, came to the office door, knocked, entered. It was just a door. In and out, out and in. But not to Cindy. To Cindy it was the yawning chasm of her fate.

And of course she knew what was going on. She was well practised in the art of pupil-teacher manipulation. She knew Mr Gibson keeping her there was part of the punishment. She'd happily have told the truth – it would have been a relief to re-live the dull three hours they'd spent at the mall, sharing a milkshake and regular bag of cold fries – but stuck here, outside the door, all Cindy was capable of contemplating was the angle of Kelly's head as she walked down the street behind her mother. And what her own parents would say. There was a brief moment when she wondered if she might still turn this to her advantage, if there was any mileage left in the 'broken family' routine. But even Cindy gave that thought little space. Given that this was the third time she'd waited outside Mr Gibson's door in as many weeks, she was fairly certain that confused and fucked-up teenager wasn't likely to cut it with her newly in-love father. And even less likely to win points with the Barbie who had bailed her out last week and lectured her father on how they should be lenient with Cindy. Talked him round until he finally agreed Cindy wasn't grounded forever and yes, it probably was just letting off steam and getting used to a new place. Talked him round until he left the room and she turned to Cindy, cat-eyed and spitting how she knew exactly what was going on and Cindy could forget it right now if she thought acting out was going to make Daddy get rid of this Barbie. In fact if anyone was going it would be Cindy. One more time and she'd be right back on the next plane to New York. And no-one needed to point out that Hannah Frier wouldn't be at Newark with a welcome home bouquet. The Barbie was just looking for an excuse to ship

Cindy back to New York and her equally fucked-up mother. All Cindy needed to do was give it up. Eventually she made it into Gibson's office, there was a storm and Cindy made it through. Took the Barbie shouting and the Daddy threats and in return made all the right promises, apologies, downcast eyes. Then she re-made herself into cheerleader queen, someone for her father to be proud of. At least that way she would get to stay and be a thorn in the Barbie's side.

Now, though, there was no Daddy to placate, no Barbie to piss off. She had no choice but to do as she was told, come when called. In the meantime, she was sitting outside the Principal's office. And Cindy wondered too if maybe part of her didn't get off on all the drama of the waiting and the meetings and the tests and the telling, didn't find some of it sickly thrilling. She'd spent an entire childhood as the rebellious one. While acting cheerleader-perfect she hadn't truly considered herself 'part of' anything, hadn't wanted to, but for the easy grease the pretence gave her life. She was used to being singled out, sent for, given bad news. In the middle of another sleepless night, with her stomach churning and hands shaking, Cindy recognised that she knew this feeling well. That she was more practised at feeling this way than she was at being fêted and accoladed and showered with praise. And she wondered if maybe she had made this up. Created a new little drama for herself. Looked back and asked if perhaps she and Kelly hadn't taken those mornings off school, not for the dull joy of hanging out at the mall, but the agonising thrill of not knowing what was coming next. And then she remembered the gut-churning slap when her fingers accidentally mapped the lump, saw the look on Jack's face as he waited beside her at the hospital. Remembered trying to force herself not to faint when she first felt the searing pain back in New York. And knew even she was not that strong. Cindy knew, unfortunately, that she had not made this up any more than she could unmake it.

The weekend passed, slowly and quickly and slow again. A foxtrot, quickstep, half-time marching beat. They both worked a little on Saturday afternoon, drank two bottles of wine before they could sleep, and even then it was patchy, uncertain, dream-infested. They went for a walk early on Sunday morning before the sun had quite cleared away the hill mist, up to the dry meadow, kicked around looking for reasons and found nothing. Stopped at the hillside bookstore for latté. Matthew was on holiday, the replacement had made cookies instead of brownies. They were dry, brittle. Healthy. Not what she wanted. Cindy found herself looking for signs, interpreting passing gestures in the wind. On Sunday night they held hands in bed and Jack kissed Cindy's face and feet and eyes and ears and nose and he kissed the small scars beneath the dressing. Over and over again. He cried. She cried. Their sleep was fitful, frightened.

Twenty-four

The room was bright. Flooded with white light from the time Janice came in to work until well after she left it. She took off her thin linen jacket, laid down her bag, put her lunch in the refrigerator, moving aside Dan's two-week-old yoghurt to do so, turned on her computer, shuffled through the files left for her while she waited for her monitor to kick in. Several papers were marked urgent. They waited in a separate in-tray. So as not to get missed. Not that all the doctors wouldn't call all of their requests urgent if they could. But there was a system, which seemed to work, no major complaints. And a well-staffed office as well; unlike the two other hospitals she had worked in, Janice Kellway was rarely so pushed for time that she worried she might make a mistake or miss some vital clue. And then again, she had been in the job long enough to trust her skills even when she couldn't trust the ease of hours.

She sat down to look through her emails, filing the personal ones for lunchtime attack, ordering the work-related messages according to her own system – everything would be dealt with by the time she went for her second coffee break of the day. Janice was meticulously efficient. And well known for it. She'd been head-hunted for this position, the histopathology department on the lookout for someone young, capable and self-possessed, ready to take on both a minor teaching role and a major position of responsibility. Janice wasn't really young, not even then – and certainly not in the interviewing board's terms – but she got the job anyway. Perhaps her willingness to work weekend shifts was part of their choice. But her husband was a builder. Weekends off were a deviation from the norm. Janice was trained to spot deviations from the norm.

Finished with the emails and her coffee, Janice collected her first file and went through to the larger room where frozen samples waited for her in a freezer cabinet, each one carefully cross-checked to match the pages she was holding. She followed the patient number to the prepared samples, checked again against the first three pages and set to work. Janice did not really look at the patient details, not the specifics. Occasionally a date of birth might leap out at her. A decade earlier there had been a woman whose birthday was exactly the same as Janice's. Not merely date but year as well. Both women turning thirty-eight. Janice going out for dinner that night with her Shaun, then skiing with friends for the weekend, Shaun's chilli washed down with lethal home-made mojitos and then on to margaritas. Not the wisest combination for a woman of thirty-eight. The other woman spending her weekend quietly at home. Waiting for the results that would make their way through the system in a day or so. Janice had signed her off as a Stage IV invasive carcinoma. Not even pretending to be sober at eleven that night, Janice raised her glass to an already-forgotten name and patient number, wishing her birth-twin health and happiness. Though she didn't expect either was likely. Janice would be forty-nine next birthday, then a big party for her fiftieth the year after. The other woman, long forgotten now, stayed forever in her thirties.

Janice liked preparing her own slides, the technical precision of going from one process to another, taking constant care, while at the same time carrying out a basic repetitive process. Throughout her residency she'd taken every opportunity to perform the most regular daily tasks. Janice had never been after glory, not interested in world-changing discoveries, content to contribute in a smaller way. She enjoyed following the whole process of her work. From freshly arrived specimen, through freezing or washing or fixing, to final analysis. She and Shaun had met as student photographers, the back-room darkroom a place they found unity despite their disparate majors, somewhere they still happily retreated to. She didn't know if her interest in pathology had been sparked by her student interest in photography, if the blossoming relationship had been part of it, or if she was simply drawn to a developing process in whatever guise it presented itself. But the path of fresh specimen, through fixative, then intricate processes into paraffin and out again, the water bath and the dyes, was similar to the process they followed in the darkroom at photo club. Slightly less kissing in the path lab, though. These days most specimens were already prepared for her, especially at the weekend when her caseload was primarily one of frozen and permanent sections waiting to be de-coded. Saturday was not usually spent waiting for an urgent delivery from an operating table upstairs. Surgeons tended not to schedule too many of their medical miracles for Saturday afternoons.

Janice set to work. She took out a CD and played The Eagles while she got on with the job. Then Michael Jackson. Then Cindy Lauper. She worked her way carefully through each of the files the secretary had left in her tray. At lunchtime she went upstairs and out to the front of the hospital, uncomfortable in the heat after the cool of the laboratory. She had her book and turkey breast sandwiches with her. She took the elevator to the top of the car park and climbed into the passenger seat of her car, opening all four doors to let out the thick heat and welcome in the slight breeze that came off the sea. She had lunch in her car whenever she could, it had the best view in the hospital. There was a staff cafeteria upstairs with tables and chairs facing the water, but the windows were set into the heavy wall. They opened neither out nor in, sealed to maintain the supremacy of the air conditioning system. And while Janice had long since accustomed herself to the daily scent of formalin in her nostrils, she preferred to try for sea breezes whenever she could.

By the time she went home that evening, Janice had worked her way through all the files she'd been left. She had entered the necessary data both in her own computer, forwarding it to the main hospital register, and on the printed reports that went directly to the surgeons and doctors and physicians concerned. Signing off each one with a careful, date-checked hand. On the way home she ignored air conditioning to open her windows wide and sing along to Elton John's 'Daniel'. Shaun was making a barbecue. If the traffic stayed this light there would be time for a swim before their guests arrived. A good day's work and no unnecessary interruptions. No necessary ones either. Just the way Janice liked it.

Cindy's biopsy results were halfway down the pile. Signed and dated and waiting.

Twenty-five

The appointment was for two p.m. After lunch Neil Austin had said. As if lunch might be possible. A leisurely break for two, a couple of hours by the waterfront perhaps. Or if she was too busy with all her vital engagements then maybe just a healthy snack, a quick bite from a Farmer's Market stall and then, all in a day's work, dash off with ten minutes spare to the physician's rooms. Cindy was being called to account. Counting down the hours.

Jack went to work in the morning at Cindy's insistence. It was his job, why they were here. (Jack listened for recriminations in 'why they were here'. Heard none but his own. As if California had made this happen, drawn her errant cells together into a single, maverick mind.) And anyway, there was nothing else to do. No point in them both sitting inside festering in a home-made stew of doubt and fear, no sleep and no appetite, too many minutes to the hour, slow seconds turning to thirds and fourths. Not that lack of appetite stopped Cindy eating. Black olive bread and salty goat's cheese, a bland, rasping cardboard on her unwilling tongue. Half-pint of pistachio icecream, her taste buds identifying the dusty pale green but nothing else. The bitter dark chocolate ginger she didn't even like, a leftover from lunch weeks ago, hidden back in the cupboard until some other out-of-town visitors arrived with palates more sophisticated than either of them possessed. Jack with his mother-love supply of Walnut Whips and Walkers crisps, Cindy's stash of clattering pistachio shells. The self-offerings she would normally curl her tongue around with desire or distaste, but now nothing. No chemical reaction at all and still filling her mouth to silence the repetitions of chattering fear.

The truth was Cindy didn't want Jack with her. Not after the long Sunday wait, heavy on both of them. She wanted him out of the house, and while he could do nothing of use, he could do what she wouldn't ask of him. He could go away. Jack's panic magnified Cindy's own to a size neither could handle. She lay in bed for an hour after Jack had left the room. He went out kissing her, kissing the air, punching the wall the minute he was beyond sight. Not sound. Intentional-unintentional. He wanted her to know how much he cared, he didn't want her to know how much he worried, his knuckles cracked against the forgiving clapboard and said the same. She rolled through the radio. Five different talk shows and not one annoying enough to be a distraction. She walked naked through warm rooms, air conditioning turned off, windows closed. Cindy was protecting herself from an outside that edged against her skin and dared her to feel. She played loud music for fifty minutes and then none for forty. Heartbeat silence. Birds, wind, a distant alarm. Burned slices of toast and swallowed down dry mouthfuls. Bitter coffee with three sugars. Showered with face turned away from the ocean. Its width made her cry. Cindy did not want to cry. Not yet. Not this morning. Not today if she could help it. Soaped her body all over but not at the site of the biopsy, the places of penetration. Careful fingers taking the path of least insistence, her unmapped skin in still starker relief.

Cindy expected bad news. She could not say this aloud to

131

Jack, would not listen to her own mind repeating the words to come. But it was what she knew. Standing under the running water she took apart her thought processes. She was thinking the unhappy possibilities because then she would not be disappointed when the physician said the news was bad. She was thinking the unhappy possibilities because some place inside of Cindy actually knew the unhappy possibility was already a truth. Noted her use of the indefinite article. At which point would this uncertain certainty turn into The Truth? Cindy wondered how many truths might be possible in the physician's office. If he dealt in single truths – this is it, what you have come for. Or maybe he preferred the card hand variety – here is one possibility, here another, this a third. Cindy didn't know which would be better. She was both ready to know now, and also to wait forever. Eleven a.m.

Drying her skin and staring at herself in the mirror. Wondering when the separation had begun. Cindy and self, skin and Cindy. Was it inevitable with age, with changing body anyway, that the real Cindy would stay hidden, closed up in some sanctuary, an inner location where she had once been safe, even as the skin around her lined and the bones that held her up became brittle? Or had this dissociation only started with the first pains? Cindy was both far inside her body and floating randomly outside it. Intensely of the flesh in a way she had not felt before, and yet constantly looking at herself as if examining an object with detached interest. Studying the legs and arms and breasts and face, torn jigsaw pieces of an old map and the key yet to be located. She longed for an ordinary conversation, the price of green apples, correct form for the bank deposit, this the right way or that? But she couldn't even trust herself on the phone. Scared words, scarred words, sacred sacrilegious sounds waited bubbling at the back of her throat. Cindy was a danger to polite society.

She kept herself inside for the morning and allowed the phone to ring through the house.

At midday Jack came home. Sipped a cup of tepid tea, changed out of jeans and into a suit and then back into jeans, another pair. Cindy was already dressed and ready. Waiting. They had little to say to each other, less use for words, fearful of both incitement and placation. Jack and Cindy sat on the sofa, watching watches, watching each other. Kissed, locked the door behind them, turning keys an intimation of prison-yard walk. Cindy was locked into this route. The only thing that would get them out of it now was an open smile on Neil Austin's face, relief in his words.

They drove together to the hospital and stared at the alien world outside the car, a lunar landscape of normal routine. In the car, Jack asked about New York.

'Babe, if you are sick, I mean really, do you want to go back?'

'To New York?'

'Yeah.'

'I don't know. A while ago I would have jumped at the chance. But I don't know now. I mean, if I am really sick,' both of them skirting around the words, skating past painful enunciation, 'then I don't suppose it matters where I am, does it?'

'Doesn't it?'

'Jack, either they can find and fix what's wrong with me, or they can't. If they can, then they might as well do it here . . .'

'And if not?'

'Then I want to be with you. Where we are doesn't matter. I just want to stay with you. OK?'

Cindy and Jack sat in the cool, bright waiting room, the one long window faced back towards the road, escape route, run-away runway. Neil Austin's large and antiseptic office was carefully lit by bulbs glowing artificial daylight, his window faced another part of the building just feet away. Meanwhile Jack's car sat outside on the open fifth storey of the car park, basking metallic in the summer sun and enjoying an uninter-rupted view of the ocean and the sky in matching Man City blue. The view inside changed on a twenty-minute rota. Another name would be called and the individual with or without anxious partner would follow a white coat and a closed file down the short corridor and into one of the equally well lit and cool little rooms off to either side.

Jack picked up magazines, held each one for a while and then put them down again, understanding by touch and osmosis that nothing inside the covers would offer adequate distraction. Cindy passed the time judging the contents of each carefully clutched file by the speed of the medic's walk, the swing of the white coat, the level of head incline as the waiting patient's name was called – a clear announcement or semi-whisper, either of which might mean good, bad or indifferent. If only Cindy had all day, all week, to stay here and watch. Look and learn. She would map their individual pat-terns if she had the time. Wishing herself all time and no time – no time until the results and all the time in the world. Now Cindy could have opened her mouth and dared the wicked words to come spilling out, here in this waiting room, with every other self-absorbed head thinking the exact same thoughts. Except that maybe she was wrong, maybe she was the only one planning bad news and phone calls to parents, tearful Kelly, Jack to hold. Maybe everyone else here was more concerned with their shopping lists, baseball scores. Then another crying wife and red-faced husband sat them-selves in front of Jack's scattered pile of magazines and she understood the fears the elderly pair were bile-swallowing back. She was creating distorted projections for everyone in the room, inaccurate scale inevitably centred on one point rather than any of the hundreds of other possible points of focus.

When Neil Austin called her name he was already half walking away from them. It was a thirty-second walk to his office. Plenty of time to choose to run away, not hear what was to be said, not allow the doctor's words to translate to body-fact. The physician led them into his room, ushered out two student doctors with a slight frown, and then made way for a new nurse to come into the room instead. Cindy liked the signs less and less.

Neil Austin was nothing like Mr Gibson, the Baton Rouge Principal. For a start, he was only a few years older than Cindy. She hoped. She didn't want him to be younger than her, several years younger than Jack. Wished that years might make him wiser than her. He smiled at her today in a way Mr Gibson had never smiled. Not even once she'd mutated into cheerleader princess. She didn't know Mr Gibson's first name, Neil Austin had offered up his own immediately. Call-me-Neil had been both friendly and careful at the brief initial consultation. A white coat thrown over his chair instead of his body, offering professional courtesy, discretion and a degree of humanity. But despite the pleasantries, Cindy knew Neil Austin was still the Principal, he had the answers before Cindy did, knew how to interpret signs she only felt to be truths.

Neil Austin smiled again. Time folding in around them. They were, all four, standing in his office now. Cindy noted his shoes. The physician was wearing heavy black shoes. Completely wrong for the weather. He had a wedding ring. Left hand holding tight to the file marked with Cindy's name and hospital number, his right hand indicating seats for Cindy and Jack. Cindy closest to the desk, a soft but unyielding

135

chair at right angles to the stacked box files, Jack beside her on a smaller more plastic version, Jack and Cindy's shoulders at the same height. Neil Austin perched on the edge of his white-coat-padded office chair, the largest in the room, a chieftain's seat, made for pronouncements. The nurse rested calm and quiet on a low stool by the door. Her hands were together, clasped in her lap. Her face immobile. Cindy wondered if the young woman's job was to stop the two of them running out of the room screaming. She wanted to ask. Thought better of gallows humour. And then couldn't stop herself.

'Are you there to stop me running out of here in tears?'

The nurse looked up, smiled, half-shrugged one shoulder. She knew what was coming. Had been at the meeting this morning, was one of the members of the team who had studied Cindy's file, her future. She didn't protest, 'Of course not.' Cindy's eyes fixed on the box of tissues by the filing cabinet, an arm's reach from the nurse's ready hand, felt her body sway forwards then quick back, a tiny letting go, prior acceptance. Grabbed Jack's hand.

Neil Austin had the folder open in front of him. He was speaking to her through the file, his voice bouncing off the pages and refracting back to Cindy. She thought he looked genuinely upset. Jack was crumpling beside her, the nurse reaching out to this falling man beside Cindy, offering him tissues. Cindy straining to understand what was being said, forcing the disconnected sound to become comprehension.

Call-me-Neil began with, 'I'm sorry, Cindy, Jack. I do have bad news for you.' And ended with, 'The very best we can offer.'

By the close of his speech the nurse had shed a few tears as well. Cindy saw them fall on to her blue pants, watched impatient hands quickly brush away the unwanted salt water.

Cindy herself was shivering, a spew of questions flowing from her wide mouth. Unfortunately Neil had an answer for every one. He spoke with careful words, the clearly enunciated phrases a medical compendium of cross-referenced sadness.

Drug therapies immediately. Probably surgery. Maybe more drugs. Diagnosis. Prognosis. Uncertain, probability, halt, resistance. Shadows, scarring, liver, blood, lungs, kidneys. Not hopeful. Unlikely. There were the x-rays and there were the scans. The reverse image, transverse image, sagittal plane, oblique plane suppositions. Then the biopsy results that backed up the hypotheses. Possibility. Postpone. Plateau. He talked of second opinions and specialists and the team that had made this analysis. Offered recourse to other doctors, a chance to check his findings. And then his certainty anyway. He was very sorry.

Jack had stopped crying by the end, but it was the pictures that eventually got through to Cindy, the scan images and the scribbled diagrams Neil Austin sketched for their better understanding. The clear biopsy interpretation. That and the mention of pain management, palliative care. One phrase that drew all the images together, whispering of carefully measured time. And then pain. And then end.

Twenty-six

Seeing as believing (LA notes)

Our maps – be they traditional Mercator projections of the world or groundbreaking 3-D humanist graphs – are believed because they are pictures. We accept what we see. Further, as we have come to rely still more on visual evidence, it is now, on occasion, the image rather than the truth itself in which we believe. Rather than being an illustration of the truth, the map is the truth. Image as leap of faith. Sometimes it is the mapping that makes things real.

What Jack found hardest to believe was the speed. Last Monday evening they had fucked in the shower. Cool water. Pliant bodies planted against the glass and chrome frame and both heads turned towards the rain driving down the half-opened window, rebound drops splashing on to the tiled floor, the orange-tinted clouds reaching way out over the sea, Jack and Cindy reaching far into each other. They'd actually fallen asleep on the bathroom floor afterwards, damp towels for sheets and pillowcases. Jack woke cold and uncomfortable, an uncharted constellation of raindrops held on the window-pane above him, Cindy curled into his chest. Two weeks ago Jack was interested in his work, enthused by various stories, congratulating himself on his choice of team, congratulating himself on his choice of partner. Cindy was working up the idea of forgotten routes and abandoned paths as essential components to personal history. In addition to that which Cindy had found lacking in California, both had also found themselves noticing unexpected pleasures impossible in New York – Jack completing a jam-free work drive seven times out of ten, home before eight and taking Cindy out for dinner by the shore. Cindy stretching her gaze from the peak of a canyon walk and seeing, courtesy of a strong wind and the early morning, her usual misty view brought into blazing kodachrome relief. They had started planning a trip back to New York a while later. In a month or so Jack expected he would feel safe enough to leave the team for a week, and Cindy thought that maybe her new town pleasures would make it possible to travel East without the whole trip being a salt-wound experience.

Last week they had been two people in love, working energetically on their respective projects, sharing disgust at federal inaction on some vital scheme, adult inertia as always overtaking their youthful fury, eating pizza and spilling beer on the sitting room floor when TV scorn-laughter became hysteria and then touch, then kiss, then sex. Later that night they had also touched on the baby-possibility conversation. The first time it had been mentioned since moving to California. Each a little coy, sounding the other out, not wanting to push or pull too far in either direction, sending out searcher words before completing a sentence, ensuring one was easy with the other's desires. And each listened with quiet pleasure to the turn of their words as last year's maybe became this year's probably, waiting for next year's yeah, ok, now. This is the right time. Yes.

Last week time had stretched from the past, through the present and into a wide-open future. Now it snapped back, catching their fingers, cracking them both slap-sharp. Now time began with Cindy ill in New York and then jumped-cut straight to the minute she'd been woken by searing pain. The future shrunk further as Cindy followed the timetable Neil Austin had sketched out for them.

Last week they had imagined they were busy, believed they had things to talk about, thoughts to occupy their minds. Now there was just one big idea, every other consideration rendered inane and pointless, dribbling away to a vanishing point of why bother. Jack's hands firm on the steering wheel, one thing he could control. Prickly fear manifesting as heat rash in small red bumps all over his chest and back, teeth clamped together, the impossibility of placatory words sticking his hopeless tongue to the roof of his useless mouth. Driving down the three-lane highway in Jack-hell where there was nothing he could do to make it better. Beside him Cindy was still shivering, a new frown line and bitten top lip as her face tried to make sense of the confusion in her brain. She sat quiet but for the tremor she could not control, weighed down in the passenger seat with new information. Her lap was an unwelcome basket of leaflets and pamphlets, photocopied sheets made clumsy with uncomfortable comforting words. A new timetable now attached to her diary and a full plastic bag at her feet. The bag was ordinary, but that it had the hospital's name stamped all over it, was made ugly by its contents, the stench of illness leaking from the cartons and bottles inside. The nurse had handed the bag to Jack as they left, the drugs Cindy was to start taking immediately. That afternoon. Three at once. Then another two before dinner. That evening before bed. Tomorrow morning. Forever. A contracted always.

After Neil Austin had taken his deep breath and said what his competent manner allowed him to say, Jack realised he had expected more. His years of too many movies had led him to believe there must be more to say, decisions to be made, options to consider. But it turned out that no discussion was necessary. The what-to-do-now deliberations had taken place long before Cindy and Jack even arrived. The medical team, several other physicians, pathologists, nurses, people schooled and skilled in this form or that had made their choices. Students had been shown the case notes and then asked which treatment they would suggest. Each one noting Neil's face for an eyebrow raise or a lip curl as the indication of pass or fail, right or wrong. Jack and Cindy were the late arrivals, come into the meeting long past the decision point. Most shocking of all was the physician's certainty. There was no possibility of doubt. The x-rays indicated a presence, the CT and MRI made it clearer, the biopsies were confirmation. Any new tests would not be to find out what was wrong as Cindy and Jack had assumed, but to see how far the disease had gone. Depth-charging Cindy's body, searching for an end, a count, something finite. Jack was angry, lashed out blame and bitterness. Neil corrected him. Unfortunately there was no fault with the New York doctors – of course it would be easier for Cindy and Jack to understand if this was someone's mistake. But in his opinion, in the opinion of his well-respected colleagues, that was not the case. The pain and collapse in New York had been an indication, a warning maybe. But there had been – at that time – nothing for the team to find. Neil had seen the notes, the explanations. He had even talked to Cindy's NY physician over the weekend, just to reassure himself. There had been no mistake then, just as there was no mistake now. Four months ago, there had been nothing to find inside Cindy. Now there was something. He and his team had found it. Searched, discovered, plotted.

Neil Austin was used to denial, wilful incomprehension.

He knew what to do next. These were intelligent people, understood many of the words and terms he was offering them. But like almost everyone else, they understood pictures even better. After all, that was their work, mapmaker, film-maker. So Jack and Cindy looked at the pictures themselves – Cindy's inner body a newly shadowed patchwork. She stared at the light-box images as Jack grasped for possibility and found himself asking about the alternatives he had never believed in before. Second opinions on the diagnosis were possible, naturally. Though Neil firmly recommended they start the course of treatment anyway, try to put a halt to some of the greater ravages meanwhile. Drugs first to attempt a containment, then assuming that went well, surgery. But he was talking extended time and containment, not cure. Neil Austin went on to say that even in the best case scenarios they rarely used the word cure. It was too loaded, too much potential for resolution in an expensive courtroom. This time he was not protecting his insurers, he was protecting Cindy and Jack against the temptation of hope. Yes, miracles happened. He did not recommend waiting for one.

And there were also any number of alternative therapies. Some of Neil's patients had used them. For a time. Instead of conventional medicine, on occasion, but he had to admit, with little success. As well as conventional medicine – absolutely, why not? Neil's voice turned softer now, conspiratorial, obliging. Sometimes he thought maybe people helped themselves simply by virtue of believing the acupuncture or the aromatherapy or the extreme diet was working. Maybe it did. And sometimes people made themselves more ill. Help, he thought, was a more appropriate word than heal. To be entirely honest, though, he wasn't usually far off – Neil Austin had something of a reputation for accurate prognosis.

142

He made a real attempt to say this with no hint of personal pride, very nearly succeeded. Then he answered the question both Jack and Cindy were too stunned to ask. Too scared to ask. Two or three months was most likely. Four or maybe even five was not totally out of the question. However, barring the miraculous – and as a sceptical medic he was never entirely prepared to do that – next spring was too far away for Cindy.

Neil Austin saw four more patients that afternoon. Good news for one man, bad for another, great news for the last two women on his list. Accepted tearful gratitude and bitter anxiety one after the other. Had another meeting, speed-read some recommended papers, half-shut his blinds against the reflected afternoon glare that was urging a headache, checked drug references for a colleague and reminded himself to look at Cindy Frier's book before bed. He knew his wife had it somewhere on her bookshelf. That evening he stopped off at the tennis court on his way home. Beat ferocious balls around a blameless court and stunned his regular partner with five unexpected aces. His wife's working day had been successful and she took them all out to celebrate, the three children neatly dressed, his youngest straining against the stiff collar of a new shirt, a bottle of champagne waiting at the restaurant. He laughed and joked with the kids, allowed their little girl to order a half lobster, knowing she would trade it for narrow strips of chicken from his plate when the red claws arrived and frightened her. He went to bed tired and not entirely sober and happy in his family's smile, forgot to look at Cindy's book. Got up before six, stumbled over an abandoned scooter on his way to the car, started again.

Jack drove Cindy home, planning to get online as soon as he could. Drag up resources and case studies and arm himself with information, possibilities. He would stop work, explain the situation, demand time off or resign if he had to. He would fix this, make it better. He didn't know what else to do. Jack couldn't imagine himself driving with Cindy missing from his side. So he wouldn't.

'We can move back, you know.'

'What?'

Cindy held tight to the loose-leaf pages resting on her thighs. Stuck in the thoughts that were racing her down an unplanned tunnel, two-way conversation seemed a long way from possible.

'I know you said no, but that was before. We can move back to New York. You'll be closer to your mother, to Kelly. Our old friends. I can leave my job.'

'You have a contract.'

'I think we've just found a way to break it.'

Cindy started to shrug and then realised her shoulders were hunched tight round her neck anyway, deliberately eased them back into place, took a slow breath. 'I don't know. I don't, I haven't . . . it hasn't sunk in yet.'

'No.'

'No.'

More silence. More slow driving. Cindy started again, an attempt to explain to Jack – who she knew to be fighting this new information with every cell in his body – that she believed Neil Austin. That even now, this early, with all the uncertainty and fear and denial rushing through her veins, there was already some part of her, the midnight pain part of her, that understood a truth had been told. 'Anyway, I don't think we can go back, Jack.'

'We can do whatever we want. Fuck them.'

'No, but . . . I like him, Neil.'

'I think he's a bit full of himself actually.'

144

'Well, of course he is. They all are. I don't think they could do that job if they weren't. They have to believe in themselves, otherwise how would anyone else? No, anyway, like's the wrong word, I don't mean like. And actually, I fucking hate him after what he's told us. What I mean is, I think I trust him. I don't want to have to find a new doctor.'

'OK. Whatever you want.'

Cindy sighed, not wanting to be in charge, forced into a place where Jack would do anything she wanted the moment she asked him. She didn't want to be the one who made the choices. Not with this as the reason.

'I don't know what I want.'

Jack turned his eyes from the road for a moment, looked to Cindy. 'I do.'

Then she smiled. They both knew what they really wanted. Another time, another place, another life. Not the one they had now begun.

'Yeah, well, assuming the doctors are right and we can't have what we want, we might as well not have it here as not have it there. Anyway, Manhattan's so dark in winter. Maybe it's time we took a break from it.'

Jack nodded, then concentrated on his driving, grateful for a teenage boy-racer in front of him, giving him an excuse to focus on something else. Cindy went back to her thoughts. The way now would be entirely new, all her own. Of course plenty of others had been ill before, at this hospital before, treated by these doctors. Obviously Neil Austin had welcomed other people into his office with that careful handshake and his sincerely sorry smile. But Cindy had not been one of them. This was her new. She looked into the future and saw only the loneliness of disease. Jack would hold her hand as they drew more blood, steady her head as she became ill in all the ways the nurse had suggested she might, pick her up after surgery and lay her down with care. Jack would be beside her through all this. But that was his limit. Beside. He could not be in the place where she was.

Cindy and Jack travelled forwards. Close enough to kiss the other's breath. Touching hands, totally separate.

Twenty-seven

Rebekah was sitting on the doorstep when Jack slowly pulled into the driveway.

'Oh Jesus fucking cunting shite.'

'What?' Cindy looked up from the third leaflet detailing possible unpleasant side effects of the two pink pills she was supposed to take before going to bed that night.

'Rebekah.'

'What?'

'She's been leaving me messages every ten minutes since I left the office. She wants me to let her go with that land story tomorrow and I promised I'd have an answer for her by three.'

'It's four thirty, Jack.'

'Yes.'

'Well why didn't you call her?'

'Oh, I don't know, maybe I've had other things to think about?' Jack shot back, pissed off with himself for not dealing with this and furious with Rebekah for making his avoidance obvious, and against all his better instincts angry with Cindy. For not understanding this was the best he could manage right now. For not promising him it was all going to be all right. For being ill. For being dying.

He pulled on the handbrake, ratcheting it up with a satis-fying scrape. 'Look, I'm sorry. I just didn't know what to tell them at work. I'll get rid of her.'

Cindy unhooked herself from the seatbelt, wondering exactly how far its life-saving properties were meant to stretch. 'How?'

'Tell her the truth. She's not going to want to hang around us with this to deal with.'

'Thanks.'

'I mean, she won't know what to say. She'll be scared. It'll get rid of her.'

'I don't want you to tell her the truth. Not yet.'

Rebekah came up to Cindy's side of the car. Cindy jumped out, eyes shining, face beaming a welcoming and sheepish smile. She threw the leaflet and other papers back into the footwell of the car behind her with a warning look to Jack. 'Hey Rebekah.'

'Oh. Hi.'

'You know, I just am so sorry you've had to come all the way out here, it's all my fault.' She took Rebekah's arm and walked her up the drive to the house. 'I had this weird thing over the weekend, felt awful all day Saturday and then even worse Sunday, real bad cramps and then puking up every-where.' She took a breath of significant pause and lowered her voice to a girl-talk whisper. 'Actually I'd been a week or so late and we were hoping – I mean I was, well you know . . . but then I started bleeding last night and just felt so ill, I didn't know what to do. Awful of me I know, but I made Jack work at home all weekend, in case I needed him around, and then this morning I called him at the office and made him come home so he could take me to the hospital, and you know what they're like . . . keep you waiting hours, and all they can say is it's a virus.'

She wouldn't let Rebekah get a single word in, all girl-friend arm-grabbing and silly giggle with impressively plausible pleased-to-see-you smile. Cindy finished up with a blame-me offer, entirely disabling Rebekah's legitimate complaint, 'Really, I've been a complete bitch the whole time, making out it was all his fault for bringing me to California. I've been such a cow – I even hid Jack's cell phone from him at the hospital. I'm so sorry.'

'Oh. OK, well, good – good that it's nothing worse and – you know – really sorry about, ah, the thing . . .'

Rebekah didn't know what to say. An implied late period had her stuttering. Admission of illness left her silent. Jack was right, she'd have run a mile if they'd whispered the truth. Cindy wondered how Rebekah would have responded had she been an interviewee; this girl after all was Jack's great hope for modern TV journalism. Cindy decided Rebekah was no doubt far more accomplished with a rolling camera beside her. For a brief moment she was tempted to throw in, 'And of course, I have just been diagnosed with a terminal disease which kind of throws a little thing like your hot news story into proper perspective'. But pulled herself back just in time. Not now. Not while part of her hoped that keeping those words to herself might yet save her.

Jack was following them up the driveway with the plastic bag, now crammed full of the explanatory leaflets and papers as well. Cindy opened the front door and pushed Rebekah through to the sitting room.

'OK, so I'm a little stupid when it comes to medications, and if you'll just give Jack and me a minute alone – no, don't worry, we'll go into the bedroom – then he's all yours. Really, it won't take a minute, and honest, I am so sorry it's had to affect you at all.'

Cindy fled the room, tears stinging the bridge of her nose. Jack followed on behind her, a mumbled greeting to his employee.

'I am not leaving you alone, Cindy.'

'Yes you are.'

'No. We need to talk about this.'

'And I'm sure we will. I can't imagine how we're ever going to talk about anything else again. But not right now.'

'We need to look through this lot at least. See what to do.'

'We know what to do. Neil Austin already told us. And the nurse. And the other one, the pain specialist? Take the pills for the next week, then another scan. Then more pills. Intravenous drugs maybe, surgery probably. I took in the timetable, Jack. I know what happens next.'

'Yeah, fine, but that's just what the hospital has to offer. There must be more we can do ourselves. We can try some alternative methods.'

Cindy scraped a dry hand over her already puffy eyes. 'Please, I'm not going to start on a mad chase after tree bark or eagle feathers or whatever . . .'

'I'm only suggesting we take a look. They can't know everything . . .'

'I'm sure they don't. Neil Austin said they don't. But not yet. Please? Just let me start on this. Give me some time to take it all in.'

'All right. But in a day or so, when we're used to it – no, I don't mean used to it – sorry, no. I'll look then, yeah? See what else I can find?'

Cindy's arms dropped to her sides. 'If you want.'

'Don't you want? You talk like you're giving up.'

'I'm talking about it like I'm getting used to the idea. That's all. You're going too fast for me right now. I just need to think about it for a while.'

Cindy leaned back against the window frame, sunshine useless against the chill running down her spine, arms folded tight in front of her, body protecting itself against the acknowledging words.

'Of course you do. I just – I need to do something useful.'

'So do. Deal with Rebekah.'

'Can't I just get rid of her?'

'Jack, she's working. She needs your help.'

'So do you.'

'Not right this minute. I don't think I even believe half of what we were told today.'

'No?'

The relief in Jack's voice was palpable and Cindy knew she had to lead him back to reality quick before he skipped off down the path of false hope and was lost to her entirely.

'Sorry, no, I don't mean that. Not like you want me to mean anyway. I do believe him. It feels like he's probably right. But even with everything he had to say this afternoon, nothing feels any different yet. Other than the pictures, his words, my sense of myself, there's no real proof. I'm not in pain. I don't look any different. It just hasn't got in. And while that's the case, you might as well get on with your work.'

'I can't work,' Jack hissed at her in shock. And dismay. Terrified by the part of Cindy that seemed to want to accept what they had been told.

'Sure you can. You're good at it. It's what you do.'

'I can't. Not now. Not if . . . he said you . . . we were, I . . . I . . .' Jack's speech ground to a halt as the tears he'd been so furious with in Neil Austin's office came back to taunt him again. 'I really fucking don't want to cry. I want to cope with this.'

'You are coping. This is coping. Believing and not believing. I'm probably in shock and that's why I think I'm fine, but for the moment I am OK. Kind of. And the thing is, you need to go to work now.'

'Why?'

'Because I need you to behave as if our lives are the same. I don't want everyone to know yet, and you work in a news-room.'

'So?'

'Well, I know a very minor celebrity in the world of car-tography hardly makes the evening news, but you think word won't get round anyway? I haven't even told my parents yet.' Cindy stopped for breath, her stomach twisting at the thought of calling her parents. 'I'm going to have to talk to Kelly. We'll need to call your mum and dad. We need time to work out what we're going to say and your job won't give us that. You know I'm right.'

Jack nodded.

'So go with Rebekah. Take her out, listen to what she has to say, tell her you need another day maybe, or twelve hours. Whatever. Look like you're thinking about her story. You said she could be good, didn't you?'

'She will be.'

'So she probably has got everything right, she just needs your OK.'

Jack nodded again, wet salt panic and fear streaming down his face, on to his hopeless open hands. Cindy wanting to hold him and kiss him and give in to her own terror. Instead she forced vertebrae to stack up, arms folded in to keep her still, holding herself together and apart from Jack.

'Go deal with this, Jack. Then come back and we'll get on with everything else together. I can't have any of them know about me just yet. I need to work out what it is I know myself. Yes? I just need a couple of hours.'

'Yeah. Sure.'

Jack walked into the bathroom, washed his face, came back, changed his shirt. He held Cindy very tight. 'We'll make this all right, I promise you, we're going to make it better.'

Cindy let him go, her body aching to hide in his. She heard him talking quietly to Rebekah in the sitting room, then there was a half-sung goodbye from the younger woman, all focus now on getting the boss on her side, the front door slammed shut. Cindy stood in the middle of the room, looking down at her body. Calves and thighs tight, hands gripping upper arms for safety, brittle nails cutting red welts into straining biceps. Slowly the tension drained and her rigid flesh let itself down, gravity and fear pulling her to the floor. She looked at the plastic bag of pills and papers Jack had left on the bed. Heard Neil Austin's words running through her head, the ludicrousness of it, the complete stupidity that it was another human being's job to tell her she was finite.

She held Jack's pillow to her face. The smell of his head, the heavy arc of his neck. She wanted to tell him that she would fight this thing, beat it. But she didn't know how to fight. And anyway, there was nothing to fight – her body was doing this to itself, making a new Cindy she didn't want. She could not fight her own flesh. Would have tried working with it maybe, but Neil Austin had been very clear when he said there were no chances. The route was plain. The only uncertainty as far as he was concerned was time. Of course he'd seen miracles, every medic had. He wouldn't rule them out. Unexplained recovery straight out of the Lazarus textbook. But as far as he and his colleagues could tell she was not a candidate for cure. After Cindy had started on the treatments she'd been offered, they would be able to be more specific about surgery. But these were treatments for time, not disease. They were giving her all they had to offer. Neil Austin had said these words to other people before Cindy, he would no doubt say them again. It was easily the worst part of his job, he did not do so lightly. He did so only when he was absolutely certain, Cindy could trust him on that.

Cindy pulled herself up from the floor, slipped off her sandals, tunnelled a way under the duvet, twisted the soft cotton around her chilled body. She was charting a new route. One she could not previously have imagined and one she would not completely understand until every unbroken path had burned itself on to her skin, into her flesh. But there was also the beginning glimmer of comprehension. Some part of her body, her flesh, her structure, that knew where it was taking her. And no matter how much Jack tried to make this new future a joint effort – and she had no doubt he would – this was her sickness. She wondered when Jack would realise she was the sick one, not him, not they. Wondered how long she would listen to him saying 'we' about her disease, her illness, her end, before he realised he wasn't coming along too. She cried. Then she dozed, woke herself with a choking sob, cried some more, whispering tears, slipped deeper down, grateful surrender to drifting limbs.

Twenty-eight

Cindy woke, disturbed by something different, another change. With blurred eyes and foggy head, she dredged herself up from unsafe sleep into the damning light of late afternoon. There had been no respite in dream, fifty-five too-brief minutes of confusion turning to fear as it hit the pillow. She realised she'd fallen asleep hoping to wake as they did in the books and on TV – wake feeling normal again, not yet knowing something was wrong. To enjoy a moment or two of would-be-ordinary before full consciousness hit her, the pleasure of an easy place where perhaps some hidden part of her entire physiology hadn't yet understood what had been confirmed only four hours earlier. She pictured the lazy beauty of passing concerns over unpaid mortgages or outsize thigh size, the easy nothingness of night's panic before a meeting with a hateful boss. She viewed daily problems through the glorious scope of proper perspective – they looked good. But in her waking now there was no relaxation of fear. She could sense it even in her sleep – the smell of dying from the inside out.

She sat up, shook her arms to bring feeling back to her numb fingers, checked the clock. Jack had been gone just over an hour and a quarter. The fact that she'd sent him away, had determinedly ignored his clear preference for staying with her, didn't make it any better that he had failed to creep back an hour ago. Jack should have been sitting at the foot of her bed, tearfully guarding her sleeping form, Prince Charming in a faded blue shirt. Cindy rubbed her eyes and tried to shake off the creeping sense of early evening loneliness, warming at the edges with a tinge of unforgiving partner-fury. It was way too early to start blaming Jack for lacking psychic abilities; Cindy knew she was not yet sick enough to get away with entirely self-centred behaviour. Maybe next week, after she'd taken the four daily doses of whatever poisons had been pre-scribed to make the progression of her disease more manageable. Maybe after surgery, when she was cut up and bleeding, when Neil Austin had promised they could offer a clearer timetable of dying. Maybe then she would have the freedom to be bitch girlfriend. Right now, they were still taking it in. Cindy was supposed to be getting used to the news and allowing Jack to do the same. And she was. She just wanted to be doing her getting used to with him beside her. The moment she woke. Ten minutes ago. Always. Except, of course, for those moments she clearly needed to be alone. Cindy looked at her messy parade of thoughts and grinned; obviously terminal illness didn't come with any relief from her contradictory nature in its bag of unknown goodies.

The grin turned to a grimace as she felt for the hospital's bag of goodies, lifted out the wadge of printed threat, the papers Jack had been so keen to scrutinise for between-the-lines miracles. She laid out the labelled bottles and boxes, her name and hospital number way too clear on each one; she did not want her identity posted on to these no-cure barriers. She flicked through colourful pages of probable side effects and less likely side effects and then the least likely but most important side effects – those demanding Immediate Medical Attention. The list was brief but frightening. When her red eyes refused to look at the words any longer, unwilling fingers made them-selves useful, popped blister packs and unscrewed childproof lids. Then Cindy held out her hand like a good girl. Yes please and thank you. Counted down the first lot of pills prescribed for her. Reached for the bottle of water by her bed. Clear water and a clutched handful of pink and white. Barbie pretty. Sick Cindy. Swallowed them down. A brief catch, slight gag reflex, more water, and gone. The routine of illness, doing what she was told. Too scared not to, while simultaneously terrified to go along with it. Taking a step forwards because there was nowhere else to go and hoping the map would make itself clear as she walked.

Cindy could have taken more time to think about this. Neil Austin had advised starting on the medication-through-to-surgery regime straight away, but he'd also suggested counselling or family discussion or group support. Hospital protocol demanded he tell Cindy that everything they were suggesting was merely that – suggestion. Though, when Jack asked him directly, the physician admitted his advice would be to start the course of drugs immediately. There was little they could do in the long run, but taking these drugs enhanced the likelihood of there being a long run in which to do that little. Cindy didn't want to have to think and she didn't want to have to talk, certainly not to any more strangers, and she didn't want to have to do anything other than just get through the next few hours. She accepted she was probably in shock and she understood that she might feel differently later. And she also understood there wasn't all that much later left to feel. She took the drugs.

Then she placed herself back beneath the sweat-damp sheets. Waiting for sleep and chemical reaction. Little pills already finding their way through her unmarked body, on the lookout for their goal. She pictured delicate pink and white, turned brutal by their meeting with her body, beginning their oesophagus, gullet, bloodstream journey, pale casing peeled back by eager stomach acids, the white powder revealed and quickly soaked up, active ingredients spun into her candy-striped bloodstream current. She woke an hour later, her skin cool and stomach queasy. Cindy lay back in bed, head too hot for the pillow, legs heavier than before, arms close to her sides, shivering despite the heat beneath the sheets and inside her blood. It was slow this feeling, a grumbling distaste rather than an actual flavour. Something in her mouth with the tone of a back-of-the-throat smell, there was a taste of saliva not her own.

The flavour of saliva not her own: first kiss, real kiss. David McLoughlin. Kelly's ex of four days earlier. Kelly had dumped him on Saturday night for Jonathan Oriel, a year older and almost a foot taller. Volunteered to pass David on to Cindy. A good kisser. He knew what to do, Cindy knew nothing. Kelly had said it was time to find out and she was going to do something about it if Cindy wouldn't. Kelly had spoken to David at lunch on Monday, taking five minutes from her cafeteria grope with Jon Oriel to whisper in David's ear. Cindy had been watching from behind a thin curtain of artfully mussed hair. She saw David's face light up as Kelly crossed the room to him, the quick pall of confusion as she proposed her plan, then a shrug, a nod, David McLoughlin turned back to something vitally important in his gym bag. Now it was Thursday afternoon and all day Kelly had been excited, expectant. Cindy had pretty much forgotten about Monday lunchtime and wondered what was hatching, but all Kelly answered was an enigmatic 'you'll see' and her fifteen-year-old's approximation of a sexy wink.

Cindy found out while waiting for the bus, queuing with Kelly to get on in the first rush, grab the back seat together. But then, just as Cindy raised herself to the first step, Kelly stepped aside and let David McLoughlin get on instead. David

McLoughlin slurring his dusty basketball boots up the narrow aisle behind Cindy. His taller boy's breath, hot with gum and after-school release, reaching to the back of her neck, tiny hairs prickling all the way down her back to the hooks of her favourite pale yellow bra. The one with the white flowers and the tiny ribbon centred on her breastbone. An arm that might have brushed hers, too warm to be accidental. Kelly smiled encouragement from where she was now sitting a whole seat ahead with Jonathan Oriel. David McLoughlin beside Cindy on the wide back seat. They both knew what they were supposed to do. This was the next step, the right move. Because Kelly said so, Cindy accepted it, and clearly David did too.

David smiled. Cindy smiled back. He ripped a page from his French book and spat his gum into it, balled it up and threw it out the window. Kelly and Jon were providing an object lesson in getting on with it. David wiped the back of his hand across his mouth, smiled again and grunted an offer, slipped his arm around Cindy's shoulders. His face closer to hers now, he muttered, 'So, Kelly said, d'you wanna . . . you know?'

Cindy didn't really know if she wanted to or not. But then it wasn't really a case of want. She nodded, opened her mouth to let fall a non-committal answer, but before the stilted breath had passed over her constricted vocal chords, David McLoughlin had stopped her mouth. By the time the bus made its fourth stop to let off the older kids on their way to the mall, just old enough to skip going home first to check in, Cindy was no longer a lips-teeth-tongue virgin. Someone else's saliva on her tongue. The taste of another fluid not her own. Marking out fresh places of feeling. One point on the axis feeding through its stumbling effect to half a dozen other sites. An unknown attempted, new ground broken.

159

Cindy was brought back to her own bed with an acid-rush, flagrantly loud belch in the designated sickroom. Neil Austin had been all too honest in his explanation that the next few weeks were unlikely to be Camille-elegant. The taste at the back of her mouth changed slowly over the next ten minutes, climbed forwards on to her tongue and taste buds. Cindy realised that what had woken her wasn't the actual flavour in her mouth – odd, metallic, though it was – but the slow churning of her uncertain stomach. She wasn't exactly nauseous, didn't want to throw up, they had said it wouldn't be quite like that, the nurse explaining further while she weighed Cindy, making sure they ordered the correct dose, perfect sizing for the little pastel pills. These days there was no need for the old-fashioned extremes. Not usually anyway, not if they were good enough at their job. And certainly not just yet, the nurse was clear about that. The pink pills were designed – ideally, hopefully – to halt the disease progress before the exploratory surgery. The fat white ones intended – hopefully, ideally – to keep her functioning, able to work, a useful member of society. Ill but not incapacitated by nausea, dying but not yet dead. Just like everyone else really. Except that she now had a schedule. Cindy lay still, tried to analyse what she felt. Hoped for ease from understanding. She found a place of comparison; this was car-sickness, sea-sickness, an inner ear upset with no obvious outer movement. Other than the world, moving on without her. She lay waiting for it to pass. It did not pass. Sipped at the bad taste water.

Left the room to her closed eyelids and travelled back to David McLoughlin. His saliva had so quickly become a commonplace in Cindy's life. From no real kisses ever, to all and every day. Back of the bus, morning and afternoon, at lunchtime in the cafeteria for an entire high school season. Tasting of fresh toothpaste in the morning and tired French verbs by four p.m., tuna sandwiches and cupcake crumb lunches. They barely spoke. There was nothing to say, they were fifteen. The kisses reached not much further than mouths, maybe a cheek, an earlobe, the hands stayed on broadening backs and narrow upper arms, fingers entwined when parental or teacher presence stilled tongues. Then David McLoughlin's father was relocated to New Orleans and there was one last lingering kiss in the hall beside her locker. His hand that strayed to the edge of her left breast, her knee that pressed more insistently against his mother-laundered jeans. Cindy never saw him again. Kelly heard years later that David McLoughlin had been killed in a road accident at twenty-one. Half a dozen drunk youths piled into a stolen van, ploughed into a waiting wall. When Kelly passed on the news Cindy wasn't sure she really remembered his face, brown eyes maybe, or hazel, hair slightly too long, dirty blonde in summer. But she knew his taste, a routine insinuated on her tongue.

Back to the bedroom sickroom. Further developments of the new taste in her throat, slow and low turn through her stomach. She lay still, waiting for the feeling to pass or to change, to become whatever it was she was going to get used to. Another half-hour on the steady bed and Cindy felt maybe this was bearable. Constant car-sick. She could do that. Do this. Be this degree of ill for this time. Until she took the next handful before bed, then the morning version. What she now understood was that this first afternoon-into-evening section was bearable. A two-hour stretch that was not beyond endurance. Until Cindy considered cumulative car-sick over a period of weeks, and found herself shuddering, her fearful stomach bending her double at the suggestion and she sent the picture away. She would cut her immediate future into manageable chunks, one routine at a time. It would not get her planning any great life changes, but it might take her through to Tuesday morning.

She lay down again, wondering when she was going to burst into wracking sobs, when the horrific nature of what she had been told that afternoon was finally going to get through to her tear ducts and make a mess of her pretty, thin face. Another slow shudder worked its way through her stomach and churned a little more bile into the back of her throat. No tears just yet. And there were more pressing concerns. Like finding a way not to choke and throw up in her sleep. Assuming sleep planned on gracing her with its presence ever again. If she wasn't going to make it to old lady swinging on the porch, Cindy thought she ought to be able to do a little better than rock star demise – even with Kelly to goad her on, a vomit-choking death had never been all that appealing.

Twenty-nine

Ten minutes later Jack walked in with flowers and sorry-it-took-so-long face. Cindy could feel the deserted girlfriend moans welling up inside her, wanted to skip the round of useless, ending-in-apology-anyway blame and recrimination, so she concentrated instead on the queasiness inside and Jack's worried face.

'How was it? Has she found the story of the year?'

'Irrelevant. How are you? Anything happened?'

'Nothing much. I slept. I cried a bit.' Cindy pointed to the boxes lined up on Jack's side of the bed. 'I took the first lot of pills.'

'Was it OK?'

Cindy frowned. 'Just odd really.'

'Well, are you sick?'

They both paused at his words, then smiled, neither going to say it, each waiting for the other to jump at the crass joke. Neither had the courage, not just yet.

'Yeah, kind of. Oh, no actually, not really sick. I took the pink pills.'

'And the anti-emetics with them?'

'Yeah. Both. Like they said to. It feels weird. Nauseous, but not properly.'

'Can I get you anything? Have you eaten? Do you want food?'

Cindy consulted her slow-churn stomach, clammy skin, the barometers of new sensation. 'I don't know. I should be hungry. We both should. Unless you ate with Rebekah?'

Jack shook his head. Rebekah had eaten. Told him her story and munched her way through a burger and fries and side dishes of coleslaw and some extra potato skins thrown in for good measure. She was excited, had been working all night, looked to be heading for another evening of the same and needed to keep her strength up. Jack looked at the menu and ordered a sparkling water. When it came the full glass was too much for him. Rebekah took it to wash down her starch overload.

Jack brought himself back to the room, to Cindy, to the new decisions they would now have to make. Not that his couple of hours with the young journalist had given him any respite from those thoughts, but now, instead of devoting only half his mind to acknowledging how abruptly his life-plan had been cancelled, he was able to look solely at the bleak picture before him, diversionary tactics no longer necessary.

Cindy was not delving too far into the uncertain future. She was addressing the immediate nature of her altered state. She was wondering about eating. How to do it.

'Maybe I am hungry. And we should have something. Flavour would be good, not bland. But not too much. I don't know if I could take too much sensation. I don't want oil, I know that for sure. Nothing oily.' She shuddered slightly. 'I don't even want to talk about it. OK then, I want . . . something with . . . ah, taste.' She lay back on the piled pillows, exhausted with thought. 'Sorry, Jack. Don't know.'

'Hold on.'

Jack clattered in the kitchen, came back with a tray, three

bougainvillea heads floating in a glass of water, a clean white plate with half a Marmite sandwich cut into thin strips.

'Marmite soldiers. No butter.'

Cindy stared at the offering on the plate. In all this time with Jack she'd looked at his home-comforts jar of Marmite and hadn't yet persuaded herself past the strange smell. Now, though, it seemed as possible as anything else. She picked up a strip of bread, held it to her lips. Took a bite. Then another.

No-milk tea and no-butter Marmite soldiers. They made a picnic on the bed, hospital papers relegated to the floor. Jack told how he'd listened to Rebekah's revelations, more impressed than he'd let the young woman know, congratulations could wait until later, he still had some status to maintain in an office from which he was likely to be increasingly absent, and withholding praise was the surest way he knew to play the king. Cindy heard his concern about the inevitable absence and tried not to flinch with either guilt or irritation. Jack would have to go into the office tomorrow, run Rebekah's story past the big bosses and then yes, she could put it out in the evening. It was her big break. He'd picked a good one.

Jack mentioned going into the office the next day with a frown. It would only be for an hour or so, he'd already worked out an excuse for both the team and his bosses. But he did have to be there, for a bit. Cindy accepted this. Had no other suggestions. Was not prepared to budge on Jack keeping her illness a secret from his work for now and so had to let him go. Wanted to let him go. And loathed the thought of it at the same time. Thinking about it rationally, she figured she probably needed time alone to process what was happening to her, to physically get used to this new routine, and at the same time she couldn't bear the thought of holding the panic at bay single-handedly any longer. She tried hard not to let the fear come out in her speech, blamed the semi-nausea, but panic escaped her mouth anyway, in a bitter aside about how important it was that Jack made sure he got his priorities just right. He took the verbal slap, didn't answer back, had been beating himself up all afternoon anyway. Let the tears fall from his stinging eyes. Cindy apologised, Jack apologised, Cindy cried. Properly now. The tears she'd been looking for. Wracking sobs, wrenching up from her turning gut and out of a forced-open mouth, lips splitting at the corners, body rocking in time to her shuddering, syncopated breath. Jack held her and prayed never again to cry before she did. They reached for each other among the debris of their careful picnic and tried not to look too hard at what was coming.

As they fell asleep, hands, thighs and feet touching, Jack offered the sensible words he'd been rehearsing in the car on his way home, 'We have to promise to talk to each other about this, babe.'

'How do you mean?'

'I don't mind if you're upset with me for going in to work tomorrow. I'm upset about it. And I'm pissed off for crying in Austin's office today and I'm pissed off that I'm not handling this better. It's all right if you mind how I'm doing. That I'm not being very good with this yet.'

'I don't think we have to be good with it yet, Jack. I don't know if I want to be good with it at all.'

'I just mean it's all right if I'm pissing you off.'

'I have permission to hate you?'

'Yeah, if you like. I want to get this right. But I'm bound to make mistakes on the way.'

Cindy smiled in the dark, started to turn into him, then her stomach flipped and she lay back, body flat, head high-raised. 'I think we can be fairly certain we're both going to make mistakes. And of course I mind that you're going in to work tomorrow. And you're not going for long. And we have no choice.'

'We just need to do our best with this, though.'

'With the story?'

'No. You and me. Not the story, the story's done. I don't have that much of a one-track mind.'

'Sorry.'

'No me, I'm apologising. I'm sorry. I want to be the sorry one.'

They laughed again, relieved to have dodged the anger.

'It's this we need to keep good, here. We have to keep talking to each other all the time. Tell each other what we're thinking and feeling, even if it is horrible, even if we're really pissed off with each other.'

'Are you pissed off with me, Jack?'

Jack paused, a semi-second too long. He rushed in with assurance, but Cindy had caught his break. 'Of course not.' He lied. 'What do I have to be pissed off with you for?' For not being better at staying alive. 'We just have to hang on to you and me. No matter what else is going on.'

'Yeah, I know. We do. We will. It's OK. Come on, go to sleep. We're both shattered.'

It wasn't OK. Not for either of them. Nor was it going to be. Cindy felt Jack against her, stroking her bare arm. Eventually Jack fell into an exhausted sleep. The bitter taste at the back of her throat and her rebellious stomach still awake, Cindy contemplated his words. His demands for complete honesty while at the very same time keeping back what he really felt. So as not to upset her. So as not to blame her. Jack wanted them to be themselves. It was a valid request. Obviously the right thing to do. But she wondered which Cindy he wanted her to be. Old Cindy or new Cindy? She doubted very much that Jack wanted dying Cindy. She knew she didn't. Nor did she have all that much desire to get through this. Getting through meant getting to the end. Sleep came, with a shudder and a sip of bile.

Thirty

That night was especially drawn out, Cindy alternating bouts of drowsy nausea with deep-sleep twenty-minute catnapping. After two hours of pointlessly lying down, Jack spent the rest of the night either sitting beside his semi-comatose partner or in the next room, perched at her desk. He was trawling the Internet for message boards and medical papers and possibility, the war zone titles Victim and Survivor spitting fear into his eyes through the blue screen light. There were plenty of suggestions and hundreds of recommended alternatives and websites, each one maybe holding the answer and, once he'd gone to them, each one offering a slightly different version of Cindy's illness – nothing exactly her age, condition, development, analysis, prognosis. Nothing titled 'The Saving of Cindy Frier'. He finally came back to bed at five; eyes burnt red from the search, he laid himself out beside Cindy, scared to disturb, scared to be away. Sleep edged inwards from his aching limbs. At seven in the morning they turned off the radio alarm's morning news – brutal international sanctions, Spanish terrorist attacks, global economic downturn – to better concentrate on the more immediate terror of the local broadcast from their bedroom sickroom newsroom. Post-2 a.m. queasiness receded, replaced by internal anxiety and toss-turn fear. Another handful of pills to take down, more discomfort edging into pain.

Each was grateful for the blue sky, the seven o'clock. While Cindy would have welcomed dark clouds and wind-swept streets as an outside reflection of her inner state, she was also thankful for the necessity of getting up. The things that made getting on with the day something she could do with little or no thought; the routine of dressing, fashion requirements converted to practicality and function. They showered together, Pacific blue no match for their own sadness. Dried and dressed in the bedroom beside each other, bodies close, still-shaking hands grazing against the other as often as zips and buttons and belts allowed. Cindy followed Jack to the kitchen and, Siamese-twin-close, they spooned and poured and placed and scraped together. Bit into dry toast simultaneously, swallowed down scraping mouthfuls. Then, empty stomachs fake-filled, Cindy swallowed her pills. The motions of getting on with it aside, illness remained anchored in place. Whatever work the little pink and white pills had been sent to do – now with a morning addition of two baby blue – was not demonstrably successful within Cindy's understanding of her body. Though she lay in bed and waited to feel the good guys fighting off the bad, she sensed instead only the nearly-familiar churn of her gut from the pink, the slight stiffening that was the holding-at-bay from the white, and then a new twist of mid-torso ache, a cool and seemingly entirely detached pain, no doubt the contribution of the blue.

She lay down, waiting to get used to how she felt. Body flat, head propped up against acid reflux. Twenty minutes passed. Then another twenty. After an hour she felt accustomed enough to sit up and ask Jack for her laptop. Five minutes later, when she'd established beyond all doubt that she could not possibly concentrate on the waving lines her eyes made of the screen, Jack took it away again. There followed another pointless question/answer/refusal session in which

Jack demanded to be allowed to stay at home and Cindy turned into the mother of a school-hating child, because I say so. He left the house under protest, bribing himself with the promise of an early return, and Cindy faced the next terrifying task. Jack had offered to make the necessary calls. Although she was aching to have him do it for her, Cindy knew this was one conversation she would have to engage in herself. Three conversations. Mother, father, Kelly. Jack could tell everyone else. These three people were only going to believe if they heard it directly from her. And Cindy had a suspicion that this was also the only way it would become true for her. Telling her mother she was dying should make a difference in comprehension.

She lay wedged against the pillows with the telephone in her hand for half an hour. Then another thirty minutes. Fifteen more. In the seventy-five minutes Jack called three times, and she dialled Kelly's number seven and a half. Hanging up before the tone turned to ring on every one. Kelly had this week off, would be getting up now, readying herself for the gym, then her afternoon, then the date she'd email-detailed Cindy about the previous weekend. The one Cindy had expressed unusual interest in, suggesting items of clothing and shades of lipstick, gratefully bubbling over any girlie details to deflect from what was really happening. Cindy needed to call before Kelly went out, wanted to let her best friend know, figured midday was better than evening, busy afternoon safer than empty night. Dialled again. The number rang. Kelly, gritty-voiced with sleep, picked up on the fourth long tone.

'What?'

'Oh damn, I'm sorry, Kelly. I thought you'd be up by now.'

'Ah no. I would. But . . . look, hold on, I'll take you in the other room.' Kelly grunted, lifted herself from the bed, staggered from the bedroom into her sitting room, pulled a rug around her naked body, raised her tone to one above a whisper, 'I have a guest.'

'I thought you were saving yourself for the big date tonight?'

'I decided to spend a little early.'

'Same woman?'

'Of course! What kind of a tart do you think I am?'

'I don't think you want me to answer that one.'

'Not without proving you know what you're talking about.'

'Easy!'

'No, it's good you called, we only went to bed at dawn and I do have a few things to do, you know, go back to bed, check out those long legs of hers in the unflinching light of day . . .'

'Kelly, hold it, it's way too early for a live girls information overload.'

It wasn't. Not at all. Cindy's knowledge of Kelly's sex life was broad and explicit and most usually welcomed. As was Cindy's reciprocal girl-boy version. But she couldn't bring herself to let Kelly detail averages and times, peaks reached, troughs ploughed. Not today. Fortunately Kelly was too tired – and too self-satisfied – to notice Cindy's unusual reaction.

'OK, sweetie. Delighted to see the West Coast inhibitions have finally caught you in their smug little grasp. What next? You giving up drinking?'

'Well yeah.' Cindy grabbed the opportunity to answer honestly, seeing it as an entry point for the conversation she was dreading. 'I suppose I might have to actually. For a bit.'

'What?'

'I don't feel much like drinking right now.'

'Good God, girl, drugs too?'

Cindy glanced over at the range of pill boxes and bottles lined up on her bedside table. 'I gave up the illegal ones already. Kelly, listen, there's something I need to tell you.'

But Kelly didn't listen. At least not to Cindy's tone. She heard the words – no drink, no illegal drugs, and vaulted seamlessly to the wrong conclusion. The opposite conclusion.

'Oh my God, you're pregnant! That's fantastic news! I mean, it is, right? I told you it would be a good move out there. Can I be the godmother? Well?'

Kelly stopped to get an answer. There was none. Just Cindy sitting alone in her bed thousands of miles away and sobbing.

'Babe? What is it? Cinna?'

Cindy finding words, 'Not pregnant, Kelly. I'm not pregnant.' Then saying it out loud for the first time, 'I'm sick. I'm ill.' Forcing her mouth to move, pushing her tongue and teeth and lips to form recognisable vowel sounds, consonants clicking into painful place, words her entire frame was life-trained to disbelieve, 'I'm not going to get better.'

But Kelly didn't want to hear this any more than Cindy's mouth wanted to say it. She was making no more assumptive leaps of logic, incapable of piecing together the whole truth from the unsaid words. 'I don't get it?'

Cindy breathing in and out, hand tight-clenched on the telephone, she forced action: brain impulse to vocal chords, chemical reactions tracing a path from the left frontal lobe, breath twisted into recognisable speech pattern, 'I'm not going to get better.'

Kelly found herself furious at what she had already guessed she was hearing, 'Christ, Cindy, what the fuck . . .?'

One more push: simultaneous impulses travelled to her primary motor area, sending off further impulses which controlled the breathing muscles, the flow of air past her vocal chords. The co-ordinated contractions of speech and breath finally permitted Cindy to offer, 'I'm going to die, Kelly.'

Silence.

'Soon. They think it will be soon.'

More silence. Attempting understanding. Shock. Denial. Disbelief. Guilt. Anger. Acceptance. Cindy slowly, haltingly, detailed the events of the last few weeks. The parts of her story she had not given Kelly in their everyday emails, two- and three-weekly phone conversations. Filled in the lying gaps. She made it very clear, offered no alternatives.

'Oh. God. Fuck.'

Kelly had one-syllable answers. And then again the choking quiet.

'Kelly?'

'Hmm?'

'Talk to me?'

Long silence.

'I don't know what to say.'

'Neither do I. But if you don't talk it sounds like you're angry with me. Come on, girl – it's not my fault, I'm only telling you what they told me. Don't kill the messenger.'

Thousands of miles of digital non-line and the bumbling words finally made sense. Non-sense. Kelly burst out laughing, 'Hah! Too fucking late!'

They laughed then. Cried. Laughed some more. Kelly launched into a series of bad taste jokes. Exactly the ones Cindy had wanted to hear, exactly the reason she had called Kelly before her parents. She needed the barbed vitriol, the cell phone, prison cell, sick-cell humour. Wanted her delicate edges buffed up, smoothed over, made clean; her pain plain-packaged before she forwarded it to anyone else. Kelly was the perfect solution. Not that she wouldn't get off the phone, get rid of the new lover, pour herself several drinks and look out her window, crying over the broken Manhattan skyline. But she knew her job. Make it better for Cindy. Put her own unhappiness in place. Be of help. Stupid jokes and silly giggling and honest tears and blatantly dishonest promises of coping from both sides. Best friend work. Best done by a best friend. They talked for another twenty minutes, Cindy extracting a promise that Kelly would go to her mother's apartment in an hour, wait until Cindy called on her cell phone and then knock on her mother's door at a synchronised minute. She didn't want her mother to be alone when she told her. Kelly agreed to be the bad news midwife. And she carried a martini hip flask in her bag.

Two hours later the deeds were done. Cindy had dodged responsibility on her first attempt, found herself calling her father's home rather than his office, explaining all to the latest Barbie. Figured those pneumatic breasts might have some use after all, give her father somewhere to hide his tears. And a certain bitter part of her took a degree of satisfaction in breaking the news to a woman just eighteen months older than herself. And then demanding the baby Barbie be the one to tell her father, Cindy couldn't possibly do it, it was too much, she wasn't strong enough. All perfectly true. When she put the phone down, she was sure she could hear the sound of snapping plastic as the current girlfriend tried to pull herself together for her coming challenge. Cindy pushed the gathering nausea aside long enough to smile relief that her illness hadn't yet eaten away at her inherent bitch faculties.

Calling her mother was much harder. There was no-one she could get to do the dirty deed. Kelly was the ready support partner, for both women, but Cindy still had to give voice to the disease. It was all wrong. The child as informant and comforter, the parent turned baby with fear and

175

imminent loss. She spoke quietly and carefully. Made sure there was no misunderstanding. Cindy's mother wailed that this was every mother's nightmare. Cindy opened her mouth to assure her it was fairly unpleasant for every daughter too, shut it just in time. This was not the moment to play pain-hierarchy. Her mother was all for getting the next plane out there, but Cindy held her off, asked for time to get used to the news herself, requested help in a few weeks maybe, after surgery. And even as she offered that alternative, she knew only too well that when her mother arrived, Cindy and Jack would be doing the caring. If terminal illness had not yet made a non-bitch of Cindy, it was even less likely to turn Hannah Frier into Mama Walton. Then, having hung up the phone promising to call again that evening, Cindy realised that for once she didn't really mind. She wanted to see her mother, would put up with the overbearing suffering which would no doubt eclipse her own; which already, even on the telephone, threatened to engulf hers. It occurred to Cindy that with the unfamiliarity coming her way, she might welcome a return to recognisable patterns. She swallowed four baby-pastel pills and three white ones, picturing irritation and argument, smother-love alternating with cold indifference, the wrong clothes, the wrong food, the wrong girl. Saw recreated once again a lifetime's pattern of inevitable, never-changing, mother-daughter suffering. And the glorious picture of normalcy it provided cheered her up so much that she washed her face, cleaned her teeth, flicked on the answer machine and went out for a walk.

Thirty-one

Cindy stopped in a natural grove. While her queasy stomach was not eased by the walk, she was relieved that the symptoms hadn't increased in her turn uphill. She'd stopped by a tree. Not all that big yet, though already wide-branched. A climbing tree really, in a few years' time, with some more strength in its branches – if she had the energy. She did not. A swing tree then perhaps, with a heavy rope and an old tyre like the one her father had told her about from his own childhood, a playmate walnut tree in the back yard of his youth. The one he never forgave his mother for chopping down after his father's death. The walnut tree simply the last in a long line of maternal injustices Cindy's father brought out for excuse whenever another Barbie risked pushing him too far into the realms of commitment. Cindy knew this wasn't a walnut she had come to rest by, but she didn't know much else about it. She ran her fingers along the trunk, wishing she'd paid more attention to her grandfather's Central Park botany lessons when he'd visited on childhood holidays. Not that this was likely to be anything other than a pure Californian native, the leaves seemed somehow too heavy, the bark too flimsy for a New York tree. This one was designed to soak up water from the ground whenever it could, from the atmosphere when the earth was baked hard and dry. This tree had dark green leaves, not the brittle gold she expected from this time of year. These leaves knew their place, had no need to fall in season, grew through the slow meld from summer past to vague winter, their coming a herald of nothing more glorious than the new season's fashions.

Cindy picked at the bark with flaking fingernails, scratched the wood beneath. If she took a saw and cut right through the centre she would be able to read its history. Darker rings for the wet years, pale ones spinning out the months passed in drought. The tree was mapping its own growth. As long as there was water and sunlight it would continue to spread itself, to travel on from its focal point in the earth, reaching roots down and branches up. As long as nothing got in its way it would continue to do so. And even then it might prove stronger than the will of the people. Certainly it would live longer than most. Cindy remembered her grandfather telling her about a long-gone family home in Vermont. The maple tree that wouldn't stop coming up through the back porch, so they just cut the boards and let it grow, up through the house, practically. It went where it wanted to, followed its own map. Outlived three generations of his mother's family before the house began to fall down around it.

Inside her body the same thing was happening, new growth stretching out and making paths wherever it could, growing in its own time. Cindy wanted to take a saw to herself, cut out the inside growths, open them up and read their story. But the ending was obvious from the opening phrases. Like Lewis and Clark charting the not-yet nation from the East Coast to the West, both start and finish lines were already in place, all she had to discover was the route from one to the other. Map the lines forwards.

Cindy had made a beginning in calling people. Before she left the house she'd phoned Jack, told him he could let his work know whenever he wanted, explain as much or as little as was best for him. Listened to his voice speaking concern and betraying fear, felt the weirdness of his absence and the under-layer of needing him constantly by her. She could, of course, expect to hear more of that concern, feel more of his unhappiness from now on. So one route was clear. There would be more worry, fear, anxiety. Cindy wondered about the feelings of denial she knew she was expected to have, how it appeared to have skipped her. Only a day had passed since Neil Austin had confirmed his own fears, and yet already she seemed to have taken in his assessment of her condition. Certainly she was in shock, definitely she felt fuzzy-headed, unclear, but there was no disbelief. Anger was there, fear of future physical pain, unhappiness that what was happening to her was also going to hurt other people close to her. But denial was plainly missing. Unless, of course, hiking through the canyons on a mild afternoon, fondling tree bark and remembering her long-dead grandfather, pushing the queasiness to one side in order to enjoy the image of herself as intrepid tree climber – unless all those were forms of denial in themselves. Perhaps keeping going was denial. Cindy pushed herself away from the tree and shook the thoughts from her. She'd told three people this morning that she was dying. Maybe that was enough for one day. Maybe she didn't have to be grief-stage perfect as well. Maybe it would be OK just to take in the daylight for a bit.

She turned up the path to walk back to the main road and home, wishing, not for the first time in her life, but more clearly than before, that future good things might be as obvious as the future bad ones. Past experience, the glory of hindsight, had taught her that even now there would be good things coming. There had to be benefits, even in a dying light. But she sincerely hoped that not all of those benefits were about becoming the Mother Theresa clone usually

179

expected of illness. With any luck – and she probably deserved a little by now – one or two of the gains might be about getting wonderfully drunk and fucking her diseased brains out and laughing behind her mother's heartbroken back. Having Kelly come to stay and not indulging in a moment's martini-too-much guilt. Having more reason than usual to demand Jack rub her back, massage her feet, go in late to work. Telling her agent to fuck off with his deadline requests – everyone knew posthumous glory and a tearful readership would make them more money anyway.

Cindy-cynic and Cindy-Pollyanna skipped hand in hand up the dappled path to the main road, the glorious Pacific, the oblivious passing traffic. And, waiting at home for the four o'clock feed, a handful of poisonous pastel pills and peaceful white steroids.

Thirty Two

At first, when the story broke, there was absolute pande-
monium. For two full days Rebekah's story was the prime
topic on news shows and talk radio across the state. It filled fat
columns in local newspapers, provided ideal fodder for leader
writers and columnists. Rebekah stood back proudly and
watched the fruits of her investigation blossom. And then,
amazed, she watched them wither on the vine. A day or two
later the story slipped further down the list of pressing matters.
A woman went missing in San Diego. A child was shot by his
best friend in San Rafael. Rebekah's story did matter. A major
secret was uncovered, a long-term scandal blown apart. And
ten days later it was entirely irrelevant except to the main
players. Rebekah was devastated. Jack reckoned it was the
making of her.

At first, when the story broke, there was absolute pande-
monium. The furore Jack had expected and Cindy had
insisted she would not allow to happen, rose up and threatened to engulf them entirely. What Cindy called 'the disease'
and what Kelly's night fears, night tears, privately termed
'Cindy's fucking imminent fucking death' spread rapidly from
West to East and back again. Phone lines went crazy, mother
and father and ex-stepmothers and in-laws and cousins
demanded doctors' credentials, old friends and new began

181

baying for time with Cindy. The hierarchy of grief sprang into action as people worked out their place in relation to each other and in relation to the Cindy-focus, what they assumed was now her special knowing, her proximity to eternity. Their place in relation to her fucking imminent fucking death.

Within forty-eight hours of telling her parents and Kelly – and giving them permission to pass on the news – there were blocked email lines as everyone from oldest friends to newest students offered condolences and tears, food and friendship. And the particularly successful herbal remedy someone's sister had used to come back from the brink of death – following cosmetic surgery. Or the native Icelandic cure for liver disease, kidney failure, heart attack, chilblains. One old acquaintance believed Cindy should never have left the safety of Manhattan. There was another cousin who wanted to pray with her – and then asked her to intercede for him when the worst came to the worst. A further ex-colleague was certain she knew exactly what Jack and Cindy were going through, and that her intimate knowledge of parental loss, childbirth, terminal diseases overcome or given in to, was exactly what these two needed right now. Health records were proffered, Cindy and Jack's answer machine was inundated with requests to rest in this beach house or that, and the quiet cool of their little home was shattered by the incessant offers of help and care and concern. Each one lovingly intentioned, each one contributing to the cumulative nightmare.

Jack's method was to turn to the Internet and libraries whenever he could, to dig through page after page in the hope of finding an elixir for Cindy's life. An elixir for his own. Cindy herself stood back in amazement and watched the friendship fruits of her disease blossom into this relentless activity. She was immensely grateful, incredibly touched, and absolutely certain that she wanted them all to go away. She wished there was no reason for this attention, found that every new message or email reminded her of just how bad things were. Stared at the big bunches of flowers that arrived every few hours and wondered how she was supposed to keep breathing in a room that looked like a funeral parlour. She was touched by the obvious concern – and hated it for the high-lighting.

Along with the would-be helpers and cure-givers, though, there was another group, homogenous yet seemingly self-selected at random from their friends and family and acquaintances. Those who felt that best practice would be to simply ignore the situation entirely. Cindy herself had a degree of sympathy with this reaction. Unfortunately she could not ignore it. The constant presence of the thing inside that had brought on her searing pain, the continual feeling of never-fading car-sickness, the rising fear of the first week as each day passed and the time of surgery and definite disease mapping drew closer – every moment the truth of her situation under-lined itself on her creased brow. Most of the people who didn't want to know were distant enough not to matter all that much. One of the big bosses and two of Jack's workmates who wanted him in the office more than the three hours a day compromise he had offered. The first cousin who sincerely believed that if Cindy simply gave herself over to the Lord – as he himself did regularly – then everything would naturally be fine, but he didn't want to talk to her to tell her and he chose to shut himself away in a prayer hour, hoping to get through that way instead. Cindy's publicist, who couldn't quite get her head around the idea that her client's time and possibility was now finite. That she wasn't much interested in going on talk shows with her disease. Cindy was mostly able to ignore these people and their fearful reactions. If they couldn't handle it, then she didn't have to handle being around them.

With the one or two who did matter, though, it was a little harder. An ex-Barbie with whom Cindy had recently managed to develop a good relationship, an old boyfriend in New York, the editor who had published her first attention-grabbing paper – the seeming indifference of these people hurt more than Cindy could have expected. And her father's version – which amounted to his calling twice a day at exactly the same time while failing to ask anything about how she was feeling or what was happening with her treatment – was excruciatingly painful. His evident inability to take in the bad news, the lack of generosity in processing the truth, reflected back on Cindy's disease. Gave her moments when she too figured she must be untouchable. Generally, of course, she knew better, was able to dismiss the lack of empathy as the masked fear it really was – even in her most frightened hours she couldn't really accept indifference at its callous face value. But neither Cindy nor Jack were strong enough to completely avoid being hurt by the fear of those who would rather not look at anything unpleasant, preferred ease to truth.

Cindy and Jack were a bad news couple living in a world which, for all its hungry feeding on ghoulish news pictures, its predilection for horror movies over love stories, preferred its death and despair filtered and carefully packaged and just a little further from home if possible. And when she wasn't hating them for being stupid, insensitive idiots, Cindy understood their predicament. She'd rather have kept her death a little further from home as well.

Thirty-three

As the first week went on, Cindy became more unwell. The constant car-sickness, a passing dizziness that veered indiscriminately from mild to extreme, the inability to sleep more than ninety minutes at a time, never deeply, never enough. Despite Jack's pleas, she was not eager to call the hospital to check that this was normal. They had a return visit booked the following Monday for another scan, more blood tests, to check if these pills – early though it was – were making any difference. If there was no change, Neil Austin had suggested they might need to take a more aggressive pre-surgery approach. That first afternoon in his office, Cindy had wondered if maybe a more aggressive approach from the beginning wouldn't be the best option anyway. Five days later, tired out from lack of sleep, drained from the careful messages left on the answerphone, she wondered how she would stand anything more aggressive. That it was coming she had no doubt. That she wasn't eager to meet it was equally certain. In addition, any contact with the place that had confirmed the disease seemed to emphasise not only her illness, but also Neil Austin's certainty of her timeline. Not that she didn't believe the medics – she had no choice, it was hardly her field of expertise – but it troubled her that they believed their own truths with such certainty. And, at what felt like such an early stage, Cindy was still trying not to focus on the dateline. She understood the words. She found the timing harder to take. She had always loved spring. Right now, even the inconspicuous Californian season-slide seemed way preferable to the alternative. Silk-acrylic daffodils prettier than none.

Cindy had taken little time to come to terms with the prognosis. But this was mostly because she had set herself very clear boundaries about what she could and could not do. She could discuss the certainty of her death. Clock-watching, though, sent her nerves blackboard-scraping. If she allowed herself to view her future weeks as finite then, on one level, placating her tearful mother, soothing her wounded father, going to the supermarket, even wasting five minutes getting in and out of bed, seemed ludicrous. She should be climbing Everest or trekking the Andes or sailing single-handed across the Atlantic. She should not be carrying on as normal. And yet alternatively, Cindy-normal was exactly what she wanted. Until the next lot of scans and then the subsequent surgery and the further biopsies which would confirm or deny Neil Austin's calendar, the timeline was, despite his professional certainty, still just a possibility for Cindy. Afterwards, she would maybe take a look at K2. Though she'd never especially cared for mountains before, she couldn't rule out the possibility that a beyond-doubt confirmation of the death-diagnosis might make a mountaineer out of her yet. Until then, in the three days of pseudo-normal remaining, Cindy wanted to go to the market, take a walk. Shower with her eyes open to the ocean, girlfriend-gossip with Kelly, even look at her own work. Acknowledging the timeline felt like giving in to it. And anyway, if there were only three months available, then of what possible use were three days? Far better to go on as if there might be three years, decades, centuries.

As she explained to Kelly in one of their now nightly

phone calls, 'Well of course I thought I understood that I was going to die.'

'You knew about this?'

'No. Not this. Although, in hindsight some things seem like maybe they were markers, but I expect we could all do that. No, I didn't know it was going to happen to me. Specifically. Just that we all die. And we all know we'll die. But now it's like I didn't ever really know it. I didn't really understand what it meant.'

'Not even when Patrick went?'

Kelly referred to their old friend who had died several years earlier. She referred to it coyly, and completely uncharacteristically, as 'went' because she had yet to say the words death or dying when talking to Cindy. Not without bursting into tears.

'No, because it didn't happen to me. Not really.'

'One of your oldest friends goes and you think it doesn't happen to you?'

Cindy shifted on the bed, raised the pillow higher beneath her head, passed a hand across her disturbed stomach. 'But it didn't. It happened to him. Sure, at the time, like everyone else, I thought it had happened to me, we all did. I thought I was affected by his death, that I was part of it. But now I feel different.'

'How?'

'Well, he died. Pat died. I didn't, not then.'

Kelly held her breath, dug iridescent blue fingernails into her palms and willed herself not to start sobbing down the line. Cindy continued; part of her knew this conversation was upsetting Kelly and part of her didn't care. One of the other changes of the proposed timeline, she worried even less about being careful, not when she had so many tears of her own still to let out.

'Kells, Pat wasn't even my partner. When he died, no part of my daily routine changed. Of course I missed him, I still do, we all do. But my life didn't alter. Not really. We were all devastated, you and me and Sam, Pat's family, but in the end, it wasn't us. At the time I thought it was about me, but now I know different. It was his life, not mine. I could still do all the things I'd always thought I was going to do, plan my life with Jack, have new experiences. I could move to California. Pat couldn't. It's about behaviour. I still behaved as if I was going to go on forever.'

'Oh.'

'I was an innocent then. A mortality innocent.'

'And now you're not?'

'No.'

'I think I'll stay a virgin in that case.'

'Yeah, I would.'

By the Friday afternoon Jack could no longer stand seeing Cindy in constant physical discomfort and he called Neil Austin's nurse himself. He came back to the room frowning.

'What?'

'I told her how you were. The dizziness, the pain and nausea.'

'And?'

'She said it was good.'

'What?'

'She said it was good. The medication is obviously working.'

'Which medication?'

'All of them. She said if the anti-emetics weren't working you wouldn't be able to get out of bed, and if the drugs weren't working you wouldn't feel sick.'

'Did you tell her I can't sleep?'

'She said, and I think I can quote her here, "Oh, but that's perfectly normal after a shock like this, she'll get used to it in time." She said they would give you sleeping pills if you like.'

'Right.'

'She sounded quite pleased with what I told her about you.'

'That bodes well for her bedside manner when I get worse.'

'Don't you worry. I'll make sure they're fucking brilliant with you.'

'I know you will, Jack.'

'They must be used to it. It's normal for her.'

'I suppose their view of good is different to ours.'

'I guess.'

'She did ask me about your book.'

'What?'

'If you're as interesting as your writing.'

'What did you say?'

'Way more so. She said she'd be glad to spend time with you in that case.'

'Hell yeah, me too.'

'She did say it with an understanding tone.'

'Cow.'

'Cunt.'

'Nurse Cunt. Very British. I like it.'

Over the weekend, away from the pressures of work – having told Rebekah it would be fine practice to cope with the fallout herself if at all possible – Jack took even more time to search out alternative methods, tales of spontaneous healing and miracle cures. While Cindy dozed and woke to groan and then fell back into a dizzy half-sleep, he printed out reams of what looked to him like possibility. And looked to Cindy like desperation.

Jack protested, 'Why won't you even look at this stuff? It's like you've already given up.'

'Not up, in.'

'What?'

'Giving up would be rolling over and saying yes, I agree, I'll die now.'

'Haven't you? You seem to agree with everything the hospital have said – you didn't even want to try for a second opinion.'

'What good would that do? Everyone says he's the best, why run the risk of taking longer to start on treatment – even if it is just keeping the inevitable at bay for a while? It's not as if I'm doing nothing. I'm taking the pills, letting them make me sicker than I felt before in the hope that this treatment will give them something to operate on when they go in. But I'm not kidding myself either, Jack. We both saw the pictures. It was obvious. Even to me. Neil Austin had maps of me and the disease was there, quite clearly. I'm not going to fight the evidence of our own eyes. I have to give in to that. I know it to be true because they showed it to us in the hospital and I know it to be true because I don't believe that kind of pain would come from nowhere. I have no reason to doubt them. You want me to stay around don't you?'

'Of course I fucking do.'

'And you want me to keep as well as possible. Right?'

'Yes.'

'Well I can only do that by agreeing that there is something wrong. If I do what you'd like me to do – behave as if they've made some awful mistake and run around like a crazy woman trying to find some other answer – then I run the risk of wasting whatever time there is. I don't want to waste any time, Jack. I want to get this right.'

'But this is awful, we have to fight it . . .'

190

Cindy clenched the fist she held crossed against her torso. 'No. I don't want to fight it, it's my own body, I don't even know how to begin fighting my own body. I don't want to be a battleground. But maybe I can subsume it. Maybe I can be bigger than this thing which, after all, is coming from me. But to do that I have to accept where we are.'

Jack shook his head, too frightened to acknowledge where they were, too hurt and angry to look up.

Cindy continued, 'You know about GPS right?'

'The satellite mapping thing they use in the jungle?'

She sighed, all too used to this fore-shortening of her work. 'Yeah. The satellite mapping thing they use in the jungle. And other places too, like almost every military application you can think of – but OK, it's famous for the jungle. Anyway, it tells you where you are. Exactly where you are.'

'So?'

'So in the past, we've always mapped using where we came from as the starting point. If I came from there, and travelled this way, then I must now be here. Now people can be out there, and imagine they're lost, and not really know how they got there – which you tend not to if you've been dropped in anyway – but using GPS you can always know where you are.'

Jack sighed, sat down on the bed, dropped his sheaf of papers to the floor. 'And what's that got to do with us?'

'Everything. Neil Austin showed us where we are. The biopsies and the scans and the x-rays are our GPS. My GPS. I have no idea how I came to be here. Neither do you. We weren't expecting this. It's certainly not where we've been heading. But it is where we are. And even though most of my career has been about working out how we got here and applying that to the future, it's not going to work in this case. I don't know how I got here, we have to give in to that. Unless we do, we can't go anywhere. There's no other way of mapping our route. You want to run around going backwards and sideways, trying to find another way out.'

'Maybe there is one.'

'Yeah, maybe there is. But the only thing that's telling us exactly where we are right now is the hospital and their machines. And maybe I'm putting too much faith in technology, but I don't see your massage woman or some dietician or a crystal healer looking into my torso and plotting the markers of my disease. I need to know where I am, Jack. And Neil Austin's methods can tell me that. And using his stuff I can then go forwards. Maybe not out, maybe not into any clearing where it will all become perfectly obvious what we have to do next, maybe all I can go is further in. But at least it's movement. And I do have to give in for that to be the case. I do have to agree that yes, this is where I am right now.'

'But there might be other things available out there.'

'Yeah, and then again we might waste the next couple of months trying miracle cures that promise everything and deliver nothing. As far as I can see, Neil Austin is promising pretty much nothing. A few months, maybe more. And I'm a scientist, I like worst case scenarios. They're what I understand. I really don't believe that I – my attitudes or whatever – made this illness. I don't know how to believe I am strong enough to un-make it.'

'So we just go on from here then?'

'That's right. And it's scary. I actually think GPS is quite scary. We've never mapped from nothing before, we've always referred backwards to our previous paths. It's going to create a massive change in the way things are done. I really don't think people have fully considered the implications of working in that way. It will totally change the way we travel and explore and discover. It's a huge leap to make – to go forwards with no thread reaching back. But right now that's where you

192

and I are. And I don't see we have any other option. I'm not prepared to give up my last few months of life to juicing and fasting and not eating what I want or seeing who I want. I'm not going to start praying to something I don't believe in. I don't want to have to make up a new Cindy because the old one simply wouldn't do any of that. I don't want to be a new Cindy, Jack. I like this one. So do you.'

'I love this one.'

'I know. And it's really fucking awful that you don't get to have her for as long as you wanted. That I don't get to have her for as long as I wanted. But I make maps. And we've been given a map of where we are now. It's pretty clear. I think we can only go forwards if we choose to believe in it.'

'Give in to it.'

'That's right. Which isn't give up and stop, it's give in and get on. For as long as there is. For as long as it takes.'

Thirty-four

The results were not good. Cindy could tell from the set of Neil Austin's shoulders that he was unhappy. What she did not know was that the tension his stiff neck signalled was not merely the by-product of her disappointing results; it was also the strain that set in when he was about to suggest a further, and more difficult, course of treatment. According to her scans, the sites of disease had neither shrunk nor, and this was the main cause of his disappointment, halted their advance, even after a week of the prescribed medication. Cindy suggested maybe they were hoping for too much in a week. The physician replied she was probably right, but he aimed for results anyway. Which was why he was now going to recommend the insertion of a central line directly into Cindy's upper chest, from which she would receive a measured dose of intravenous chemicals every day for the next week. She would come to the hospital each morning, have the drugs pumped into her by one of the specialist nurses, and then she would go home to bed. He was very clear about the go to bed bit. The intravenous drug version of the little pastel pills made at least a minor difference in all but the most extreme of cases; it was also far harder hitting, and was going to make Cindy very ill.

'I thought I was very ill now?'

'You are. But without the symptoms of being very ill.'

'I still won't have them when you give me these new drugs, though, I'll just have the symptoms of the drugs.'

'That's right.'

'So you want to make me more sick than I've been for the past week – which by the way, hasn't felt quite as nothing as you seem to believe – in order to make me better?'

'Not make you better Cindy, no.'

Cindy was just detached enough from the news to note the speed with which her doctor jumped on the word 'better'. Clearly there was no way anyone in the hospital was going to risk saying anything that might suggest a cure in her case. She would have laughed at his litigation-induced paranoia, if she hadn't felt so ill. And scared.

Neil Austin continued to explain, 'We hope this tougher version of the treatment will halt some of the progress of your disease. At its best it often gives the surgeon something to remove, and if not, then at least it will allow us to determine more clearly the extent of your illness.'

'By making a hole in me and having someone pump drugs into me every day and guaranteeing I'll be so sick I won't be able to get out of bed?'

Neil Austin remained calm in the face of her mounting anger. 'What can I tell you? It's a blunt instrument, I've admitted that much already. It's also the best we can do. In cases such as yours we've found the more we deal with the disease before surgery, the greater the chance of . . .' Cindy and Jack waited while he searched for a word that had no resonance of 'cure' attached; it came with an uncertain shrug, 'Buying you some extra time.'

'At the cost of making me more sick.'

'For now, yes.'

Cindy and Jack sat in the office, a soft ticking clock above their heads. Cindy had seen the queue out in the waiting room, knew for certain she was not the only person Neil Austin would be giving bad news to that afternoon, noted the doctor's unsuccessful attempts not to clock-watch while she brought herself to accept this new recommendation.

Then she unhooked her hand from Jack's. 'Not much choice is there?'

Cindy could feel Jack's relief beside her. Much as he had been searching for alternative solutions, his whole being was still willing her to jump at any chance offered – no matter how unpleasant it was for her to go through. Or for him to watch.

Neil Austin was shaking his head. 'No, you do have a choice. You don't have to do any of this. I'm simply offering what I believe – what the team believes – is the best course of action.'

Jack nodded. 'We know that.'

They stood up to follow the nurse who was already on her way out of the office and into the treatment room, the faster to get on with the job. Cindy looked back at the doctor who was shuffling her papers aside in order to get on to the next of his late appointments. 'Doesn't stop me hating you right now.'

Neil Austin didn't look up, but he had a resigned half-grin as he waved her away. 'Tell the nurses. They love a good doctor-baiting session.'

Putting in the line hadn't hurt. Not really. The young nurse – too young nurse, Cindy thought – explained that, as well as the more common side effects, the drugs they would be using over the next week were also likely to irritate her skin, burning her veins from the inside out. In the old days she would have come in every morning and they would then have been searching for a workable vein, one willing to take the medication in, dealing with Cindy's nerves and the veins closing off, jabbing her repeatedly until they found a safe way in. With this method, she went home with the small plastic canula in her, the top sealed off, needle threaded through. Thereby saving Cindy from six days of having a new 'sharp stick' made each time she came in. Not to mention the time, hassle and strain it saved the medical staff. And actually, it hadn't hurt much. Wasn't really like pain. Preparation for pain perhaps. Cindy had a local to take care of the initial invasion, then the central line was threaded into a vein in her upper chest near her collarbone. Against a chest wall that was, not long ago, covered with a soft layer of skin-smoothing fat. Now her bony breastbone poked through, a relief map of veins easier for the nurse to catch. Then they were ready.

This was more like it. Cindy recognised this picture she was now part of. Taking the little pastel pills at home, fending off Jack's requests to look at websites and library books, even the conversations with her parents and Kelly and other friends – none of the actions had looked like they were supposed to, looked like the sick people on TV, in the movies, until now. But now there was the nurse, and the tray of medication, and the line in her vein, and the row of people all lined up and waiting for the same. Some reading while drugs dripped in to them, others sitting scared or just tired with friends holding their hands. In one corner a man lay – old or young, Cindy couldn't tell his age from his creased face, hairless head – eyes closed and moaning quietly, clear liquid dripping into his arm. And now she was sitting here in this treatment room, sunshine muted through the thin curtains, these people too ill for bright light, too inside to notice outside. Cindy looked down at her shaking, scared hands, the line by her collarbone, the wristbones sticking out where only a month ago she'd had flesh – how could she not have noticed this creeping weight loss? She was like them. She was like the sick girl she'd seen in the wheelchair on her first visit to the hospital. She was the sick girl. And now the tears rolled down her face, Jack mopping them away as they fell. The nurse was slowly and carefully pumping in the measured liquid, Cindy was slowly and carefully taking in the fact of her disease with it. The syringe was changed and another liquid went in, and another, and Cindy felt her stomach churn in protest, her veins hot and itching as it began to travel through her, find its way in. The nurse finished up with a fat syringe of the anti-emetic, a vapour-flavour tugging at the back of her throat. The final drug was supposed to stop Cindy feeling the full effects of the poisons that had already been pumped into her. But it was too late, the colourless liquids had gone into the central line and Cindy had taken in their strongest message.

As she lay on their bed, trying to find a place that eased the constant sense of nausea, she tried to explain to Jack.

'I had absolutely believed Neil Austin. Seeing those scans and the pictures, I believed what he had to say. I believed I was ill.'

'But?'

'It was an intellectual understanding.'

'And now?'

'Now I've spent an hour-and-a-half sitting with those other sick people and looking at them – the hair-loss skinny ones like they're out of a Holocaust photo, the others puffy from steroids who actually look even sicker somehow, all of them smelling ill, smelling like hospitals – and I'm them.'

'No you're not, you're here. With me. I wouldn't leave you in there.'

'That's not the point, Jack. I've been kidding myself.'

'You're the one who said you believed what they were telling you.'

'I know. I do. I don't mean like that. I did believe them. I just had this stupid idea that maybe I was better than everyone else. I could be sick and not suffer. I could be terminally ill and not end up like everyone else does. I thought I didn't look like them. My illness didn't look like that. Like the pictures you always see. And I had this stupid fucking idea that if I didn't look like them then, somehow, I wouldn't be one of them. I might be dying, but I didn't have to be a victim as well. But I do. And I am.'

Cindy started crying again and Jack lay near her, not close enough to disturb her aching skin, not so far she couldn't feel him. A nauseous tremor ran through her from head to toe and he pulled the blanket over her shoulders. Cindy cried herself to a restless sleep, waking every now and then with a shudder, a mouthful of bile. Jack wiped her lips and kept watch and was waiting when she opened her eyes.

By the third day they had a routine. In the morning Cindy found the main part of the nausea had subsided, but she was weak and tired. She would wake a little more after a shower – careful of the line, noting the shower drain for signs of falling hairs (there were none, it was too soon) – and then her spirits would plummet again as they drove to the hospital. As the drive progressed Cindy would become more agitated, dreading the next two hours, and yet trying to ignore it, because even acknowledging the nausea to come made her body shudder. At the treatment room there were always delays and they were persuaded by the nurses that the best thing would be for Jack to leave her there while he went in to work for a while, he should then come back in the late morning and pick her up. That way he would be able to take her back to the car and get her home and into bed. Cindy was always drowsy after treatment, the first two hours the best really, while the anti-emetics left her sleepy and unaware, before the sickness set in properly. Then, once she was fully awake and Jack had found something she could manage to eat, he would go back to the office for another hour, two at the most, his cell phone on at all times.

Jack would happily have taken time away from the office, but that the programme carried on. One good story was not going to make their reputation. Jack had picked a good team, but even they couldn't work entirely without leadership. Still, he would only have gone to the office in the mornings if that was the case, but it quickly became apparent – certainly by the end of the second morning when she actually kicked him out of their bedroom – that Cindy still needed time to herself. Despite her weakened state and constant nausea, she wanted some time on her own. She was used to working by herself, being alone much of the time, the intrusion into her privacy that sickness had brought was not welcome. In fact, the worse she felt, the much less likely she was to appreciate another phone call or well-meaning visitor. Beyond her own need for solitude, though, she also needed time. Cindy was beginning to understand the disease. Taking time to read up on it – not the heal-yourself books Jack had come up with, but the ones that explained what was happening to her, the books that mapped her body. Cindy lay in bed, holding the sickness back and learning the paths of her body, the routes of her disease. Beginning to call it her disease. One of the nurses had told her that some people take months to truly believe in their illness. Cindy acknowledged she did not have months. And she also had a faster way in. The books on anatomy and physiology became a route-planner, the central line a gateway.

The week was long and hard and showed both Cindy and Jack just how much more they could take than they'd expected. She had not thought she could be so patient a patient, give in to being looked after, allow Jack to both mother and father her and then still kiss her goodnight. For his part, Jack had not known he could clear up so much vomit, wipe so much bile, drive so many miles, and still be happy to do the same another day.

And though the days dragged slower than they could have believed, the week of intravenous drugs finally came to an end and another set of scans showed a definite change for the marginally better. Tiny good news in a dying paradigm. Cindy was granted seven days' freedom from both the central line and any other medication until surgery. Time to build up her strength again. As predicted, she had spent the previous week loathing Neil Austin – and enjoying the nurses' mocking Austin impressions – and then, when he came into the treatment room and confirmed this would be her last treatment, she decided instead that he was entirely loveable. Her relief at the news almost blocked the feeling of sick irritation as the nurse pumped in the last of her daily drugs, and she asked the physician if all his patients succumbed to Stockholm syndrome, the victim coming to love the captor who is entirely responsible for their welfare.

The young nurse holding the syringe smirked and Neil Austin shook his head. 'No, mostly they still find a way to hate me. But then, we usually find they hate the surgeons even more, so in comparison I end up looking like the good guy.'

'Unless you cure them?'

He nodded. 'Oh yeah, then I'm God – Doctor Kildare played by Brad Pitt.'

The nurse sniggered. Cindy asked, 'Even for the men?'

'Especially for the men.'

He signed off her forms and walked away, leaving the nurse

to remove the central line. Cindy almost felt sorry for him, with no chance to play the healing saint to her ailing patient. Until the first wave of nausea hit and she remembered she'd always thought Doctor Kildare was a bit crap.

Thirty-five

In the lead-up to the surgery, Cindy and Jack's carefully nego-tiated and successfully balanced relationship came under some serious strain. Cindy wanted permission to be ill – and she wanted to be treated as perfectly well at the same time, regard-less of how weak and drained the IV drugs had left her. She didn't want to pick up the telephone, receive emails, open the front door, speak to her mother – and she wanted Jack to behave as if nothing was any different. The week that followed should have been easier, at least after the extremes of nausea had worn off, but while it was impossible to behave as if nothing was happening, she didn't want every moment to be filled with her fear of the future either. She was counting the hours and ignoring their passing. Her own view of what was happening to her changed from one minute to the next, and she wanted Jack both to anticipate her changes and ignore them. Jack himself wanted the old Cindy back, and he wanted to swaddle the new one in cotton wool kisses. He wanted her to be well, and part of him wondered what she had done to get this, what he had done for her to get this, which one of them was to blame. They were stumbling in the dark, some-times finding each other and sometimes not.

The night before she went in for surgery, Jack curled his body around hers, tried to zip her into his skin, hold her inside.

'You know what I was thinking on my way home today?'

'How gorgeous I am?'

'Always.'

'Yeah, well I don't think you should count on my gorgeousness for that much longer.'

Jack shook his head, kissed the nape of her neck, hoped he sounded convincing when he promised Cindy that how she looked didn't matter at all. And it was true it didn't matter to how much he loved her. But it wasn't true it didn't matter. Jack hated that she was looking so ill and Cindy knew it.

'OK, so what were you thinking?'

'Well, I spent most of the morning in staff meetings. Trying to share out work without making it look like I'm giving it all away.'

'Did it work?'

'I doubt it. But I don't care all that much either. Anyway, listen, I was driving home and thinking about three months' time. For us.'

Cindy's body stiffened, her heart beat a little faster beneath Jack's hand. 'Uh-huh?'

'About how I just don't know where we're going. There's no plan.'

'No.'

'And I hate that.'

'I know you do. I'm not too pleased with it either.'

'I was driving, and I know the route home now, really well. But when I first came out here I kept getting lost. When I was working late, those canyon roads could get really dark by the time I came back. I was remembering back then and I thought that right now, it's like we're Hansel and Gretel, you and me. Stuck in the woods with no idea when the old witch is going to jump out and get us.'

Cindy eased her back more firmly into Jack's body, pulled

his arms tighter round her thin waist. 'Then it's lucky I've barely been able to eat. We've still got all those pistachios. We can use the shells to make a trail.'

She ignored the three months. There was nothing to be said about them. They were impossible, uncharted waters. Besides that, her clearest thought that night was about pain. The very present, physical pain of having her body cut open.

Jack and Hannah Frier waited in the relatives' room. Cindy had not wanted her mother there. Had not wanted to worry about someone else seeing her, having to be strong for yet another sad face, but Hannah had flown down anyway. And Jack had not expected to want his mother-in-law beside him, except that now, in the waiting, it felt surprisingly good to have another person who was as scared as he was. His misery comforted by company.

Neil Austin brought the surgeon to see her as she lay in the hospital bed that morning. Introduced him as her new hate figure. Cindy thought it was strange to be handing her body over to someone she'd met so briefly, would have said so, but that the surgeon clearly had better things to talk about. Incisions, scar tissue, pain management. How Cindy felt about her upper torso, were horizontal or vertical scars preferable? Non-existent was preferable. Time for the scars to heal and another summer for them to matter on the inside or outside of a bikini was preferable. Cindy commented that she didn't care about latitude or longitude. The surgeon didn't understand, and talked primarily to Neil Austin anyway. Cindy wanted to ask if that was because he found it hard to chat when the patient was in a hospital gown, but that most of hers was covering her face. The doctors' deliberations over, she was joined by the anaesthetist and then rolled away to the operating room. She was surprisingly happy to leave – her own tension and her mother's mounting hysteria seemed to be rubbing off, even on Jack. The sooner this was over, whatever it was, the better. Cindy kissed Jack and held his hand until the trolley reached the door, then she left them behind, overhead fluorescence pacing out her path.

The operating room was not much like the *ER* version she'd been expecting. Much smaller. And no music. Cindy's new hate figure did not like music. His assistant – younger, less experienced, more female – usually listened to Van Morrison if she could, Brahms if she had to enjoy someone else's classical. Today there was silence, but for the devices keeping Cindy breathing, the anaesthetist's machinery, the clatter of the clutter of people, the metal and rubber crowded in around Cindy's body, ready with fresh instruments, fresh blood. The assistant made the first incision, her hand careful and steady, too slow for her senior's liking, lacking style in his opinion, but she was competent, painstaking. The rest proceeded according to plan.

Face and lower body covered, skin iodine-swabbed, Cindy opened up, stretched out, blood sucked wherever it welled up and obscured the view, Cindy-body poked into and dug about. Skin, muscle, tissue, blood, ribs, organs moved until the hunted seam was carefully uncovered. Then the disease deliberately measured, its apparent course solicitously noted. After the minimum of consultation, the surgeon made a brave choice – exhibiting his flair and his assistant's fear – by cutting out a chunk of unwanted new-born flesh, the disease that was creating itself, fresh-formed blood vessels, newly created tissue. A delicate procedure, removing only enough to take the disease, taking just enough to leave good margins, spilling nothing. The assistant would have left this piece, scared she would miss something, knick the wrong place, damage more than the removal would offer as solace. She would have been right to leave it had she been operating; with that degree of fear she might well have made a mistake. But the senior surgeon was doing the removing and, with those skills and that arrogance, he had taken the right option. Fortunate Cindy. The surgeon's choice gained her a precious fortnight, sent fourteen saved days off to pathology for analysis. Ninety minutes later there was no more new to be seen. They had as much information as they would gain this time. Instruments were counted, swabs blood-weighed, a fine line of stitches caught into bruised skin. Cindy was put together again.

The more and less experienced surgeons washed up side by side. He went for a round of golf with his broker, the assistant went for lunch with Neil Austin – as yet their burgeoning affair amounted only to long looks and possibility. Hope on her part, resignation on his. Jack and Hannah were told things had gone well and they waited while Cindy was taken to the recovery room. Neither of them understood what was meant by 'well', though they smiled gratefully at their informant anyway.

Cindy oozed in and out of consciousness, gagging on the blood in the back of her throat. After ten minutes of the recovery room nurse calling her to wake up, she came round properly and immediately wished she hadn't. She was morphine-nauseous now and was eased forward to throw up into a kidney-shaped steel bowl. An hour later Cindy woke back in her room, Jack and her mother both staring down at her. There was dried vomit in the corner of her mouth, crusted blood and iodine had left high-water marks across the unbandaged part of her chest, and a dark purple bruise marked the IV point of the anaesthetic, which was now replaced by a saline drip.

Hannah leaned in, her face looming down over Cindy's,

filling a field of vision that searched for comfort from Jack. 'Hello, my beautiful baby.'

Cindy frowned out of puffy eyelids, still gummy from the surgery, opened a sticky mouth to speak and squinted down at herself, the mess that was herself. She smiled at her mother, dry lips cracking with the effort. It was marginally less painful than laughing.

Thirty-six

Cindy reached beneath the gown and felt her body, stretching fingers itching to touch hitched-up skin. No sense of its own, the scar tissue, a fat and red lump of old-made-new crust, could not feel her fingers, though her fingers could not keep from feeling the seam. Her hands continually strayed to the wound even though she knew it hurt to touch. Not physically hurt, not the insensitive upper layer, thickened with scab and dried blood, but underneath the bruised muscle, the flesh mourning that which had been carefully cut out. Mourning the missing part of itself. Own flesh gone bad. Grown wild. This raw scar, a six-inch-long chunk of skin and flesh and muscle the crowding doctors had pulled open and then sutured back together, was a narrow raised mound. Like the burial mounds she'd seen in the west of England, long burrows to hide and honour the dead. Cindy brought herself up from her antibiotic doze with reaching hands, teaching herself a fresh layout.

She mapped the new site on her torso. The triangulation marked from scar tip and then across from left breast to right, a plumb line to the base point of the swollen red which was the new wound covering. Neil Austin came to talk to her, explained the surgeon had removed as much of the disease as he could – suggesting, though not confirming, that there was more they had charted but left in place. The pathology report on the removed tissue might suggest they should open her up again, make another foray into her speed-growing cells, but any decision would have to wait for the results to come back. Cindy wondered how long they would bother opening her up. Her flesh was running faster than she was, the surgeons could not cut deep enough to get it all out; it was, after all, Cindy they were trying to cut out of Cindy – where was the route plan for that? The doctors were trying to map out the good and bad in her, but it was the same body, same flesh. This was an internal coup, no boundaries to keep the inside out of the inside. Neil Austin looked at Cindy's face, her blank listening, overt acceptance, covert pain, and assured her that post-operative depression was common. After the fake, nauseating high of the morphine, it was usual to come back to an unhappy reality feeling unhappy. Cindy figured that as long as she was still concentrating on trying to sit up in simple pain instead of absolute agony, the nebulous charm of happiness was way down her list of concerns.

Hannah Frier stayed in LA for five nights, sleeping on the sofa and marvelling at the view from the shower as she got in Jack's way at every here-to-help turn. Each morning she drove Cindy's car to the beach, walked along the shoreline praying to half a dozen gods governing a variety of misrepresented faiths, and then patched up her tear-torn face, walking into Cindy's hospital room with a false smile and a failing heart. She sat by the bed while her daughter slept, poured water for her when she woke, told parentally-corrupted versions of childhood happinesses, and re-told her mother-myths, as much for her own sake as for Cindy's. Fortunately for both women, Hannah's need for money was far greater than her ex-husband's, and she flew back to New York and her job – no paid time off other than for actual bereavement, her only child's terminal illness being the

210

wrong side of death for company policy. She flew out of LA almost two hours before their natural mother-daughter love was overcome by their natural mother-daughter antipathy, boarding the plane just before the goodbye wave turned into a semaphore of relief. Cindy's father called. Asked for the surgeon's name, inquired after her insurance policies, how long she would be in hospital and when the next results would come through. He told her she was doing well and to keep it up. He failed to ask how she felt. Her mother told her she loved her every ten minutes, her father's girlfriend assured her he loved her too. Cindy calculated both declarations into a genetic balance.

After a week in hospital Cindy discharged herself, bored and tired and sick of being around sickness. The medical team would have preferred to keep her in for another few days, but they understood her desire to get out, get on. The pathology report had come back, the results were not good, but they were accurate. They almost exactly mirrored both the surgeon's expectations from what he had seen beneath her skin and Neil Austin's original prognosis, with maybe the fortnight gained from the removed tissue extended to three weeks. Under those circumstances, the staff were used to patients preferring home to hospital.

It was dark, very early morning, the rain from a late evening storm still cooling the sea-breeze air. Jack pulled himself from sleep, trying to interpret the noise. Reluctantly following the sounds up from dream-state, the only place he'd felt any calm during the week, he returned to the unsafe bedroom. He had been woken by the sound of clattering bottles, objects thrown about, drawers and cupboard doors slammed none too quietly. Cindy was moving around the dark room, as fast as her still-weeping scar would allow her to travel, collecting the detritus of the past few weeks. Her stiff arms were loaded down with pill boxes and bottles and wound-dressing materials and scissors and Band-Aids and get well cards and dying flowers and hospital information sheets and medical reports and printed out emails of love and support and concern.

'Cindy? Is something wrong?'

'Everything's wrong, Jack. I'm dying.'

Jack groaned, too tired to play the word games that came with Cindy's moments of fury. 'Apparently so. But I meant something specific? Something I can actually help with?' He looked at his alarm clock. 'It is two thirty in the morning.'

'Oh well, in that case I'll go back to bed and get in a good night's sleep. That's a great way to live out my last days. Snoring.'

'Well it's probably as sensible as what you're doing right now.' Jack looked at the pile of rubble forming in her arms. 'Um – what are you doing right now?'

'I don't want it. Any of it.'

'No. I'm just too knackered for clairvoyance at the moment. You don't want any of what?'

'All this stuff, mess, clutter. I hate it. I don't want our bedroom to look like a hospital room. I'm not in hospital, I've been in hospital and now I've come home and I don't want it. I fucking hate all this. It stinks like sick and tired and old and ill. And dying.'

Jack got out of bed. 'OK. Well . . . you're not old.'

'Yeah, and I don't need constant reminders that I'm all the rest either. I'm not happy, Jack.'

'Of course you're not happy! You're ill. No-one expects you to be happy.'

'But I want to be happy. I'm sick of being sick. And tired of being tired.'

'I know.' Jack forbore to say he'd had enough as well. Cindy

212

dumped the cascading armload at his feet. 'What do you want me to do with this?'

'I don't care. But I don't want to see it. It's bad enough that my body tells me constantly how sick I am, that it hurts to move, to sit up, lie down, it fucking well hurts to breathe, for God's sake. I don't want the house doing it to me as well. I will not have my bedroom made into an emblem of disease. I can't sleep in this, there's nowhere to rest when I have to look at it all the time.'

'I'll put it away.'

'Don't put it away. Throw it away. I don't want any of it in the house.'

Jack looked down at the pile at his feet. 'I think that'll be a bit difficult. We do kind of need the scissors.' He kicked a faded bunch of tulips aside. 'And I might cut my finger one day. I'll hang on to the Band-Aids if that's all right with you.'

Cindy was heading back to bed, her fury dissipated, pain returning. 'Whatever.'

'But OK, I'll dump all these letters and cards. It's true, you really do have crap friends. How incredibly insensitive of them to send you messages of love and concern.'

'I don't want their fucking concern. Or their love. I want them all to be sick and dying and having a shit life – shit end of life – so they know exactly how I feel.'

'Not Mother Theresa tonight then?'

'Only if she hated the whole world and everyone she knew and her entire wasted life and died fifty years too soon . . .'

'Not that I know of.'

'And spent her last two months in pain, and was bitter and nasty and bloody horrible to everyone she knew.'

'And ghastly to live with.'

'Because no-one understood how crap it was.'

'Or how scared she felt.'

213

'Not scared. Just fucking bollocking angry.'

'Bollocking. Nice touch.'

'Piss off, Jack.'

'OK. Shall I dump this lot now, or in the morning?'

Cindy pulled the sheet closer around her. 'In the morning.'

'That way we'll be able to see what we need to keep?'

'Don't push me or you'll find yourself in that pile.'

Jack climbed in beside her, waited for something sensible and wise and loving to occur to him. Two minutes later he realised he'd waited too long and came out with the best he could manage, 'You know, you don't have to be good at this.'

'I do so,' Cindy moaned.

'Why?'

'If I'm not good at this you'll all be horrible about me at the funeral.'

'We might be horrible anyway.'

'I'll come back and haunt you.'

'You don't believe in ghosts. You won't know what we're saying.'

'Oh yeah. Shame.'

They slept then, until the alarm went off, reminding them of daylight and continuity and the handful of newly pre-scribed pills waiting to go down.

Jack took the morning off work to lie in bed with Cindy and hold her. In the afternoon, she sat at her desk – not with any particular intention of working, more just to be there rather than lying in bed and adding a physicality to the unwell she already felt – while Jack went to his office for the first time in three days. Email and home-working and long telephone conversations were all very well, and had certainly become the mainstay of his input over the past month, but his physical presence was more pertinent. In an already established work-place, being seen to be there would still have mattered, but with a new team and a new programme it was vital. While he had all the sympathy his workplace could muster, Jack's problems were his own. His colleagues weren't selfish, but they were ordinary. Jack's present life was a place of fear and stasis, everything on hold, with no real sense of what the future would be once this moment passed. The people in his office, however, had to keep going. And, some of the time at least, they needed Jack with them for that to be possible. So Jack went into work and turned up with doughnuts and chocolate bars. He lifted a stack of files from Amber's desk and sorted them into 'No', 'Never' and 'Fuck Right Off!', he talked to four lawyers in fifteen minutes, cleared thirty-four emails from his computer, and made a date to go for a beer with Douglas. He had a long overdue coffee with two of his immediate bosses and threw out a dying pot plant. He joked and laughed with his team, yelled down the phone at the inefficiency of someone's else's staff, personally took over the edit on a tricky piece that no-one seemed able to get just right. And he thought of Cindy constantly. Wondered how she was, if she had changed the dressing on her scar yet, if she'd managed to do any work. He hoped she had achieved enough to make her feel the day hadn't been wasted, and that she was now back in bed. He wanted her sleeping. He wanted her body to be healing from the onslaught of the surgery and for the new medication to be working while she rested. He was a whirlwind in the building and made his presence strongly felt. And he really wasn't there at all.

That evening he opened the front door to silence. Just turned dark outside, the curtains were wide open and the lights still off. Jack found Cindy curled up on the sofa, head in hands. This wasn't to plan, not part of the 'treatment scale' Neil Austin had predicted. Given that the pathology results after surgery were much as expected, she was supposed to be starting to feel a little better. She was on a different regime of pills for now. There was a suggestion they would maybe return to an IV form if these didn't seem to be working, but that would of course have to be weighed against quality of life; a week more of constant illness, or a week less. Neither Cindy nor Jack were ready to start thinking like that, though the physician warned them the time for those decisions wasn't all that far off. For now, though, they'd been granted a reprieve of sorts. Cindy needed to recover from surgery before trying any more invasive medication, then when she was feeling stronger the hospital would take another series of scans, see if they couldn't update their calendars. There was still no hope for spring, though Christmas and the New Year were more than likely. Given that Jack came from a Jesus-free tradition, and that both he and Cindy found Thanksgiving more than family enough, neither were quite as thankful as Neil Austin might have hoped.

Cindy didn't look up when Jack came in and his skin froze around his stalled bones. As much as Neil Austin could promise anything, he had been confident that Cindy's first post-operative weeks would be both lucid and non-hospitalised. Jack was flooded with an immediate cheated fury and then, when Cindy eventually raised her head to look at him, the third time he spoke her name, relief. Joy. Extreme, rampant, adrenaline-pumped joy. Still there. Breathing, time passing, not stopped. Not yet.

He turned on the light. She'd been crying. And sleeping. Tired, gritty eyes hid beneath rubbed-raw lids.

'What? What's happened?'

Jack picked himself up by the scruff of the neck, took his ineffectual question and punched it hard in the face. He stood there hating his own fear and waiting for an answer.

'It's the babies.'

'What babies?'

'The ones we're not going to have.'

'Oh.'

Cindy had started mourning her future. Jack could barely bring himself to mourn Cindy; he couldn't possibly add in to the grief something as unreal as potential children, wouldn't allow for any other intrusions into their life. He was already having to share this too-little time with her parents and Kelly and all the others who'd suddenly realised their lives would not be complete without one more afternoon, another five telephone calls with his partner. He was damned if he was going to waste half an hour on their never-made babies as well.

Cindy pointed to a magazine on the floor. 'I was reading this. Surrogates. Frozen embryos. I could leave you some eggs.'

Jack exhaled, almost laughed with nerves and held-back tears. 'Great. Just what I want. Leftover you.'

'Or they could clone me. Freeze my cells until they know what to do.'

'Even better. They'll figure that one out in about twenty years. Why not do both? Grow a brand new you. We'll leave the clone with your octogenarian parents until it grows up into now-Cindy. And then I can marry her. She'll be twenty, I'll be nearly seventy. That's a perfectly normal age gap for an LA couple.'

'And you could bring up the frozen embryo together.'

'How right you are. I certainly won't be too old to be a dad by then.'

'Chaplin did it. Picasso. Saul Bellow.'

'Of course they did. And no-one had any moral qualms about it at all. Babe, you're a genius, we'll just clone you! What the fuck have I been getting so upset for?'

Cindy stretched out on the sofa, scratched at her daily-thinning hair, rubbed her eyes again. 'I have no idea.'

'Me neither. Good. Seeing as that's sorted, you can stop your bloody crying. Drink?'

'Yes please.'

They turned up the lights still brighter, kissed, beat off Cindy's incipient nausea with Kelly-strong martinis, watched trash TV, ate home-delivery Thai. Held hands. Made bad taste jokes about cryogenic eugenics. Pushed the future away for another night.

Thirty-seven

Kelly left the airport with three bottles of champagne, stopped at the first Californian supermarket she could find and bought the largest and most expensive bottle of tequila available, slamming the tequila and champagne into a bag of ice in the back of the car. It was a rental, she figured with the amount of insurance she was paying, melting ice should be the least of her worries. She then made a further pre-telephoned detour on her way through LA – grateful as always to her assistant – and arrived on Jack and Cindy's doorstep with red and gold flowers, chilled alcohol, and a ludicrously large bag of grass.

She held the gifts out to Cindy, took in her friend's weight loss, lined face and yellowing, shadowed eyes, and whispered, 'I've heard it might be good for you.'

Then she burst into tears. They smoked a quick joint out on the deck before the next wave of tiredness overcame Cindy. Kelly exchanged pleasantries in return for Cindy's detailing of the unpleasantries, and in the listening Kelly became both sadder and more hopeful. This really was happening, just as she had been afraid to admit to herself since the day Cindy had called with the news, and all through their daily phone calls. There truly was a closing down of time. But Cindy had not changed. She was the same person, just with a clearer knowledge of her own boundaries, the edge of her skin.

Later that afternoon, with Cindy asleep, Kelly and Jack sat on the deck and finished the second bottle of champagne.

'Is there anything I can do, Jack?'

'No. Yes. Being here is good. She wanted to see you. We both did.'

'I mean is there anything I can do for you?'

Jack shook his head, paused, looked at Kelly, stopped himself speaking.

'What?'

'Stupid wishes. Nasty thoughts. Can't seem to help myself at the moment.'

'You'd rather it was me?'

'No, of course not. I only meant . . .' Then Jack stopped himself explaining, stopped himself lying. 'Fuck it, yeah actually. I would. I would rather it was you. I would rather it was only touching me at one remove. I'd rather it was anybody than her.'

'That's OK.'

'No it isn't. But it is how I feel.'

Hannah Frier's return visit also came armed with gifts – beads and incense, crystals, flower remedies and half a dozen coffee enemas. Despite acknowledging the expense to her cash-strapped mother, Cindy wasn't able to accept the gifts as lovingly as she might have liked. She took the crystals – in the sitting room only, not their bedroom – refused the incense, welcomed the flower remedies (preserved in brandy, after all), and told her mother exactly what she could do with the enemas. For a woman who rarely left Lower Manhattan unless she absolutely had to, Hannah Frier was infused with a good deal of Californian cliché. After an hour of poor-baby/poor-Mummy forced understanding, followed by a brief argument totally unrelated to illness, each woman individually decided to let it go. They knew who they were, role-playing wouldn't change that. They went for a slow walk along the beach, Hannah collected shells, quoted Whitman on the wet sand. To make her mother happy, and maybe even for herself, Cindy prayed with Hannah at dusk. That night, to make Cindy happy, and certainly for herself, Hannah held her daughter as she threw up and wiped both their faces after the tears and then lay in bed beside her only child, stroking Cindy's hair until she fell asleep. And though the distance from his partner's skin made his own burn through the night, Jack left the two women to rest together.

Cindy's father arrived with a brand new girlfriend. Brunette. Apparently the last one hadn't been able to cope with his current proximity to mortality. The new woman was small, practically flat-chested compared to his usual round of pneumatic Amazons, and she had her own business importing South-East Asian art into the country. As they shared coffee and the cinnamon loaf the girlfriend had apparently baked all by herself, Cindy whispered to Jack that the shock of her 'I'm-dying-Daddy' phone calls had clearly thrown her father way off course. And laid a ten dollar bet that the new young woman would be blonde within two days of the funeral. Peter Frier obviously saw a peroxide partner as way too frivolous in the present circumstances. The woman was, however, just turned twenty-four. And her name was Heidi. Cindy tried not to laugh at her father and choked instead on the inequality of it all. She had long ago realised that she expected so much more from her mother than her father, forgave him long before she did Hannah. But the coffee enema/Heidi combination was so very like each of them, so much exactly who they both were, that she almost couldn't bear it. Love clarified inside disease.

They went out for Thanksgiving lunch, the estranged parents, the new girlfriend, the best old friend, and the happy couple, one of whom had to be helped from the house to the car, to her seat and back again. Who sipped cold water throughout the meal, ran her dry-skin finger along the condensation runways that lined the heavy glass. While the others worked their way through broad plate entrées, Cindy tore bread to fine shreds to make it easier to chew, to get it into her swollen stomach. She pushed a dark bloody steak around her plate – red meat to raise her red blood cell count according to the hospital, red meat to confirm her death wish according to the horrified vegetarians scattering the restaurant. For all that Hannah, Peter and Kelly spent the entire meal negotiating with each other who had the greatest claim to Cindy's attention and at which point her gaze was to be relinquished and passed on, they actually managed an enjoyable meal. A funny meal. Warm, if not sparkling, conversation only occasionally stalled while other people picked up Cindy's lost words. Pain and medication were robbing her of basic nouns. The first time she'd been unable to locate the simplest word – 'it holds liquid, has a handle on the side, for hot things' – Cindy and Jack had been terrified at her loss of 'cup'. Now it was a barely noticed feature of regular conversation, a charade-in-passing and then on to the next phrase. Though it still scared Cindy.

Heidi turned out to have a good sense of humour as well as a sharp eye for line detail. Jack and Kelly liked the young woman, and even Hannah and Cindy warmed eventually. Though Cindy confided to her mother in the bathroom that she suspected both Jack and Kelly liked Heidi for reasons closer to Peter's own, than for her elegant turn of phrase when describing eighteenth-century Malaysian earthenware. Then Cindy retched again into the porcelain bowl and

Hannah shushed her with a cool hand and an unchecked sigh.

Where passing illness could not stop the meal, the restaurant staff did. It was five o'clock, they had dinner tables to set and a new menu to begin preparing. The visiting diners reluctantly rose from the table, unwilling to break the spell, not wanting to return to their position as strangers in LA, the reason for their presence magnified in a hotel room, underlined by Cindy's slow progression to the door. They walked into the damp afternoon and headed off in different directions. There were arrangements for the next day and the one after that. Jack was taking his exhausted partner home to bed.

Jack walked Cindy to the car, the others waved from the street. Kelly and Hannah both watched Peter walk away, a proprietary hand on Heidi's tiny, low waist. Kelly wanted to touch that waist too – not Heidi's specifically, just anyone to hold, someone to remind her of skin and continuance. She headed back to her hotel to change and then made for a bar downtown. It was a bar she'd been warned against. It made most sense. Hannah wanted Peter's hand on her waist – his hand specifically. Not because she still loved him, and certainly not because she could imagine loving him again, but because in the touch between the two of them lay a spark of their daughter. It was just over two months since diagnosis. They were holding their breath, hoping to still time.

Kelly went out and got horrendously drunk. Way too drunk for California, way too drunk for New York even. She picked up a holidaying English-woman, a would-be actress, not thin enough and still too pale for American television work, but good enough for Kelly to kiss and lie beside and be drunk with and hold to her, hold into her, imaging that maybe the inebriated sex could reach in and rip out the part

223

of Kelly that was dying too. Looking for solace and finding a fuck instead.

Hannah went back to her hotel room and offered to swap. My life for hers, my past for her future. She trawled the heterodoxical canon she normally offered her petitions to, but couldn't find anyone or anything ready to make a deal.

Peter and Heidi went back to their suite. Heidi wanted to sleep and Peter wanted to go out, sightsee, play tourist. She lay down to take a nap and he channel-surfed with the sound on mute, flicked through the stack of specialist magazines she always carried with her, read the opening two sentences of her bedside novel four times. Peter could feel sadness and pain welling up inside. So he changed clothes and went to the gym, tears escaping in sweat.

Cindy and Jack went to bed early. The sun had only just fallen beneath the water line.

'All today I kept hoping it might change.'

'How?'

'I don't know. Both my parents here and Kelly and you, all together, part of me had this stupid idea that some miraculous healing thing might happen. They'd give us their blessing and you'd kiss me and I'd wake up and it would all be over.'

Jack's throat constricted. 'Over?'

'Not over over, idiot. Sick over.'

'Sorry.'

'Yeah. Bad boyfriend.'

They kissed. Cindy closed her eyes. When she opened them it was all still there.

Jack spoke first. 'You did really well today.'

'No I didn't.'

'Yes you did. It was a long lunch and everybody wanted your attention and your parents were doing what they do when they're together, and you did really well to keep sitting at the table for that long, let alone smile and be as good as you were.'

'I just couldn't speak.'

'I know.'

'They're only here because I'm ill, my disease is the reason my parents are in the same room for the first time since my book launch. And there's nothing to say, Jack. All I have to talk about is being ill, it's all I do now.'

'You can talk about being ill. That's why they're here. They won't mind if you talk about it.'

'I mind. I mean, of course I want it to be acknowledged – at least my father's had to acknowledge it with them all being here together. It's way better than him pretending it isn't happening, than basically ignoring me. But I've been reduced to just being sick. Like I'm nothing else.'

Jack nodded. He couldn't think of anything to say that would make Cindy feel better, everything she said was true. Other than the few hours he made it into work, pretty much all they did now was take care of her disease. And even at work, he never stopped thinking about Cindy.

She was still talking. 'It sits on my tongue and even when I want to talk about something else, it gets in first. I can't have a conversation without qualifying it through my illness. Everything I say filters through it. It's filled up my mouth.'

225

Thirty-eight

Ten days after her parents and Kelly left LA, Cindy went back into hospital. The constant nausea and lack of sleep had taken their toll. She was shattered and frightened and infected. Intravenous medications threaded their way through her slowly collapsing veins, body wired up to an array of plastic tracery. Cindy slipped in and out of feverish sleep, certain she could feel the combination of drugs as they made their way through her body. One branch tracking down stray cells, on a blind search-and-destroy mission that attacked her own defences in the process, the other sector coming along behind, mopping up the wracked ground, setting down new tracks and fresh props, only to have it all knocked down again when the drip bags were changed six hours later. And all of it inside Cindy. All of it being Cindy. To the hospital staff it was normal for the drugs to kill off healthy-Cindy as well as sick-Cindy – a 'collateral damage' that so easily rolled off the tongues of government aides discussing far-flung conflicts in places only Cindy's detailed geography understood. The arbitrary terms 'good' and 'bad' no more comprehensible than the multi-coloured fever dreams that assailed her whenever the staff rounds and visitor lists gave her more than five minutes to sink again into heavy sleep. She lay in bed and waited to get better. Because they told her she would. From this infection anyway. She lay there and, when awake and quiet, waited for meaning. A Terra Australis to balance her known world. Then fell asleep before any answers could reach her.

With the news of her hospital return, both parents flew straight back into town, Peter without Heidi to hide behind this time, Hannah prop-free. They alternated hours sitting beside her bed, waiting for Cindy's short moments of lucidity, each hoping it would come in their own watch. Other friends flew in too, Kelly came for the weekend. Jack was happy with the show of people and jealous of the time he was having to yield. He wanted Cindy to know how well loved she was, and he wanted her to keep all her hours for him alone. In order not to find the public presence any more annoying than the limits of his patience, he booked out her evening visiting times for himself, and went to work in the day, stopping off first thing in the morning and at lunch to see Cindy. Eventually, though, the constant trickle of muted visitors, all trying to grieve in the corridor rather than beside Cindy, finally reinforced the looming time limit. Three weeks before Neil Austin took him to one side and said it was probably time, Jack told his bosses he would not be coming in any more. Turned off his cell phone, handed over the pager to his PA, they could not call him for any reason. There were no earth-shattering matters that might need him, he was on indefinite leave. He knew the office would be a different place when he was able to go back to work. And he knew he would be a different person anyway.

Cindy came out of hospital after ten days of IV antibiotics. The doctors had suggested maybe it was time to stop the disease medication – and Cindy jumped at the offer. She was on another level of illness now. The infection that had brought her into the hospital appeared to have cleared up, but she was very weak and Neil Austin warned that while they were OK to send her home, she would no doubt be back soon; in

227

hospital they had stronger painkillers. He wanted Cindy to know that she would need them.

Peter Frier found a two-bedroom apartment close to Jack and Cindy and invited Hannah to stay there with him for as long as was necessary. He did not tell her he had only taken the lease on a monthly basis, there was no point underlining what they both knew.

In the back-to-front house Cindy and Jack created a new routine. They woke up with the later sun and he would give her drugs: painkillers mostly, and anti-infection prophylactics. Cindy's body was beaten down, she needed all the help she could get. People came to see Cindy in the morning and then again in the afternoon. They fitted in their visits around Jack's timetable. There would have been visitors there all day every day if he had allowed them, but he knew how quickly Cindy tired. Hannah and Peter and Kelly were welcome whenever they wanted, everyone else had to go through him, and he didn't care in the least if they thought him controlling and selfish. Cindy herself would have been happy to see no-one but Jack, maybe her mother and father occasionally, Kelly sometimes, but the past weeks had plainly emphasised her new value. It wasn't just up to her. Cindy may have been the one dying, but everyone else was also part of the process. Much as she wanted to hoard herself in their house, Cindy was aware of her duty to see people, to welcome friends. She was close to pushing through that membrane, her bony hands were relics carrying special knowledge even before death – perhaps even more so because she was not yet dead; the twenty-first century inability to accept an afterlife meant Cindy had to parcel out her saintly favours while still breathing.

Now that there was nothing Jack could do to make it better, his caretaker caress came into its own. He bathed

Cindy, holding her to him in the wide shower room, his back to the ocean, her shadowed eyes facing the sea. He changed the dressing on her scar. The disease and then the infection had slowed her healing, the wound, stretched over her thin frame and her increasingly swollen belly, was still raw, sometimes bloody, often weeping. Jack wiped her face when she threw up, took her to the toilet, washed her down after the night sweats, the day terrors. Initially there were moments when the grossness of her body and her pain repulsed him, but he knew the partitioned mess of bone and sore skin and weeping wound was the whole of Cindy now, and that there would soon enough come a time when he would give anything to be able to wipe acid vomit from her throat, stained piss from her legs. He didn't want to give himself cause for any more regret than was inevitable, so Jack held himself still through the revulsion, it passed and he continued. And in between the nursing he reminded himself to kiss her dry lips, to stroke her transparent skin.

One afternoon, when the visitors had left and Cindy had slept long enough, they tried to make love. The effort was hungry and sincere, but everything was painful for Cindy, everywhere he touched her was fearful for Jack. And then they were laughing, at the vigilance with which they were protecting her failing body, the return-to-virgin status that death awarded her flesh. The laughter turned to tears, into a smile then back to a kiss and slowly to skin and bone and mouth and teeth, the smell of desire masking the scent of Cindy's decay.

Thirty-nine

Cindy and Jack were sitting on the beach. It was eleven in the morning and not only had the cloud cover not been burnt away by the risen sun, but the gentle grey of the early morning had mutated into a fat gathering, threatening freedom from the water-retention stupor by mid-afternoon.

They had been for a short walk. Very short and very slow. Just the way Cindy liked it these days. Just the way Cindy was capable of these days. From the house to the car to the shore, then shoes off and along the water's edge for ten minutes. Rest for five and back again. Bony toes and over-arched soles massaged by the warm, wet sand. While in hospital the last time she had given in to Jack's pressure for her to see a massage therapist a couple of times a week, but though the woman was good and blessedly silent, Cindy still preferred her feet soothed by the natural world. The therapist who came to their house certainly offered her 'natural' oils and aromatherapy concoction, but as Cindy handed over Jack's fifty dollars for forty minutes of her time, she could never quite get over the feeling that this woman didn't really approve of her, even as she took the money. Whether it was paranoia or not, Cindy sensed a degree of censure that she hadn't given her disease-ridden body into entirely alternative care. And she could understand the woman's disappointment. Sometimes Cindy wondered herself if her mother's regularly suggested colonic irrigation and juice fasting and crystal healing and any one of the thirty or so alternative therapies Jack had researched for her might not have been the very one to do the trick. The system that would have had her running down the beach this morning and stripping off and throwing herself into the water in vibrant, glowing, disease-free health. Except that Cindy hadn't known which particular single-regime treatment would be the one for her. She hadn't been able to guess from the websites and the leaflets and the books which of the often completely differing theories was going to tackle her disease and make her better. Because each one said they alone were right. Each one promised a miracle cure – but only if she followed their path to the letter, with no deviations and complete faith.

At least the medical doctors didn't guarantee either complete or lasting cure. She quite liked their 'we-know-how-little-we-know' honesty. With Neil Austin there was less chance she'd be blamed for not having enough belief in her own power to heal herself. She had looked through the books Jack had brought home, and the websites he'd bookmarked in the first foggy weeks when he'd been trying to make it all better, before he realised better was out of his hands. It was astonishing how many of those offering 'I-Fixed-Myself: You-Can-Too!' workshops tended to be based on self-diagnosis rather than medically assessed disease. How often they had avoided the very tests that would at least prove to a sceptical Cindy there had been something truly wrong with them in the first place. And how often they charged five hundred dollars a workshop. There was one other great draw to the traditional method – not an awful lot of the alternative therapies offered morphine for pain control. These days, Cindy was a great fan of pain control.

She held Jack's hand as they turned upwards from the shore to the car park behind the dunes. Usually she wanted to

231

return to the car and home, the safety of her own things, known spaces between her increasingly tender body and other objects, those that bruised on touch, marking their trajectory on her increasingly fragile skin. But today she held him back.

'Can we sit down for a while?'

'You're too tired to get to the car? I could carry you?'

'No, I just want to sit down here for a bit.'

'We have to be at the hospital at four. And you need to eat something before we go. I've got some soup waiting at home.'

'I know. And there's pills to take and organic juice to drink and my mother coming later, but I'd just like to sit by the water for now. I'd like not to have a timetable for a bit.'

'Oh. Right. Sorry.'

Cindy sank into the sand just above the water line. The tide was going out, they were safe from any but the bravest of waves. She smiled at Jack and held out her hand to him. 'You didn't do anything wrong. I just want to stop for a while. I want to do something that isn't on the schedule. OK?'

Jack flopped his body down beside hers. Flopped in attitude but not in reality. Did his best to make it look as if he was just throwing himself down, did his best to hide the care with which he held himself every moment he was around Cindy, fearful of hurting her, scared of breaking her. Two elderly women ran past them. One much taller and thinner than the other, deep in conversation, both shouting to be heard over the roar of the surf and their own panting. The thinner woman was in front, she held her hand out to the larger woman behind her and they ran on, one pulling the other, laughing at a joke the bigger woman shouted from behind.

Jack watched them run on. 'Do you think they're together?'

'I hope so.'

They smiled then and Cindy lay back on the sand, Jack resisting the impulse to check the ground beneath her for shells or stones or anything else that might make it through her translucent skin to the relief-map skeleton beneath.

'What's next, Jack?'

'Home. Painkillers. Lunch. Then we go in. Check out the results from your scans.'

'No. I know that. I mean, what's next?'

'If the scans don't show any improvement?'

'None of us expect the scans to show improvement. Even that little student Neil's got in doesn't expect my scans to show any improvement.'

Jack was surprised. 'The smiley one? She's given up too?'

'Not given up. The poor girl's just accepted the limits of her job. She's only a kid. Last time I saw him alone I told Neil she was a bit young to be taught the facts of life.'

'What did he say?'

'Baby doctors are never too young to learn they're not God.'

'He's right.'

'Often.'

Jack studied the dark clouds, they were definitely coming faster into shore now. He didn't want to risk Cindy getting soaked, no matter what it was she'd stopped to talk about.

'So what do you mean, what's next?'

'When I die, Jack. What's next?'

'Oh.'

'Well it is going to happen.'

'I think we both know that.'

Cindy lifted a thin hand to the shore. 'This keeps going. The water. In and out all the time. And the trees, and the hills, they all keep going.'

'And you won't.'

'No, I'll stop. But something's got to happen to me. Energy transfer, matter decomposition.'

'Have you changed your mind about heaven?'

Cindy sucked in her breath and smiled. 'I've tried, but no, I just can't imagine it.'

Jack shook his head. 'Me neither. I wish I could. I think it might be easier, maybe. Believing you were just somewhere else. That I could . . . you know . . . see you again one day.'

'We should become Buddhists.'

'Why?'

'Kelly's Buddhist friend told her you meet the same people lifetime after lifetime. You could be my son next time. Or daughter if you like.'

'Nah. I'd just take more of this if that's OK.'

'That's OK.'

They sat for a while longer until the wind picked up and the blackest clouds began dropping their load a little way out to sea. Even the excessively cool surfing boys started to head into shore. Jack helped Cindy to her feet.

'I wish I believed in ghosts. I could come back and watch you.'

'You don't need to, I won't be chasing anyone else, Cindy.'

'No, I didn't mean it like that. I meant I'd come and see how you are. How you're coping. It's going to be harder for you later.'

Jack looked down at her thin frame, her swollen stomach, yellowed eyes. 'Well, it's hard for you now.'

'It's hard for both of us now.'

'Yeah. It is.'

Cindy slept a little that afternoon and then they drove together to the hospital.

As Jack helped her out of the car, she pointed out a young woman walking by. 'She's cute.'

He shrugged.

'Come on, don't you think she's cute?'

'These late-night conversations you've been having with Kelly – are you trying to tell me something here?'

'Yeah, Jack. I'm gay. I'm in love with Kelly, have been all this time and figured I'd wait until I was dying to tell you.'

'That's nice, dear.'

'Kelly thinks so.'

They walked slowly along the corridor to the waiting area. Cindy opened her mouth to speak, Jack silenced her. 'I'm not interested.'

'In what?'

'In whatever you have to say.'

'You don't know what I have to say.'

'I think I do.'

'What then?'

'You want to tell me it's OK if I meet someone else. That I'm young. That I should love someone else again. Am I right?'

'I thought I was being very generous and giving. How did you know?'

'Cindy, you are being generous and giving. And controlling and . . .'

'How is that controlling?'

'It's what you do. You want to map everything out. Work out what's going to happen next, be certain of the future. You want to know where we're both going, it's what you always do. Only you can't do it for yourself, so now you're trying to do it for me.'

'Oh.'

Neil Austin's nurse called them into the office and they got up to follow her, Cindy leaning heavily on Jack.

He whispered in her ear as they followed the woman down

the corridor, 'Not that I'm not grateful you understand. I appreciate the gesture.'

Cindy nodded. 'Yeah, well what you didn't know I was going to say was I do want you to meet someone else. But not for a while. Two years absolute minimum. I want two years in black. And tears. Every day.'

'Is that all?'

'Minimum. I mean it, Jack.'

'I'm sure you do.'

'So?'

'Done.'

Cindy grinned and they reached Neil's office door. 'Good. Now put on a big smile, Neil's not looking forward to this.'

'No. I guess it's hard for him too.'

'Fuck that. He's not dying. He's been making me even sicker.'

'The treatments made you sick, Cindy, not Neil.'

'Yes, I do know that, Jack. I just want a little play. Before he gives us more bad news. Come on.'

Cindy started up an infectious giggle and attempted a bright bounce into Neil Austin's office. It actually turned into a cough and a semi-stumble, but was certainly enough to make the physician's heart sink. Which was Cindy's aim. Still able to force a change, make a difference. Dying, not yet dead.

Forty

Neil Austin had the news they were expecting. Go home and wait. Cindy could have a self-administered morphine drip for as long as Jack was able to care for her at home; after that they would admit her again to the hospital. Though she didn't mention this out loud, Cindy had no intention of hanging on long enough to be admitted again. She didn't want to die in a morphine-induced haze, nor did she want to die in a bed that was not her own. The house might face the wrong way, but it did at least have open windows. The hospital windows were hermetically sealed, and mostly facing inwards to the other hospital buildings. Cindy knew they wouldn't let her die in the car park, even though it had by far the best view, and she wished disease on the unthinking architect who had chosen air conditioning and building regulations over the patients' view.

It was early afternoon and Cindy had a craving for icecream. Pistachio icecream. The parents had just left, Kelly was coming over later in the day. Jack had to go, Cindy couldn't wait. He tried four stores before finding one with pistachio, and made it home again through a sudden out-of-nowhere traffic jam within ninety minutes. Every minute a flagellating hour for Jack. He walked into the house and called her name. No reply. He went as usual straight to the bedroom. Cindy wasn't there. The bed was empty, covers pulled back, her balled-up tissues of dried and drying tears and snot and phlegm exposed, faded islands on the white sheets. Adrenaline flooded his stomach, bitter taste in the back of his throat, his breath catching against his constricted vocal cords as he called out to her, 'Cindy? Where are you?'

No reply. Jack running into the bathroom, out on to the deck, fumbling with doors and locks.

'Cindy?'

The last run into her office. Opening the door she'd kept closed for the past week, refusing to work, no point, no future, why begin something now?

Cindy was sitting at her desk, sheets of paper surrounding her, computer glowing bright, half a dozen books open and pages marked.

'Fucking hell! Why didn't you answer me?'

She swivelled round in her seat, face gaunt and surprised, a smile marking the usual line of her dry mouth, eyes bright for the first time in days. 'Sorry, I didn't hear you, I'm working.'

Jack wanted to slap her for terrifying him. To leap for joy that she was sitting up on a chair and not fallen down in the crumpled heap of blood-and-finished he'd been picturing daily, hourly, for the past three months. To hold her forever. Then he registered the smile. 'Working? On what?'

Held himself in. Didn't want to make it too special that she was working, didn't want too much enthusiasm to crowd her fragile hold on possibility.

'I'm trying to map myself.'

He looked at the papers around her, the heavy reference books, each one marked with a dozen or more bright slivers of paper.

'How do you mean?'

'There's this map in Hereford Cathedral.'

'Hereford, England?'

'Yeah.'

'You've been to Hereford Cathedral?

'No I haven't. Research. I've read about it, seen copies. It's famous.'

Jack snorted. 'Really? Something in Hereford is famous?'

'To mapmakers.'

'Just the select few then.'

'That's not the point. Anyway, it's a mappamundi, map of the world.'

'Ancient or modern?'

'Middle Ages, a representation of what they knew then. But it's not like a conventional modern map, it's full, it says everything.'

'How do you mean?'

'Look.'

She held out her hand and pulled him to the desk. Jack felt the papery warmth of her skin, the energy she had for this moment. Tried not to cry. She was pointing to a page, her cracked and grey fingernails sharply outlined against the glossy black and white. 'The known parts of the world are in there, but also the unknowns. "Here be monsters." That kind of thing. And other places people had heard of and not yet been to, this one here, see? He's this Priest-King that no-one knew existed for definite and yet everyone believed he did. Or wanted to believe he did.'

Jack looked at the man in the drawing. 'He looks like Father Christmas.'

'He was way better than that. More like a cure for the common cold.' They both laughed, easy, silly laughs. 'According to the teachers then, this Prester-John had the power to make the world a better place.'

'Quick, let's go find him.'

'They tried. They weren't even really sure where to place

him. Some maps had him in Ethiopia, others way further down the continent.'

'And you want to map this bloke into your life?'

'No. He's an example. And anyway, he would only have made things better according to the mapmakers. He might not have done any good for anyone else. It's all very subjective you know, mapmaking.'

'Yes, darling, I do know. Christ, you start work again and suddenly I'm the thickest person in your class.'

'Most thick.'

'Thank you. So what's this Father Christmas bloke got to do with you?'

'Nothing really, he's just the sort of thing that goes in. I thought I could try to map my life. Put it all in. A mappa-mundi.'

'Mappacindy.'

Cindy grinned, the cracked lips pulled tight against her teeth. 'Yeah. Who I am, how I got there, here. Everything I know. And the things that I know I don't know.'

'Like a painting?'

'No. Like a map.'

'It looks a hell of a lot like a painting to me.'

'That's because you don't know how to look at it.'

'Well no, I wouldn't.'

'It's OK, babe. I like the slow students. Look, it's just a map. A representation. A form of the truth.'

Jack looked at the outlines she'd drawn on the pages, the diagrams on her whiteboard. 'So how far have you got?'

'Not very.'

'Why not?'

Cindy shook her head. 'I'm scared.'

'What of?'

'Scared of getting it right. Scared of getting it done.'

Jack frowned, not understanding.

Cindy took a breath, another, held down the shudder, the physical touch of her fear. She continued, 'Scared that if I do it right, if I get it done, then it will be finished.'

Jack still didn't understand. 'And?'

'Then the map of my life will be done.'

'Oh.'

'And I'll be done too.'

'Yeah. I see what you mean.' Jack reached around her, her shoulder blades cutting into his forearm. 'It's probably OK to do it. You're probably not that magic. Not really.'

'I guess not.'

'I love you.'

'I love you back.'

What he really wanted to say was, 'Keep going, finish it. It's a map. It tells me where to go. It means I'll be able to find you.'

Wanted to say it, but didn't.

Forty-one

Cindy died that night. It was much less dramatic than Neil Austin had predicted, than the likely scenario he'd taken care to outline honestly to Jack, and with slightly more delicacy to Cindy. Contrary to both expectation, and its usual course, the disease did not reach Cindy's lungs first. There was no painful drowning in her own body fluid, lungs fighting to find air as they turned to liquid, insistence on a return to the hospital as the only place she could safely die. The inexorable forward march took a deviating route and turned from the norm to offer a gentler end, found her heart instead. There was no quake or fit, no shocking gasps for breath, no unendurable pain. They were asleep. Cindy folded into herself, left arm out from beneath her so as not to rub against the too-slowly healing scar tissue, Jack's longer body folded around hers. One moment Cindy's heart beat normally – slower than usual, with the odd forced beat, certainly – but as normally as it had since the invasive treatments had begun. And the next moment it failed.

Cindy had worked on the mappamundi for almost three hours, taking time to rest and try to eat with Jack while she thought of more that should go in, and then returning to her desk and the plane table she had set up for herself to sketch on. She worked on it freehand, in coloured pencil, sticking on extra pages where necessary, turning them over when the route tracked further than the page allowed, scribbling notes to herself. This was the first draft, she needed to get it all in, trace her continuing progress. Conception in a half-remembered bedroom her mother had once told her about, a confession she'd not wanted to hear. Kindergarten three long blocks from her parents' first apartment. Miss Kale in the entrance class. School and teachers, friends spinning off to paths of their own. A big break at Baton Rouge, Kelly in sharp focus, an array of pink-shaded Barbies. From there a spiral of learning routes, colleges and universities, travel, lovers, potential and past partners all spinning into each other. Some incidents started new narrow trails of their own, thin branches that widened into fat roads merging with the present day. Others simply stopped, lost friends, lost days. The varying colours of minor celebrity and major certainty. A twisted route that traversed the globe and kept coming back to New York. Crossing the Kelly path again to find Jack, Jack and Cindy lines merging and splitting, then braiding into each other. A narrow side line dating from Cindy's New York collapse, it appeared to go nowhere. Then another big leap across to California. In miniature detail she described the canyon routes she had made her own, the café, Matthew Amos who'd made the brownies and kept his childhood maps. Then the beginning of disease. Biopsies, pathology, surgery, prognosis – a pale thread reaching back, along the California route, through canyons and lattés, twisting inside childhood and Baton Rouge, London and Japan, linking first kiss and last line of coke and second fuck and third heartbreak. Linking each moment to this disease, to the first collapse, to now. Tying it all in together. The mountain view and the shower room ocean.

She broke off for half an hour to have coffee with Kelly,

slept briefly, welcomed both her parents into her bedroom, worked again, dozed on the sofa, and then had a late supper with Jack. Her appetite was pathetic, but she welcomed the Marmite soldiers anyway. Bit the heads off three of them. She was foggy throughout the rest of the night, occasionally pulling herself up to look at the map, put in a line or word or icon, mostly just making notes about what else she would add in the morning. At ten she let the maximum dose of morphine drip into her racked body, an hour later she threw up what little contents her stomach possessed. Jack turned out the light at eleven thirty, they lay in the dark together holding hands, touching feet. Cindy drifted in and out of conversation and eventually turned on to her side so Jack could wrap himself around her sleeping form. He kissed the back of her neck. Jack was exhausted and, like Cindy, slept deeply for several hours. When he woke up it was because he was cold. Because she was cold.

Forty-two

Endmaps: reaching consensus (Cindy Frier, Dis-Location, notes 1997)

There comes a time when we have to stop mapping. Accept that we have made the picture as clear as it is in our power to do, with the resources and knowledge and research available to us in this moment. The chart is as accurate as it can be at this time. And that's it. We must give up and hand our findings over to the mapmaker, the one who will turn our drawings and analysis and discoveries and uncoverings into a real picture, a readable graph. Sometimes it is difficult to know when we have reached this point. We keep thinking there is more to be found, more to be laid down, and there probably is. But that is for another map. This one is done. It is time to give in.

Acknowledgements

Thanks to: Shelley Silas, Antonia Hodgson, Stephanie Cabot, Melanie Lockett, Esther Douglas, Lauren Henderson, Maki Jagose, Ray Mears and the Members of the Board.